This

is

NOT

an

Office Romance

By Eloise Fox

Burning Chair Limited, Trading As Burning Chair Publishing
61 Bridge Street, Kington HR5 3DJ

www.burningchairpublishing.com

By Eloise Fox
Edited by Simon Finnie and Peter Oxley
Cover by Burning Chair

First published by Burning Chair Publishing, 2024

ISBN: 978-1-912946-40-2

For H

CHAPTER ONE
Emily

Emily sat on her bed, quietly sobbing, tears running down her cheeks. Her breathing came in ragged bursts as her mind raked over the same thoughts again and again. As she tumbled through her memories, the light outside slowly brightened enough to interrupt her and, taking a deep breath, she reached for another tissue. What no one ever tells you about grief, or depression, or whatever this was, thought Emily, was the way it jumbled the mind. How it stopped the natural flow of thoughts, creating hurdles and circles, never letting the mind fully stretch its legs. She felt sad for how she used to be, unsure whether she ever had been happy, and convinced she never would be again.

As she stood up, the morning sun shone across the North London gardens beneath her bedroom window. She practiced the exercises that her new therapist had given her. She focused on the small things: the faded green plastic swing, the grey squirrel darting along the fence top, the cat curled up on a shed roof. After looking at herself in the small bathroom's mirror, she decided to wash her face and reapply what little make-up she used. Only in her mid-thirties, and she already had grey circles around her eyes. Maybe they worked with her dark gothic hair and pale complexion, she thought, trying to be positive.

Gently shaking her head, she moved to the full-length mirror in her bedroom. With a conscious effort to fit in, she had deliberately toned down her outfit. No more New York power dressing; instead a simple, but elegant, suit with minimal jewellery. As she picked up her satchel (a satchel for goodness' sake, her Fendi handbag now languished in the wardrobe) and her house keys, she looked back round at the empty hallway and could feel a sob rising inside her that took all of her willpower to push back down. Not now, she firmly told herself. Enough.

Emily sighed as she closed the front door to her house and made her way down the short garden path. Walking down the unusually sunny London street, her frown lifted as she started to think of all the steps she had to take between where she was now and the new job she was heading for. As her therapist always said, the steps were the key; like putting one foot in front of the other. She just needed to focus on task after task to get to where she needed to be. She was determined; she would succeed.

She heard a familiar beep and took her phone out of her pocket to see that she had a new voicemail. Putting the mobile to her ear, she heard the familiar voice of her mother.

"Hello sweetie. We just wanted to wish you a *great* first day in your new job," the message said, emphasising the word 'great' in an artificial way that prodded Emily's already fraught nerves. "We're so excited for you, aren't we David?" A muffled "Yes, absolutely," could be heard in the background from Emily's normally quiet father.

Her mother continued. "Look, we know that it's…well…no, we *understand* how difficult it must be, but we…"

Emily ended the voicemail. It was too much for her. She knew they meant well and they loved her dearly, but she needed to get her head in the right frame of mind before she got to the office, and this wouldn't help.

She rooted around in her bag, found her earbuds and started to listen to one of her favourite playlists. Before long, as the sun rose even higher over a bustling city, Emily Taylor found that, with each new step forward, her heart was lifting.

*

As she got closer, Emily found the City of London to be buzzing with noise and colour. The wave of chaos instantly took her back two years to a life she had buried deep in her mind. To a time when she would rise early in her Manhattan apartment, grab a coffee from her favourite downtown stall, and then settle into her office overlooking skyscrapers and most of the city.

Things had changed a lot since then, including Emily herself. Since the accident, she had flown back to rural England to be near her parents and had stayed in the countryside for almost the whole time. Now back in a major city, she found the assault on her senses both startling and exhilarating. She was back and at last she was moving forward, but it was still slightly overwhelming.

It was only two days ago that she had moved into a new house in a London suburb that she had rented online, and she had spent most of her time indoors making it 'right'.

Now she was here in the midst of the buzzing City, and it was equally daunting and thrilling. The sights and sounds of masses of people hurrying here and there. Red buses, black cabs, blue rental bikes—she found the whole dizzying scene intoxicating. To come here, to start a new life, to prove to herself that she was the kind of woman who didn't shy away from challenges. But as she walked through the towering buildings and bustling streets, she felt a little niggle of doubt: was she ready?

As she turned onto Liverpool Street, she smoothed down her skirt and adjusted her matching jacket. She knew she looked the part and was ready for battle. Her heart was pounding. This was the first day of the rest of her life and, even though she had taken a job at a smaller firm, she was still joining one of the most prestigious law firms in the City. She knew many lawyers who would have killed to join Harrison & Associates.

She reminded herself that she had to get the balance right—

before her world fell apart, she was one of the most respected lawyers in her field and her new company was lucky to have her, but she also mustn't come across as entitled or stand-offish. She would more than hold her own against any of their team, but even so, she was thrilled to have landed such a position with such a firm. Yes, they were smaller than most, but they had built up an enviable reputation of having the best lawyers and being able to pick and choose the best clients. They had gone through some troubling times recently, but they had restructured the business and addressed their problems head-on. More than that, she would be working directly for the infamous founder, Darius Harrison—a legend in the industry—and she couldn't wait.

As she neared the office, her senses heightened. She drew in the sights and sounds of the city, loving the life that they represented. Cars honked their horns, people rushed past her on the pavement, and the smell of coffee and pastries filled the air. Emily inhaled deeply, her eyes sparkling. This was just what she needed; why had she waited so long?

She left the main road and made her way through the winding streets, her heels clicking loudly against the pavement. The buildings loomed above her, a mix of modern skyscrapers and ancient landmarks. Emily couldn't help but feel a sense of awe at the City's history.

Lost in her thoughts, she suddenly heard a screech of tyres and a sickening thud. She spun around to see a car on the opposite pavement and a cyclist lying in the road, his bike several metres away. Instinct took over as she rushed over to the cyclist, who was on the ground, groaning in pain. Emily knelt down beside him, trying to work out what to do.

"Are you okay?" she asked, her heart racing.

The cyclist moaned and tried to sit up, but Emily gently pushed him back down. "Don't move, you might have injured your spine. I'm going to call an ambulance."

By this time several other people had rushed over, including a young man who knelt opposite Emily and said to the cyclist,

"I'm a doctor. Can I see if you are okay?"

The cyclist nodded and laid back on the road as the man started poking and prodding him. "Tell me when it hurts," said the man.

Whilst this was happening, Emily fished out her phone and dialled 999. As she spoke to the operator, she tried to keep the panic out of her voice. This was not how she had expected her day to go. She explained to the operator what was happening, then turned her attention back to the cyclist. "Can you tell me your name?" she asked, trying to keep him calm.

The cyclist nodded weakly. "It's Tom. Thank you for helping me. Thank you both." And he smiled weakly at the doctor.

Emily returned his smile. "Of course, Tom. We're going to get you some help." Turning to the doctor, she handed him the phone and added, "They would like to talk to you if that's okay?"

"Sure. I'm Anjay by the way," said the man, taking her phone and giving her a smile in a slightly flirtatious way.

"I'm Emily," she replied.

Tom groaned and pointed to his leg. With his one free hand, Anjay pulled Tom's tracksuit up slightly, exposing a deep cut on the calf. He updated the operator, and his tone became very formal as he demanded an ambulance quickly. Emily quickly took off her scarf and used it to apply pressure to the wound, which received a thumbs-up from Anjay.

"Keep talking to me, Tom," Emily said, trying to distract him from the pain. "What do you do for a living?"

Tom grimaced as she applied pressure to his wound. "I'm a bike courier. I guess I won't be doing much of that for a while. Where's my bike?"

Emily looked around said. "It's just over here; someone's put against the wall for you. You're doing fine. You'll have plenty of time to rest up and catch up on Netflix. Just focus on getting better for now."

Soon, the ambulance arrived, and Emily watched as the paramedics loaded Tom onto a stretcher and into the back of the vehicle. She gave him a reassuring smile as they drove away, feeling a sense of satisfaction that she had been able to help. As she straightened her jacket and picked up her bag, Anjay came over and said, "You were amazing just now. Most people wouldn't have been that calm under pressure. He was lucky you were there."

"Will he be okay?" Emily asked.

"Yes, his leg is fine. The only thing I was concerned about was the bleeding, but the paramedics have that under control. He should make a full recovery."

"Is that what you do? Work in A&E with emergencies?" asked Emily.

Anjay smiled. "No, I couldn't hack that. I'm a surgeon. I focus on hands. I couldn't help but notice but you have beautifully slender fingers."

Blushing, Emily replied, "Oh, I bet you say that to all the girls," to which they both laughed.

"Look, I really don't normally do this, but do you want to grab a drink some time?" Anjay asked.

Emily froze. She hadn't even considered this. She had only just come out of her self-imposed exile and started to re-engage with society and here she was, day one of her new life, being asked out by a rather dishy surgeon. Her blunted instincts told her to say no and run away, but the old Emily was still inside her and before she knew what she was saying she replied, "Yes, that would be lovely."

"Great," said Anjay and punched his number into Emily's mobile. "There's my number. If I call it now from your phone…" Suddenly, from Anjay's pocket, Emily could hear a tinny version of Lady Gaga's *Poker Face*, which made Anjay blush. "Err, best you forget that bit," he started laughing.

Emily also chuckled and took back her phone, saying, "Look, it's great to meet you, but I should go."

Anjay smiled. "Me too. I'll text you later. It was great to meet you, Emily!" And with this, he turned away and walked down the street.

Emily paused. What a strange start to the day. Getting out of the house; helping a cyclist; meeting a possible date. Okay, but now she needed to focus, she told herself.

As she finally approached her new employer's headquarters, Emily's nerves kicked into overdrive. She checked her reflection in a nearby window, smoothing out her hair and unnecessarily tucking in her already tucked blouse. She wanted to make a good first impression; after all, this was the job of a lifetime. Taking a deep breath, Emily pushed open the door and stepped into the lobby, ignoring the butterflies in her stomach. This was it: the start of her new life in London.

*

As Emily entered the lobby of the impressive building, she thought back to how she had got there. She had video conferenced her way through the interviews, so this was the first time she had actually been in the offices, and they were exactly as she'd hoped. She had worked in her fair share of offices across the States, and she knew how important an impression they made, so was pleased that this one lived up to her expectations. Arriving after rush-hour meant she was alone apart from the grey-suited reception staff. Her heels clacked in loud echoes across the large space until she approached the reception desk, where a well-dressed woman greeted her with a warm smile.

"Good morning. How may I assist you?" the receptionist asked.

Emily inhaled deeply. "I'm Emily. Emily Taylor. I'm here for my first day at Harrison & Associates."

The receptionist checked her list and nodded. "Ah, yes. They are on the top two floors, twenty-nine and thirty. Let me just call up to let them know you're here."

Taking a seat, Emily only had to wait a few minutes before one of the lifts opened and a younger woman in her twenties came through the large security gates, smiling. As she reached Emily, she thrust out her hand.

"And you must be Emily," the woman announced happily. "I'm Annabel and I work for Darius. After all the emails, I feel like we know each other already," she said lightly and gestured Emily to follow her through security to the lift.

"I hope you don't mind, but I have to say that we're all absolutely thrilled that you're joining the team," Annabel beamed. "Even Darius, and that is very rare!"

"That's very kind of you."

"I'm sure you get this all the time, but the work you did on the Dawling case was amazing. I wouldn't say I'm a major feminist, but you were absolutely brilliant and made me proud to be a woman," Annabel gushed. "I hope it was okay me mentioning it?"

"No, not at all. Although that was quite a few years ago now…" said Emily politely.

"We couldn't believe it when you accepted the job here. You're going to give us a kind of edge on top of everything else we've got. It's so cool. By the way, you're going to love it here. It's so completely awesome."

"Great," said Emily and, feeling like she need to say more, added, "That's…well, that's what I'm hoping for…"

The lift doors opened onto a wide reception area with floor-to-ceiling views over the London skyline.

"This way," gestured Annabel and they walked down the wide corridor, arriving at a large set of wooden doors. Annabel knocked firmly and opened the door. "Emily Taylor for you, Darius," said Annabel, stepping to the side to let Emily walk into the large office. "Can I get you something to drink?" she added.

Emily stepped into the office, taking in its remarkable size and view, but quickly moving her appreciation to the furniture, which would have been more at place in a stately home. From the leather sofa to the grandfather clock, this was all assembled by someone who had not just money, but taste in how it should be spent. It was also a clear contrast to the rest of the building, and Emily wondered what this focus on the past and the classical said about its occupant. Emily quietly asked Annabel for a coffee, who disappeared with the request.

"Good morning, Ms Taylor," said Darius, stepping out from around his large mahogany desk to shake Emily's hand. "It's a pleasure to finally welcome you on board," he added.

"Thank you. Thank you so much. I'll be honest. It's been a little while since I've been in a corporate setting. I'm just taking it all in," she half-laughed. "Oh and please call me Emily, if that's appropriate?"

Darius smiled back in response. "Thank you, Emily. And I completely understand about getting back into the rhythm of things after taking a break. You just take whatever time you need to climatise to our hectic environment."

Emily focused her attention on Darius himself. He was definitely older looking than on the VC screen, but still looked very well for someone in his late fifties. He cultivated an eccentric academic uncle image, with tweed suit and well-trimmed white goatee. Even though he was going to be her new boss, after the various calls they'd had and her experience of dealing with a wide variety of *'important'* people in her previous life, she felt reasonably relaxed in his company.

Darius gestured towards one of a pair of leather armchairs and they both sat facing each other with the views over London to their side.

"I think it's fair to say that your joining has created quite a buzz in the office, Emily," Darius said. "It's just what we need right now. As you know, it's been a tough time for all of us here, from the pandemic and the economy and so on, to the bully boy tactics of our competitors. Not to mention the..." Darius paused.

"...the sexual harassment cases?" Emily added, fixing her gaze on him.

Darius almost imperceptibly shifted uncomfortably in his

seat. "Well, yes...those." He let the words hang in the air.

Although not reported widely in the media, it was common knowledge amongst lawyers that Harrison & Associates had gone through a bruising few years. A series of complaints had arisen about several of the senior partners and, when Darius hired an external company to investigate, they unearthed some of the worst behaviour in corporate life: bullying, harassment, even accusations of inappropriate behaviour on business trips. It had shocked the market that this well-respected company had allowed such activity to go on in its ranks. But, in his defence, Darius had got ahead of the problem. He had ruthlessly cut out the 'bad apples' and provided generous compensation to anyone affected. He had brought in new advisors on inclusivity, and made sure all staff were trained in a new code of conduct, with a whistle-blowing line for anyone who witnessed bad behaviour.

And the recruitment of Emily was the latest move in this transformation of the business. Emily had made a name for herself mainly in the US, representing a wide range of successful women who had been discriminated against by the patriarchy. She had an enviable reputation as someone who would challenge the status quo to get equity for women, and in most cases ensure they got the money they deserved. From entertainment artists who received a lower royalty share than their male equivalents, to C-suite executives who were offered less favourable contracts because of their gender, Emily had fought hard for all of them to get what they deserved. She was the best, or had been, until she stepped away from that life.

Now here she was at Harrison & Associates, and she was determined to make a go of it again. Whilst many of her clients had moved on to new legal representation, she was determined to build up a solid client list again. She knew she had to take a few steps down and would be at a lower level in the corporate world than she was used to. But it didn't matter. She loved her job and, regardless of everything that had happened—maybe even *because* of what had happened—she was looking forward to throwing herself into her work again.

Darius regained her attention by looking up and staring straight into her eyes to emphasise his point, "But, I am determined—*we* are all determined—to pull this company through the tough times and get it back to where it should be. Hence your appointment, along with some other critical changes. I am convinced that we can become the market leader again if we focus on the right things and get the perception to match the reality."

"And that's where I come in?"

"Exactly. That's where you come in. Only by having people of your skills and experience will we succeed. As we discussed, we need new blood and different perspectives. I want a firm that reflects our diverse client base, not one stuck in Victorian times."

Emily could feel the passion glowing around him like a halo. He was as driven as anyone she'd ever met, and she couldn't help wonder what he would—or more importantly, what he wouldn't—do, to get what he wanted.

They talked energetically for near on half an hour about where the company was going and what Emily's role would look like. Darius was extremely open, and he even told her about the idea of taking over another company, but Emily knew he was choosing his words very carefully. As he spoke, she could tell that he was shifting into autopilot and, although he spoke eloquently, she felt he was like an actor speaking well-rehearsed lines whilst his attention was focused on some other distant item. She didn't judge him for this as she too, having done her research and already well aware of most of what was being said, was lost in her own thoughts.

She also felt a loneliness emanating from him. As if he was a visitor from some other place and didn't follow the same ways as everyone else here. Only one degree out, but clear for all who were looking for it. She imagined that some of the more traditional City lawyers would be unsettled by someone who didn't follow their rules and fit their acceptable mould. This was what made

Darius special, and how he had differentiated himself, but Emily also wondered if this isolated him from everyone else?

She knew what that was like, more than most. She had been in the centre of the crowd for years, but since the tragedy, since her life fell apart, she had been truly alone.

*

"So, hopefully that's all clear, and all we need to do now is get you a pass for the building," said Janet, the representative from HR after she had taken Emily through all of the paperwork relating to her new job. "If you follow me, I'll take you to the dreaded security office…" she gently laughed.

As the two of them walked to the lifts they chatted about a variety of things, including Janet's teenage sons, who were quite a handful, and the best places to go and grab coffee nearby. Emily really liked Janet and immediately felt at ease in her company. As they got out of the lift in the basement of the building, they were presented with a subterranean world of exposed concrete blocks and pipework. They walked down a narrow corridor until they could see the security office up ahead.

"Look, I wasn't sure whether to say anything," said Janet, stopping abruptly in the corridor enough distance from Security so no one could hear, "but I've seen your file. I obviously knew about you before, but I also now know the details of what you've been through. And, well, I just wanted to say that I can only imagine how hard it is to come back to work after time off. So…" She swallowed and lent forward to touch Emily's arm gently. "So, if you need anything, anything at all, then just let me know. I am here to help."

Emily was struck dumb, and it was only after a moment of realising what Janet had said that she tried to reply, but instead could feel her eyes welling up. Unable to form a reply, she just nodded.

A panicked expression covered Janet's face and she exclaimed,

"Oh, I'm so sorry. I just wanted you to know that both Darius and I are rooting for you, and we will support you in any way we can."

"Thank you," Emily finally replied quietly.

"Oh no, I'm such an idiot. I've shaken you up, right before your security pass photo!"

They both started laughing and made their way into the large but low-ceilinged room full of security monitors. A large, older man sat at one of the desks and greeted them efficiently as they entered.

"Morning, Gary. Emily here has just started and needs a full access pass to our floors." Turning to the door, Janet said, "Emily, if you don't mind I'm going to leave you in the capable hands of Gary, who I'm sure will get a great photo of you. Won't you, David Bailey?"

Gary turned out to be a lovely but quiet individual and, a quarter of an hour later, Emily left the office resplendent with her new pass swinging round her neck.

Once in the lift, she checked her reflection to make sure she looked as composed as she now felt. It was fine. She was fine.

As the lift doors pinged to indicate the ground floor, no one entered and the lift doors started to close, but just as they were almost shut, a firm hand appeared in the middle and as the doors reopened, in strode one of the most handsome men she had ever seen. He was tall and broad-shouldered, with dark hair that fell in soft waves over his forehead. His deep brown eyes had an intensity even in the dim light, and Emily could feel her heart skip a beat.

Emily quickly composed herself and nodded, stepping back to let him in. He also pressed the button for the thirtieth floor and, as they rode up together, Emily couldn't help but steal glances at him. She felt a sudden connection, a spark of electricity that she couldn't explain. She felt she had to say something so she blurted out, "So, do you work at Harrison & Associates too?"

The man turned to look at her with a fixed, mildly curious,

stare as if being rudely awoken from his thoughts.

"Yes. Yes, I do. When you say 'too', do *you* work at Harrisson's?" he said, in a mildly condescending tone.

Emily could feel her heckles rising as she took offence at the man's response. The spark she had felt immediately doused by what she perceived as the micro-sexist response of this patriarchal figure. God, she had forgotten how the business world was stuffed with dinosaurs like these.

She folded her arms and turned away, determined to not even dignify the man with a response.

The man's eyes widened, and he looked as if he was about to say something. Then the lift pinged and they arrived at their floor.

As the doors fully opened, the man quickly stepped out into the bustling office, and Emily realised that she had stopped breathing. She looked over at the reception desk and, no sooner has she turned back to see where the man was, he had already gone, lost in the sea of people rushing around the office.

Emily couldn't shake the underlying feeling that she had just had one of those *moments* that life throws at you. It was disorientating how quickly the attraction that she had felt for the man had shifted to frustration with his tone-deaf response. Anyway, she dismissed it as being a silly, momentary attraction to a clearly handsome, if possibly unfriendly, man. It had been a long time since she'd had a 'crush' on someone, and it felt ridiculous to give the man even a second thought. But as she walked over to find Janet again, she couldn't help but wonder if fate would bring him back into her life ever again.

CHAPTER TWO

Jack

Jack stepped out of the elevator and made his way quickly to his office on the other side of the bustling law firm. He had just been in a lift with a strikingly attractive woman, but he wasn't the kind of man who would be so crass as to chat her up just because she looked attractive. He did try and engage her in conversation but felt uncharacteristically tongue-tied in her presence, and she had seemed to turn away rather than engage. It was strange, but he couldn't shake the feeling that he had seen her somewhere before.

As he walked down the deeply piled carpeted corridor, he tried to focus on the important cases that lay ahead of him, but his mind kept wandering back to the beautiful dark-haired woman he had just seen. There was definitely something special about her; there was something like a jolt of electricity that had gone through him at the mere sight of her. Jack shook his head, trying to clear his thoughts. He had work to do, cases to win, and he couldn't let a random physical attraction distract him from his job.

Entering his large corner office, he settled into his chair and started going through his emails on his tablet. Shortly after, his

PA Sarah, strode in behind him. "Well, well, well, look who's finally gracing us with his presence," she said, smirking. "Did you enjoy your exciting networking breakfast meeting?"

Jack rolled his eyes. "Nice. Listen, I need to ask you something. Did you happen to see the woman who was in the lift with me earlier?"

Sarah's eyes widened in delight. "Oh my word! Jack Braun checking out some lift totty!" she said, grinning and suggestively walking round his desk. "Do tell. Who's the lucky lady?"

Jack's face flickered with embarrassment then quickly composed itself. "It's not like that. There was something about her. I just… I thought I might have recognised her."

Sarah perched on the edge of his desk, still grinning. "Oh, I see. You're smitten. Well, I hate to burst your bubble, lover boy…but I would politely point out three small facts…" she said holding up three fingers to indicate her points, "One: I don't know anything about the woman in the lift, so I'm guessing she was here for a meeting. Two: if she is beautiful and smart, she naturally wouldn't be interested in someone like you. Three: *you are engaged*, dear boy. Or did your fiancée suddenly slip your mind?"

Jack scowled. "Very funny. You know what? You can be really annoying sometimes."

Sarah shrugged, still smirking. "Of course, that's what you pay me for. I'm just doing my job. Keeping you on your toes; someone has to."

He smiled gently, unable to stay annoyed at her for long. Sarah was often cocky and irreverent, but she was also one of the most efficient and hardworking people he knew. And despite her teasing, he knew she had his back.

"Fine, fine," he said, throwing up his hands. "You win. But if you do happen to hear anything about the woman in the lift, let me know."

"Will do, boss. Now, if you'll excuse me, I have some important PA duties to attend to," she said, giving him a playful salute as she sauntered out of the room, leaving Jack shaking his head to himself. Despite her sometimes infuriating personality, he knew he was lucky to have her on his team.

Jack settled back into his chair, feeling a bit more relaxed. As he glanced at the stack of paperwork on his desk, he couldn't help but think about the woman in the lift again. He ran his fingers through his hair, trying to clear his thoughts. Just then, his mobile rang. He stared at it, and then after a moment's consideration, answered it, and was immediately greeted by his fiancée, Kate.

"Hey babe, how's your day going?" she asked.

Jack forced a smile into his voice. "Oh, you know Same old, same old. Just another thrilling day at the office."

Kate laughed. "Well, I hope it's not too boring for you. I was just checking you hadn't forgotten that we're going shopping tonight. I was thinking we could go for dinner afterwards. Maybe that new Italian place you've been wanting to try?"

Jack hesitated for a moment. He had a feeling he was going to be working late again tonight, but he didn't want to disappoint her.

"No, of course I hadn't forgotten," he said finally. "I'll see you there, and dinner sounds great."

"Okay, no problem," she said. "See you later; love you."

"Love you too," Jack replied, hanging up the phone.

He sighed and leaned back in his chair, feeling a sense of unease settling in his stomach. He couldn't shake the feeling that something was off, that he was missing something important. And he couldn't help but wonder if the woman in the lift had anything to do with it.

*

Later that morning, Jack looked up from the stack of papers he had been concentrating on and, sighing, he rubbed his temples. He was making frustratingly slow progress through the reams of contractual papers that formed his current case. De-focusing his eyes and looking out of his office window, he snapped out of his thoughts and came back to his surroundings with a jolt. He needed coffee and to stretch his legs, so he rose from his desk and strode towards the kitchen area, still mulling over the vestiges of the documents he had been pouring through.

The office had employed a full-time barista who was deaf, a great guy called Stu, and so Jack stared at the menu to ensure he was able to sign the right order with his hands. He was so caught up with this and thoughts about work, that he didn't even consider the person in front of him in the queue who was waiting for Stu to finish making her coffee. It was only as she turned round, sipping her coffee, that Jack realised it was the woman from the lift, who recognised him at the same time.

"Oh. Hi," she said.

"Hello," replied Jack and, after a pause, added, "I didn't actually catch your name."

"I'm Emily," she replied, and Jack felt her eyes piercing into him as she explored his face for a reaction.

His pulse raced, which annoyed him as he saw no reason for it, but taking a moment to regain his composure he offered a slightly defensive, "I'm Jack. Jack Braun. I'm one of the partners here."

And then, before Jack could work out how to avoid an awkward silence, there was a loud knock from behind Emily which startled them both. As they turned back, Stu's smiling face greeted them and he gestured to the menu.

"Oh, I'm so sorry," said Jack and made the hand sign for a double espresso.

"You do that well," said Emily, at which Jack politely smiled. "Have you always been good with your hands?" she added, which caught Jack off-guard. His raised eyebrows prompted Emily to smirk. In response, and for the first time that day, Jack genuinely smiled and the crack in his formality brought out an equally warm smile from Emily.

"So, when you're not hanging around in lifts, do you actually work here?" asked Emily.

"Ah, yes. Sorry if I was a bit aloof earlier in the lift, you caught me deep in thoughts."

"Happy ones, I hope?"

"Just a tricky case I'm closing out. What about you? Are you thinking of joining the firm?"

"I've just started today."

Jack nodded, and then his expression changed. "Of course, you're Emily Taylor! How can I have been so stupid? I just wasn't expecting someone so…"

"So…?" asked Emily after a pause.

Jack regained his composure. "Well, uhm, it's great to have you as part of the team."

Jack took his coffee from Stu's outstretched hand and signed a thank you to the barista. He nodded to Emily and walked away, his heart rate far higher than it had any right to be.

*

Jack sat at the long, polished table in the conference room, surrounded by some of the other partners of the law firm. Seamus Hayes, one of the older partners at the firm, was lecturing the others on the latest changes to financial fraud regulations: a dry, technical subject that Jack couldn't seem to focus on. It didn't help that the large, overweight, grey Seamus had a way of speaking that was irritatingly condescending. Jack knew he should share the respect that the legal community had for this character, but Jack just didn't care for the pomposity, the casual discriminatory remarks he then excused by being from another time (Jack particularly hated the way Seamus referred to the woman in his team as "his girls") and the complete absence of teamwork with the other partners.

But Jack knew that Darius kept Seamus on board as he was one of the highest fee earners in the business. He had built up a solid client base who kept bringing their business to him, and that amount of income can give the benefit of the doubt to many questionable behaviours. When Darius purged the firm of the bad apples just over a year ago, many thought Seamus would also go, but there was no evidence that he had done anything wrong and Darius had made it clear that Seamus would stay. Jack's approach was to stay as far away from him as possible, so it pained him to have to sit quietly and listen to this windbag drone on.

Jack's mind drifted on to Emily Taylor: the way her eyes sparkled, the sound of her laugh, the way her hair fell in loose waves around her face. He had only met her briefly, but he was already slightly smitten. He was now worried that he had been too formal with her, too stiff-collared. Would she think him just another boring suit?

As the meeting droned on, Jack found himself doodling in the margins of his notes, drawing little caricatures of her. He knew he needed to snap out of it and focus on the discussion at hand, but he couldn't seem to shake the image of her out of his mind. He tried to tune back into the conversation, but it was like listening to white noise. Suddenly, his thoughts were interrupted by Annabel, Darius' PA, who knocked and put her head round the door asking if Jack would come to Darius' office.

Relieved, Jack got up and followed Annabel down the corridor, which brought back memories of being led down the wood-panelled corridors to the headmaster's office at his Prep School. He shook off the memory with an almost perceptible shudder and entered the office.

"Jack, I wanted to talk to you about this financial fraud case we've just landed," Darius said, his eyes never leaving Jack's. The head of the firm was a formidable man with a piercing stare and a reputation for being tough on those at the firm, but Jack had worked for him loyally for over a decade now and they had a mutual respect for each other, as well as there being something of a paternal relationship between them.

Darius continued, "We've been digging deeper, and we're starting to uncover some possible links to Russian organised crime. Have the team briefed you on this?"

Jack pushed aside his own worries about the case. "Yes, it's definitely something we need to keep a close eye on. We don't want another Kuvropol on our hands."

The head of the firm nodded, his expression inscrutable. "Agreed. I'm glad to hear you're taking it seriously. Mariya Svravipona is a new client, and I had some initial concerns given she's Russian, but she checked out as clean of any of that gangster rubbish. But I don't want our fingers burned on this, right Jack? I need you all over it and one whiff of crap, we're out. Understood?"

Jack nodded. "Of course. It has my full attention."

Darius sat back in his chair. "Good, good. But that's not all I wanted to talk to you about. We've a new partner starting today—Emily Taylor."

Jack smiled, "Ah yes, I've already met Ms Taylor."

"And?" Darius turned his focus towards Jack.

"Good. All positive. She was, er, younger, than I expected, but very, er, positive."

"Excellent," Darius said, bringing his fingers together in a steeple. "I think she will be a great addition to the team."

"I fully agree," replied Jack.

"And how are things going at home, Jack? With your fiancée and marriage and so on?" Darius asked, suddenly switching gears.

Jack felt a flush of embarrassment rise in his cheeks. He had never been completely comfortable discussing his love life with his boss, or anyone outside of his closest friends for that matter, but Darius was like a father to him in many ways and was just being supportive in his own way.

"It's, well…it's going well," Jack replied, trying to keep his tone neutral.

The head of the firm leaned back in his chair. "That's good

to hear. A happy home life can be a valuable asset in this line of work."

Jack tried not to roll his eyes. He knew Darius was just trying to make conversation, but when he was at his clumsiest, it was hard to take him seriously.

"Is there anything else you wanted to discuss?" Jack asked, eager to escape the awkward conversation.

Darius shook his head. "No, no, that's all for now. But keep up the good work. I expect great things from you."

Jack nodded, relieved, and made a quick exit from the office. He experienced a twinge of annoyance at the way his boss had pryingly switched the topic of the conversation, but he tried to push it aside and focus on the task at hand. The financial fraud case was complex and daunting, and he knew he needed to give it his all if he wanted to succeed.

*

That evening, throngs of couples glided between the sparkling bright shelves of cutlery and dinner sets, as Jack traipsed behind his fiancée in a high-end department store in London's West End. He was trying his best to feign interest in the various crystal stemware and designer cutlery thrust into his face. He had never been particularly interested in material possessions, and the idea of compiling a wedding gift list seemed like a pointless exercise to him. But he didn't want to disappoint Kate, who seemed to be thoroughly enjoying the experience. He tried to put on a polite smile as she cooed over each item, imagining what their life together would be like with all these beautiful things.

As they moved from department to department, the tension between them grew thicker. She would shoot him annoyed glances whenever he seemed bored or uninterested, and Jack would feel his temper rise whenever she insisted on adding yet another expensive item to the list. Every item added to the list seemed like another nail in the coffin of his way of thinking and his freedom. Not freedom from Kate, but freedom from the material and banal. He felt himself being dragged down by all these trinkets.

"Let's pause a bit," said Kate, turning to him. "Come on, let's pop in here." She grabbed his hand and lead him into the small champagne bar in the store. They sat at the end of the small bar and ordered a glass of Tattinger each and, after a pause, Kate looked deep into his eyes and asked what was wrong.

Jack eventually answered, "It's nothing. Honestly, just work and so on."

Kate's face showed concern. "Really? You just seem so… distant."

"I'm sorry. I really am. You know I'm not much of a shopper, and places like this turn me cold."

"As long as you're not having second thoughts, Mr Grumpy," she said, smiling.

Jack straightened up, took her hand, and said, "Of course not. I love you."

A look of relief flickered across Kate's face, and she turned the conversation to wedding details and their respective families. At this, Jack couldn't help but feel a pang of sadness as he thought about his own parents, both of whom had passed away in his teens. They had never seen his career achievements, or the life he had built for himself. His fiancée's family, on the other hand, was a picture of perfection. They were wealthy and successful, with strong family ties and a seemingly endless supply of love and support for one another. They loved Jack and he loved them, so much so that he felt that they were a key part of his decision to propose to Kate a year ago.

They finished their drinks and, with the alcohol softening his mood, he was able to relax slightly. As they made their way through the store again, Jack tried to hard to focus on the life that lay before him and consider how lucky he was and would be. But before long, he once again began to feel increasingly trapped. He was getting married in a few short months, and he still wasn't sure if this was what he really wanted. For reasons he couldn't explain, the woman he had met in the lift kept creeping into his thoughts, and he couldn't shake the feeling that something wasn't quite right.

His thoughts were interrupted by Kate's voice, pulling him back to reality. "Jack, are you even listening to me?" she asked, her voice again tinged with annoyance.

"Yes. Yes, of course. I was just, um…" He said, trying to focus on her words, but with his mind constantly drifting.

As they moved on to the next section of the store, Kate started to complain again about his lack of enthusiasm. "I know you don't enjoy this, but couldn't you throw yourself into it just for me. You don't have to be so quiet and grumpy all the time," she said, tossing her hair back in frustration.

"I'm not grumpy," Jack replied, trying to keep his voice even. "I just don't see the point in all of this." He waved his hand around indicating all the shelves of homeware.

Kate huffed, unimpressed with his response. "Well, I see the point in it," she snapped. "We're getting married. We need to start building our life together. Oh, for goodness' sake!" she stormed off down one of the aisles.

Jack felt a pang of guilt as he watched her walk away. He knew she was right, of course. But he just couldn't help the feeling that this was all wrong.

CHAPTER THREE
Emily

Emily stood outside the tube station, a combination of anticipation and nervousness fluttering within her. It was a few days after her first day back at work and she had agreed to go on a dinner date with Anjay, the compassionate doctor she had met when they had both helped the injured cyclist. Memories of their shared act of kindness and their easy camaraderie lingered in her mind.

As Anjay approached, a warm smile graced his face, instantly putting Emily at ease. Their eyes met, and she felt an immediate connection. They exchanged pleasantries and, as they walked down the street, they discussed how their days had gone. The conversation flowed effortlessly, punctuated by laughter and shared anecdotes.

Anjay had chosen his favourite Italian restaurant for the meal and, as they settled into a cosy corner table at the restaurant, the soft lighting and gentle music created an intimate ambiance. Whilst Emily had been used to the high-end restaurant scene in Manhattan, she still loved the charm of these small, family-run, trattoria that you could find just outside the busy centre of London.

Emily admired the twinkle in Anjay's eyes as he spoke, his passion for his work as a doctor evident in every word.

"I still can't believe that accident. That poor cyclist. I'm glad we were both there to help," said Emily, as he played with the cutlery in front of her.

Anjay looked up and into her eyes. "Me too. It looked like a bit of a nasty break, but I'm sure he'll be okay. I'm planning to swing by the hospital to check in on him and I'll let you know. Anyway, as tragic as it was, there was a positive side; after all, we got to meet each other."

Their connection deepened as they delved into personal stories and experiences. Emily found herself drawn to Anjay's genuine and compassionate nature, but she still found herself cautious about sharing too many pieces of her own life.

"So, Anjay, what made you choose a career in medicine?"

"Well, growing up I always wanted to make a difference to people's lives. I initially thought I wanted to be an engineer like my father, but there were several doctors in my family who I thought of as heroes. When it came time to choose a career they were a big, and I have to say positive, influence. They showed me you could help people and the community more than any other job. It inspired me to pursue medicine and help others in the same way."

Emily smiled, warming to the passion Anjay had for his job. "That's so lovely. It takes a special kind of person to dedicate themselves to such a challenging career."

"Thank you. It's not always easy, but it's incredibly fulfilling. Speaking of which, what about you? What led you to your line of work?"

As the evening wore on, they both enjoyed the conversation, each sharing anecdotes and views. Emily was still cautious but couldn't help feeling a growing sense of comfort in Anjay's presence—a familiarity that transcended their brief acquaintance and one that she'd not felt for some time.

As the evening progressed, they savoured their meals,

engaging in light-hearted banter and moments of shared laughter. However, the weight of their respective emotional struggles started to enter the conversation like a dark mist rolling towards them from the corners of the room. As Emily started talking about her new job and rebuilding her life, she could see Anjay's smile slip and a flicker of sadness cross his expression.

"Are you okay?" she asked, worried that she had said something to annoy him.

"Emily, I must admit something. The truth is, I'm still struggling with things in my past. I was separated and then divorced last year, and I didn't cope with it very well. I now accept that my marriage ended because I was always consumed by my work, but last year I was angry and hurt, and…well, I wasn't a great person to be around. I still love my wife and I think I always will. I've only been on one date before and that didn't work out well because I just couldn't commit because I'm…I don't know, I'm just broken. I still feel so raw emotionally, I find it hard to open up and trust."

Anjay sighed and looked down at the table.

"I'm so sorry, I don't want to be dramatic but I just don't want to mess you around. I should never have asked you out…"

As he trailed off, Emily reached out her hand "Hey, it's fine. Really."

"I'm so, so sorry. I thought now was different and that you were different and that *I* was different, but now I realise that I still need time. You are so perfect and I've had a great time tonight, but what I realise is that I'm just going to end up messing you around and I really don't want to do that."

Emily listened attentively, her heart imbued with empathy. She surprised herself at being able to put aside any frustration and annoyance. Understanding the pain of unresolved emotions, the longing for closure and healing, she squeezed his hand.

"Oh, I'm so sorry. No matter whose fault it is, it is always hard on everyone when a marriage comes to an end. I won't say I know what you're going through; I don't, but I know the pain that I've experienced and…"

Emily stopped as the lump in her throat became too big and she quickly withdrew her hand and grabbed her glass of water, partly to hide her face and to help her control the tears.

"Emily? Are you okay?" asked Anjay, leaning forward.

She silently nodded her head and looked down at her lap.

"Do you want to talk about it?"

After a few moments, Emily looked up at him, "I can't. I just can't."

Anjay recognised a fellow victim of heartbreak, and they sat in silence for several minutes.

Emily broke the silence, "It takes courage to open up and I love the fact that you've shared your pain with me. Especially as we've only just met. But, and I kind of hate myself for saying this, I'm not going to be the person that fixes you. I'm not sure I'm strong enough for me right now, let alone supporting someone else."

Anjay stiffened and his expression hardened. "I don't need someone else to *fix* me. What I need is time to heal. I can see this was a mistake."

"Oh my. I'm so sorry, Anjay. I didn't mean it like that. What I meant was that I think you're great and if we were both in a good place then maybe there could be something between us, but let's be honest we're both…."

"Damaged goods?" said Anjay, a smile slowly returning to his face.

Emily exhaled gently and then also smiled. "Yes, damaged goods, indeed."

"Look, I'm sorry. I didn't mean to take offence and I certainly didn't mean to come on a date with no hope of it going anywhere. I just really liked you and wanted to see where it went."

"I feel the same," said Emily, feeling her eyes getting moist.

With sadness in his eyes, Anjay said quietly, "Look, you're a very special woman. But as much as I've enjoyed tonight, I'm not ready. I see that now. To meet someone as amazing as you and not want to take it forwards…Well, it means that there's more healing I need to do and, from what you say, maybe both of us need to."

As the evening drew to a close, they savoured their final moments together, the realisation slowly settling between them that their paths were not yet aligned.

Amidst the bittersweet conclusion of the evening, the two lost souls shared a heartfelt goodbye. They thanked each other for the laughter, the companionship, and the glimpse of what could have been. Their eyes reflected a mutual understanding of the paths they needed to travel separately. Emily walked away sad but also with a newfound gratitude. In Anjay, she had witnessed resilience and strength, mirroring her own struggles. This encounter had taught her that even in the midst of heartache and emotional upheaval, there were others who carried their burdens with grace and resilience.

With each step forward, Emily carried the knowledge that her journey was not unique. The world was populated with so many souls seeking solace and healing, just like her. And with this realisation, she found a renewed sense of hope, knowing that, as she continued to navigate her own healing, she would encounter kindred spirits along the way.

*

The sun streamed in through the large windows of Darius' office, and Emily noticed the dust motes dancing in the sunbeams above his expansive oak desk. Emily and Jack sat in silence waiting for Darius to arrive. They hadn't spoken more than a greeting to each other since they first met in the office a few days before, and now didn't seem like the right time to have a proper conversation.

Suddenly Darius stormed in and looked at them both, his expression unreadable. He pulled back his chair and stood behind his desk. Emily couldn't help wondering if he was actually going to sit down before he spoke. She had seen way too much of this kind of postering during her time in the US for it be effective, so she ignored it, instead picking off an imaginary speck of dust on her jacket.

"Thank you both for coming in," Darius began, his tone serious. "I have something important for both of you."

Emily felt a flicker of interest. This could be interesting, she thought to herself. Whilst she had only been at the firm for a few days, she was very keen for her first heavyweight case.

Darius grabbed his chair and sat down. "As you know, we have a new client, Mariya Svravipona, and we are restructuring her business 'empire' to move it onto a more robust footing. Well, she has been pleased with our work to date, so has brought us a new challenge. She is concerned that her husband and business partner has been embezzling money from various companies and doing it through a holding company they have in Bermuda. She wants us to investigate from both a financial fraud," Darius gestured towards Jack, "and a divorce angle," he then nodded at Emily.

Darius opened the leather writing pad in front of him and added, "There are, erm, concerns that all is not quite legal, and the business partner will disappear with the money."

"Who is the business partner?" asked Emily quickly.

"A Sergey Kuchovski. We've not come across him before."

After a moment's pause, Jack frowned. "With all due respect, I think it would be better if someone with more experience worked with me on this case."

Emily's expression instantly turned to shock, and even Darius raised an eyebrow. "And who would you suggest?"

"Well, one of the more senior partners, perhaps," Jack said, his voice hesitant. Turning to Emily, he dispassionately said, "Ms Taylor, this is nothing personal, but a matter this, well…delicate, needs someone with deep experience of international finance."

"I'm not sure short-changing my career in one sentence could be *more* personal, Mr Braun," retorted Emily coolly.

Emily was ready to launch a tirade of arguments, when Darius held up his hand quickly and said, "Stop. Stop. I've already made my decision. This is a complex case which will need both our best financial crime and civil litigation capabilities, and that's the two of you. Unless either of you still disagree?"

Emily shook her head, her heart pounding. She had been hoping for a chance to prove herself, but she didn't want her first opportunity to be one where someone like Jack Braun had doubts about her ability.

Jack didn't say anything, but his expression was grim as he stood up to leave the office.

As they stepped out into the hallway, Emily could sense Jack's anger. "I can't believe this," he muttered. "Darius is making a big mistake."

Emily's frustration boiled over. "What the hell is that supposed to mean?" she demanded.

"Honestly? It means that you're not ready for a case like this," Jack said, turning to face her. "It's nothing personal, but you've only just come back to work and this isn't one of your Hollywood types getting a better divorce payout. This will be complex, and I don't want to be responsible for any mistakes you make."

Emily's cheeks flushed with anger. "How dare you! I've worked on cases like this before and dealt with complexity that would have you reeling, you egotistical prick!"

Jack's whole face looked shocked, and he struggled to respond.

Emily stepped into a nearby empty meeting room and turned to Jack shouting "In here. Now!"

As Jack entered the meeting room uncertainly, Emily slammed the door behind him.

She stepped right in front of him and raised her voice aggressively at Jack, "Right, Mr 'Team-player', maybe you could explain to me how you and your financial crime buddies are going to file dissolution proceedings, negotiate their way through whatever pre-nup is in place and get all of our client's money back? That is, even if you can find the money in the first place?"

Jack stood dumbfounded; he hadn't been spoken to like this for years.

"No? Okay, how are you going to get an interlocutory injunction to get the money frozen when you don't even know where this Sergey guy is?"

Jack started to reply, but Emily cut him off, thrusting her forefinger in front of his face.

"No, I didn't think so. So, look here, Braun. Let me do my job and you do yours. I am very good at what I do and don't need to prove myself to you or anyone. I had a client list you could only dream of and more successes over the past decade than most lawyers would achieve over their whole career. So, if you ever tell me that I'm '*not ready*' or if I even smell a whiff of you getting in the way of me or my team, then I will come for you and serve up your balls on a gilded plate. Do you understand me?"

She didn't give Jack a chance to reply, flinging open the meeting room door and storming off down the corridor.

As she turned the corner, she started to breathe heavily and, ducking quickly into the ladies' toilets, she found herself hyperventilating. *What the hell*, she thought, *am I having a panic attack?* She locked herself into one of the cubicles and sat on the toilet, focusing on calming her breathing. She used the exercises that her therapist had taught her. The adrenaline that was coursing through her body slowly receded, leaving a metallic taste at the back of her mouth. After what seemed like eternity, she could feel her body coming out of the shock.

Only then did she start to think about what had just happened. She was horrified that she had just spoken to a fellow senior partner like that, especially given she had only just started. But then she considered it more; sure, she had possibly been a bit strong with her points, but everything she had said was true. Well, apart from serving up his testicles on a plate.

She found herself chuckling at this, partly embarrassed at how direct she'd been. But she had been through too much to put up with people under-valuing or disrespecting her. Whether it was a sexism thing or something else, it didn't matter. She knew who she was and what she was capable of, and people could either accept that or get out of the way. As she was painfully aware, life was too short to not be direct and honest with people.

Hell, she felt good; energised like she hadn't been for so, so long. She freshened up and walked back to her desk. As she sat down, ready to prepare for this new case, she suddenly realised one thing: the old Emily was coming back.

*

Later that afternoon, Jack and Emily arrived at the sleek offices of Mariya Svravipona's company in West London, taking note of the opulence around them. The receptionist, a young woman with long blonde hair and a welcoming smile, showed them into a large boardroom that had the feel of a library, with the walls covered in bookshelves on three sides and the other containing a large window with a view of the stately Victorian redbrick buildings across the street.

As they waited for Mariya, Emily considered saying something to Jack about their confrontation earlier. They hadn't really spoken since, and this meeting with the client has been arranged by Jack's PA, Sarah, who had come over to introduce herself. She seemed nice, but Emily had picked up an undercurrent of something loaded in how, rather than what, she said. Jack hadn't been around when she planned to leave the Harrison & Associates office, so she had jumped in a black cab alone, and it was only when she pulled up outside the building that she saw Jack pacing the street deep in conversation on his mobile.

My word, thought Emily. *He still looks fabulous.* As he moved, Emily could see that his well-cut, probably Saville Row-tailored suit, covered a well looked after physique. Emily couldn't reconcile the way she felt in his presence, which held this undeniable animal magnetism, with the cold and deeply objectionable manner in which he acted. She needed to put the attraction to one side, or she was going to get steamrollered by someone who didn't give two hoots about her feelings. After all, she was Emily Taylor, successful lawyer; she didn't need this man's attraction.

As she had walked towards him, all she'd received from Jack was a quick nod, before he turned and entered the office, which Emily followed him into.

So, they waited in silence, which after a few minutes was broken by the receptionist reappearing with a tray containing a coffee pot and cups made of delicate bone china, which she set down on the table before leaving the room. Jack and Emily sipped their coffees apprehensively, feeling like they were about to be in the presence of someone very powerful.

Finally, the door opened, and Mariya strode into the room. She was a short woman, with delicate features but shocking peroxide blonde hair. She wore an expensive trouser suit that was perfectly tailored, but the large amount of gold jewellery and the way she carried herself made it clear that this was a woman who was as used to the streets as she was the boardroom.

Mariya 's face was twisted in anger as she sat down and eyed both of them closely. Jack started to speak, but she interrupted loudly. "I don't have time for your British introductions and whatever," she said gruffly in a thick Russian accent. "I've been betrayed by that piece of scum husband of mine, and I want to know that you're going to find my money. You must stop him from disappearing with it into Russia."

Jack started to explain the process that the team would follow, but Mariya interrupted him again. "Blah. Blah. I don't care about your corporate nonsense," she barked waving her heavily jewelled hand. "I want action, and I want it now. What are you going to do?"

Jack's face stayed impassively still. He had to deal with all manner of clients in his work, and his normal strategy was just to let them expend all the energy until they were ready to talk sensibly about the matter.

Not receiving an immediate response, Mariya stood up and started pacing the room. "Do you know how much money is at stake here? Do you know how long it took to make that money? Can you even think what I had to do to make that money? The sweat. The sacrifices..." she said loudly. She then turned and, gripping the back of her chair with both hands while sinking her long nails deep into the leather, she hissed, "You sit there, in your expensive suit, calmly talking of 'process' and 'claims' but what I want is vengeance. Yes, I want my money, but I want more. I want him destroyed." She froze, staring deep into Jack's eyes, scanning them for something... Maybe weakness?

Emily couldn't bear the tension in the room, and couldn't see how these two strong characters were going to stop posturing and start working, so she cleared her throat and spoke directly to Mariya.

"Ms. Svravipona, let me speak plainly. We understand how important this is to you, and we're going to do everything we can to help," she said calmly. "We know how to do this; we've done it before and we'll do it again for you. But to be successful, there are lots of tedious steps we need to get through, and we need you to be comfortable that we're getting on with things. I know it's frustrating, but we'll get results. If you want your money, you just need to trust us. We know what we're doing and, whilst this may appear slow and boring, it will get you the results you want."

Mariya cocked her head to one side as she considered Emily. In a gesture of acceptance, she sat back down and spread her hands palm down in front of her.

Jack relaxed ever so slightly and tried to regain control of the conversation. "My colleague is right. We understand your frustration, but we need to follow the proper procedures to make sure we have a solid case against Sergey before we take any action."

Mariya snorted. "Procedures? You lawyers and your procedures. Sergey has already taken over twenty-five million from the company. You think he's going to sit and wait for you to finish your paperwork? No, he's going to run back to Moscow and disappear with my cash."

"We'll do everything we can to prevent that, Mariya," Emily interjected, trying to keep the situation from escalating further, and checking that her client didn't mind her using her first name. "But we need to work together and gather the evidence before we can take any action."

Mariya's eyes narrowed, studying Emily for a moment before turning back to Jack. "And you, are you as effective as you look? You are young man. Do I not need a wise, old head to take care of this?"

Jack clenched his jaw, feeling his anger rise at the condescending tone. "I may not be the oldest partner in our firm, but I have a lot of experience in this area and have worked on a number of similar cases, many for individuals from your background. And with Emily's expertise beside me, I am very confident we can handle this."

Mariya leaned forward, her voice low and menacing. "You better be right. My money is at stake, and I won't tolerate mistakes."

"We understand the seriousness of this situation," Emily said firmly. "Rest assured, we will do everything in our power to bring Sergey to justice and recover your funds."

Mariya 's face softened slightly, and she leaned back in her chair. "I hope so, Miss…?"

"Emily. Just call me Emily."

Mariya's expression finally cracked into a smile. "Emily. I am counting on you and Mr Braun. Do not disappoint me."

"We won't," Jack said firmly, meeting Mariya's gaze.

With that, Mariya stood up and walked out the door, signalling the end of the meeting. The receptionist reappeared shortly after and escorted them out of the building. Once they were outside, Emily let out a long breath, feeling the weight of the case settle on her shoulders.

*

As they walked down the street, they both appreciated the silence between them; they were both slightly punch-drunk from the encounter with that powerful woman. Eventually, Jack slowed his pace so he was level with Emily.

"That could have gone better," Emily remarked, walking beside him.

"I can't believe you did that," Jack said, his voice rising. "You completely undermined me in front of the client."

"What are you talking about?" Emily replied, incredulous. "I was just trying to calm her down. You were just making her angrier."

"Well, *I* was just trying to explain the process to her," Jack retorted. "You had no right to step in like that."

"I had every right," Emily snapped back. "I'm on this case too, you know. It was my opinion that the best course of action was to act like a human being and connect with her on a personal level."

"Well, I don't think it was your place," Jack replied, his tone icy. "And you should have let me handle it."

Emily rolled her eyes. "Fine, Mr Know-It-All. Next time, I'll just sit quietly and let you do all the talking. Perhaps you'd like me just to sit there and take notes for you, sir?"

"That's not what I'm saying," Jack said, exasperated. "I just think we need to present a united front to the client. We can't have you contradicting me in front of her."

"I wasn't contradicting you," Emily said, her voice rising again. "I was just trying to make her feel heard and understood. And it worked, didn't it? She calmed down."

Jack shook his head, still fuming. "I don't know why Darius paired us up on this case. You clearly don't respect my authority."

"That is absolutely not true," Emily protested. "But I do question *your* view on *my* authority. I'm not desperate to lead this case, but I won't just sit back and take orders like some brand-new graduate trainee. Right now, we need to work together to get this case sorted."

They reached a busy street corner and stopped walking, glaring at each other.

"I can't believe we're arguing like this," Jack said, his tone softening. "We're supposed to be a team…"

"Then *you* need to act like we're a team. Your grumpiness might work with others, but it doesn't wash with me. I've dealt with bigger and uglier bullies than you in my time."

Jack sighed and looked away. "Look, let's draw a line under today. We can meet first thing tomorrow and I'll try and accommodate your input more… If you promise to calm down."

"Calm down? Calm down? I *am* calm, you…you…"

"I just meant…" said Jack hurriedly trying to dig himself out of the hole, then he suddenly stopped, muttered, "Oh, forget it," and walked away down the road.

Emily watched as Jack disappeared around a corner and started to question herself. Had she been too hard on him? No, he had to learn to respect her as the experienced lawyer she was.

Oh my word, thought Emily. *This is going to be seriously hard work.*

CHAPTER FOUR
Jack

Bloody hell, she is so *infuriating*, thought Jack as he walked away from Emily. He hadn't felt this emotional for as long as he could remember; it was as if his heart and head were at war. The more he got to know Emily, the more he found her attractive; she was smart, beautiful, but more than that she just had this effect on him. But his head fought this, reminding him that, not only was she deeply annoying, but she was a work colleague, and one who had only just returned to work after a major trauma. He didn't know the details, but occasionally she had a haunted look in her eye, which he recognised. She had seen tragedy and been shaped by it. His head was right, it would not only be inappropriate for him to even think about Emily in that way, it was also completely immoral given that he was engaged. Engaged. OMG, did he deliberately hide this away in his thoughts? It was like a debt hanging over him.

He had to keep his emotions to himself, something that wasn't usually a problem for him. But there was something about Emily that he just couldn't shake off. The more he pushed away his feelings, the bigger they were when they came back.

He instinctively looked at his watch and with alarm he

realised that he was running late to meet Nate. He quickened his pace as he walked down the street.

Twenty minutes later, Jack arrived at the exclusive private club in Pall Mall, where he had arranged to play squash with his old university friend, Nate. Entering the club and nodding to Charlie, the porter, he breathed in the homely smell of leather and wood polish. Walking past the grand foyer, he slipped down a wide staircase with mahogany wood panelling, towards the changing rooms in the basement.

As he strode towards his locker, he saw Nate tying his laces. His friend looked up and smiled at him. "Ah, Brauny, how the devil are you?"

Jack smiled and shook Nate's hand warmly, replying "Very well, Nate-y, very well. And all the better for seeing you."

They exchanged friendly insults and banter as they got ready and then made their way to the courts. As they got ready to play, Nate gave Jack a straight-man look. "You ready to lose again, old man?"

Jack laughed. "I don't actually recall you ever beating me. I think you may be the one who's going to be in trouble."

The game began and they were evenly matched. The ball flew back and forth between them, with Jack making quick, agile movements to return Nate's shots. Sweat dripped down their faces as they exerted themselves, trying to outdo each other. They pushed themselves to their limits, knowing that only one of them could emerge victorious. They moved quickly around the court, breathing heavily despite their obvious fitness. Nate had always been a skilled player, but over the years they had played, Jack had always kept up and sometimes even overtaken him.

As the game progressed, the comments got harsher, but still in good spirits. "You're not as fast as you used to be, old man!" Nate yelled as he returned a shot.

Jack panted in reply, "We're the same bloody age, you fool!"

Their competitive nature was evident, but they still

maintained a sense of humour throughout the game. They knew how to push each other's buttons, but never took it too far. Both were determined to win. Jack was ahead by a few points when Nate made a crucial mistake, missing the ball and careering into the wall. "Damn it!" Nate exclaimed.

"Looks like I'm going to win this one," Jack said with a grin.

Rubbing his side, Nate smiled. "Not so fast, buddy boy. We're not done yet."

Each of the last few points became more intense. Finally, Jack hit a perfect shot into the back corner that Nate couldn't return. "Game!" Jack declared.

After a long and gruelling game, Jack had finally emerged as the winner, but only just. They both stood bent over and holding their sides panting.

Eventually, when he had caught his breath, Nate walked over to Jack and held out his hand. "Well done, matey." Jack shook his hand and they both laughed as they wiped the sweat from their faces.

"Now that was a close one," Nate said, grinning.

"Yeah, you almost had me. Good job you're getting slower," Jack laughed, still panting slightly.

As they left the court, they showered, changed and headed to the bar upstairs to grab a drink and catch up.

*

Jack and Nate walked up to the private bar at the back of the club's top floor, with a stunning view of the sun setting over this part of central London.

"So, how's Adele?" Jack asked, taking a sip of his Barolo.

"She's doing great," Nate replied with a smile. "In fact, I have news…"

Ever the showman, Nate let the pause develop between them with a glint in his eye. "Adele's pregnant. We'll be adding another member to the family at the end of the year."

"Oh wow. Congratulations, old chap," Jack exclaimed, slapping his friend on the shoulder and clinking his glass against Nate's. "I'm really, truly happy for you. That's it, though. Middle age here you come!"

Nate grinned. "Yep, it's a lot of work, but it's worth it. Being a father is the best thing that's ever happened to me. It's also brought Adele and I even closer. I know that doesn't happen for everyone, but for us, having Tommy and spending time as a family has been the happiest moments of my life."

Jack nodded and frowned almost imperceptibly, taking another sip of his drink. "And how's work been?"

"It's been busy," Nate replied. "But I can't complain. I love my job, and it pays the bills, you know?"

"Oh, I hear that."

"And what about you, matey?"

"Fine. It's all…fine" Jack said, leaning back in his chair.

Nate raised an eyebrow. "Really? That sounds far from convincing."

"Oh, I don't know. I just feel I'm not making any progress. I'm doing the same stuff I was years ago. Same old, same old. Up until this week, I felt like I was stuck on autopilot just going through the motions and getting the right result. Everyone happy but me…"

Nate sighed and looked Jack straight in the eye. "You need to pull yourself together, matey. You have no idea how lucky you are. Great job, great fiancée, great life. You just need to get your direction back."

Jack looked away over the city. "You're right. Of course, you're right. But…"

"And how is the wonderful Kate?" smirked Nate.

"Easy, tiger," Jack said, with an edge to his voice. "She's fine. Look, I know you guys don't completely take to her. Sure, she can be an acquired taste, but she is all the things I've ever wanted: smart, funny, beautiful."

"C'mon Jack, don't be so bloody sensitive, I'm only joshing.

She's great and, when you first started dating, she really brought you out of yourself. It's only that she can be a bit full-on sometimes and we worry for you. You're like a brother to Adele and me, and we just want to see you happy."

"I know. I know. It's just that…"

"Just what?"

Jack shifted in his seat and ran his fingers though his hair. "How did you know, Nate?"

"Know what?"

"That Adele was 'the one'? How did you get to a point that you knew?"

"Honestly? I didn't. Very few people do. You have to take a leap of faith. But that's not the same as having genuine doubts."

Nate could see that Jack had lost the colour in his face and his pained expression looked grey. "The thing is, I just don't know what I feel. And I'm so used to making big, complicated decisions at work that I find it inconceivable that something so small as whether I should marry an amazing woman like Kate should have any doubt about it. What is wrong with me?"

"Jack, there is nothing wrong with you. Nothing at all. You are just having wedding jitters, that's all."

Jack nodded and drank deeply from his glass. The two of them sat in silence, engrossed in their respective thoughts and just being comfortable in each other's company.

"And what happened this week?" Nate said breaking the silence.

"How do you mean?"

"You said, everything was boring up until this week. So what happened this week?"

Jack froze, only just realising what he had said. When talking about his life, he had inadvertently mentioned Emily. Had he done it consciously? He was suddenly painfully aware that something had shifted and that she had made a bigger impact than he could have imagined or wanted.

Nate stared at him. "You okay, Jack?"

"The past week, it's been... interesting," Jack said, choosing his words carefully.

The reality was that Jack didn't know what to think or feel about the past week. He neither had the time nor inclination to bring his feelings up to the surface and consider them. All he knew was that he had been shunted on to a different track by Emily entering his world.

He looked up and realised that he had been lost in his own thoughts. "A new lawyer has started at work."

"Oh. New competition for the mighty Jack? Who is he?"

"No, no, not like that. Her name is Emily Taylor," Jack replied quietly.

"*The* Emily Taylor? The feminist lawyer, Emily Taylor?"

Jack nodded and Nate blew the air out of his cheeks. Laughing, he said "Now I get it. You're smitten!"

"Absolutely not," said Jack, a little louder than he expected.

Nate raised his hands as if surrendering. "Okay, okay, I'm not going to give you a hard time."

Jack untensed slightly. "It's not like that."

Nate just grinned.

Jack's expression lightened slightly. "It's just that...well, she brings something different to the firm," he said, a note of hesitation in his voice.

Nate raised an eyebrow. "To the firm?"

"Yes, the company needs talent like her," Jack mused, stroking the stubble on his chin.

Nate took a beat and stared at his friend before continuing. "Look, Jack, you and I have known each other since we were at school. So my 'job' is not to dress things up or pander to your massive ego, but to tell you how it is." He paused to make sure Jack was taking this in. "And really, despite all of the corporate rubbish that you've just spewed out like a PR machine reading out the company policy on diversity and recruitment. Despite that fact that your life is complicated. Despite you being unsure about your upcoming marriage, which by the way you looked when it came up, is making you ill. Despite *all* of these things, there is one thing that I am convinced about, which I don't think you, in your highly intelligent brain has actually figured out, and that is…"

Nate couldn't resist inserting another dramatic pause.

"The one thing is…that you have a little crush on our new friend, Emily Taylor."

*

The following day, Jack was at his desk going through the large pile of papers in front of him and occasionally making comments in his notepad, when he found something of interest. At a knock on his half-open door, he looked up to see Sarah, his PA, grinning at him. Jack gestured for her to come in and she proceeded to enter and sit in the chair on the other side of his desk.

"So, I've been asked if you have time for an extremely important person," she said with a smirk.

"Who?" Jack asked distractedly, still partly lost in his thoughts.

"What if I was to say that this was someone who you were getting to know and others—not me, I stress—had noticed you had a soft spot for?"

Jack sighed and stared at Sarah, his icy mood thawing as he took in her friendly smile.

"I think such comments, even shared, would contravene our HR policy on workplace etiquette and would probably result in some form of disciplinary action."

"Disciplinary?" said Sarah, raising one eyebrow. "Sounds painful."

"Only as painful as the door to the firm hitting one's rear as they were rapidly exited."

"Ouch," said Sarah in mock shock. "Of course, I know you're joking…"

"Do you? Why?"

"Well my suspicions were first raised when you quoted one of the firm's HR policies, which I know for a fact you couldn't locate even if your life depended on it."

Jack smiled and reflected that there were very few people that could raise his spirits quite like Sarah. She was not just his PA; she was also a good friend and like the sister he never had. He had been honoured to 'give her away' at her wedding several years before, and he trusted her like no one else in the world.

"So, whilst I would be more than happy for this guessing game to go on forever, who was it that wanted to speak to me?"

Sarah pretended to flip through the notepad in her hand. "Oh, where was it? Oh yes…" She looked up, staring Jack straight in the eye. "Emily Taylor."

Jack held Sarah's gaze and deliberately kept his poker face.

"There, I knew it!" Sarah exclaimed.

Jack calmly turned in his chair, "Knew what? Now let me think, Emily Taylor. Emily. Taylor. Oh yes, the new lawyer that's helping me with the Svravipona case. Yes, I think I know who you're talking about."

Sarah laughed. "Jack Braun, that nonsense may work outside this office, but I can read you like a cheap novel."

"One with a good twist at the end?" Jack replied, now also smiling.

"I'm not sure. It's a bit slow in places." And, at that, Sarah winked at him as she got up and left the room. As she did so, she loudly whispered over her shoulder, "She's in her office, *if* you're interested…"

*

Jack found Emily's office door open and, gently knocking, entered the room, which was notable by its small size and lack of any furniture save the desk and chair at which she sat. As he entered, he could see that Emily was also poring over piles of documents and spreadsheets. She looked up at Jack and let out a sigh. "This is going to be a nightmare to trace. My team have pulled together an initial view but there are so many shell companies and offshore accounts to sift through," she said, dispensing with any pleasantries.

Jack leaned against the wall, suddenly very conscious of his body language. "Yes, it's not going to be easy. But I've seen more complex set-ups. We just need to follow the trail of money." He looked straight at her and couldn't help but notice just how beautiful she really was.

Not looking back at him, she nodded. "I was thinking we should go to Bermuda. Speak to some of the people in the office there and actually see what records they've kept. There might be something off-line there that we're missing here."

Jack looked serious as he contemplated this then, with an irrepressible smirk, said, "Bermuda. Well, it'll be a tough one, but if I need to go then needs must. I'll keep you updated on what I find."

"We don't know each other well, *Jack Braun*," she said, emphasising his name for effect. "But if you think for an instant that I will sit here twiddling my thumbs whilst you get your hands on critical documents in Bermuda then you're not as smart as you look."

Taken aback slightly, Jack stiffened. "Well, if you think it's really necessary…"

"Look," Emily adopted a tone that made him feel slightly uncomfortable, "I'm not some junior that you can push around. I know what I need to do on this case and my gut tells me the Bermuda office will have the information I need. This isn't a holiday, and it's certainly not my choice given I've just started here, but I will do whatever it takes to make this case a success."

Jack tried to lighten the mood. "Sure, sure. I get it. Well, we should update Darius at some point so he doesn't wonder why two of his team have suddenly disappeared to the Caribbean."

Emily smiled at him, and it seemed genuine. Jack was struck

by how the unexpected expression created a warm glow all around her. She was usually so serious and focused, it was nice to see her let her guard down even slightly.

Just then, Sarah walked in. She took one look at the two of them and raised her eyebrows.

"Is everything okay?" she asked.

Jack nodded. "Yes. We're making progress. Emily has just had a good idea about going to Bermuda."

Sarah smiled. "Sounds fun." She winked at Jack when Emily wasn't looking. "By the way, Darius asked me to remind you that he wants an update when you've made some headway."

Emily and Jack both rolled their eyes. Even though Darius managed the whole firm, he was notorious for being all over the details of every major case.

"Yes, we were just saying the same thing," Emily said, attempting a smile.

Sarah turned to leave, but not before giving both of them a wide smile.

"I'd better let you get on," said Jack.

"Yes, thank you." And Emilly buried herself in the papers in front of them. Jack felt as though he had been dismissed and walked out not quite knowing how to react. Normally it was him who was accused of being cold and formal, he thought to himself as he returned to his office.

*

Jack stood at the doorstep of Kate's house, his mood lifting as he looked forward to spending some quality time with his fiancée. Just as he was about to ring her doorbell, the door opened and out came Kate's cleaning lady, an older woman that Jack had met a couple of times. She smiled on seeing Jack and left the door open for him to enter, before saying her goodbyes and rushing off. Stepping in, Jack removed his shoes as Kate normally insisted on, and made his way to the kitchen at the back.

However, as he approached, his footsteps slowed, and he unintentionally overheard a conversation drifting through the partially open kitchen door. It was Kate's voice, but the tone and words she used caught him off guard.

"Oh, Jeremy, you are sooo bad. Stop it!" said Kate flirtatiously.

On hearing this, Jack froze with curiosity and something else he couldn't place.

"No, you are. No. *You* are!"

Jack's heart was thumping and his stomach lurched as he became uneasy about the nature of this call.

He stood paralysed, not knowing whether to interrupt or wait for Kate to finish her call; but in the moments he was frozen he heard Kate talk very openly with the other man.

"Well maybe I will wear something shocking. Something scandalous..." she said, laughing.

Increasingly concerned, Jack opened the door wide and strode into the kitchen as if he had just arrived. Kate's face went from wide smile to horror in an instant and this, coupled with a shift in Kate's tone, made him feel a pang of discomfort.

Kate quickly ended the call, still startled she looked up and locked eyes with Jack. Her expression morphed from surprise to guilt in an instant, as if caught in a compromising situation.

"Jack, I didn't expect you so soon," she stammered, her voice tinged with a hint of unease.

Jack, struggling to suppress his own emotions, tried to maintain a calm composure. "Who were you speaking with?" he asked, his tone betraying both curiosity and concern.

Kate's defensive stance took hold, and a flicker of annoyance crossed her face. "Oh, just a friend from work. No one important," she retorted.

Jack's heart sank. He had hoped for an explanation that would soothe his concerns, but Kate's defensive response only fuelled his unease. He had always believed in their trust and open communication but, in that moment, doubt began to seep into his mind.

"You seemed on very close terms with this 'friend'?" Jack pressed, his voice betraying hurt and confusion.

Kate's eyes narrowed, and her defensive stance shifted to something more aggressive. "Why are you interrogating me?" she shot back, her words laced with a coldness he didn't recognise. "I have friends, and I can talk to them without having to justify it to you."

Jack felt a wave of shock and disappointment wash over him. He had hoped for understanding, for an open dialogue that would mend the fracture that had suddenly appeared between them. Instead, he found himself facing a side of Kate he had never seen—a side that was defensive, dismissive, and even hostile.

He took a step back, his heart heavy with the realisation that the person he thought he knew so well had revealed a hidden aspect of herself. The foundation of their relationship, once strong and unshakable, now felt fragile and uncertain. As Jack stood there, his mind swirled with emotions—hurt, confusion, and a lingering sadness. The awareness that their relationship might not be as solid as he had believed pierced through him, leaving him at a loss for words. Silently, he turned away from her, unable to bear the tension that hung in the air. The image of the woman he had once loved was starting to blur, clouded by the revelation of this darker side.

"I've made some stir fry for us. Do you want to open a bottle of white?" Kate said, her voice bringing Jack back.

"Sure. Sure," nodded Jack, trying to push away his dark thoughts in the hope that he could turn things back to normal.

They sat in near silence eating their meal, exchanging the smallest of talk and never really looking at each other. Their exchange of words hung like a dark cloud over the table.

"I won't stay tonight. I've got an early start and I've got to get some things ready for a business trip next week," said Jack as they were loading the dishwasher.

"Oh. Oh, right," said Kate solemnly. "Where are you going?"

"Bermuda," replied Jack, trying to lighten the mood with an ill-timed smirk.

"What? Are you kidding?"

Jack couldn't tell if Kate was happy for him or outraged that he was going somewhere nice rather than some cold, industrial city.

"Who are you going with?"

Jack cleared his throat. "It's for this Russian case I'm working on. Bermuda is an infamous offshore tax haven. We think I might find out some answers by being there on the ground."

Kate could sense there was something he wasn't saying, so pressed on. "And you're going on your own, are you?"

"No, actually one of the new partners is also coming."

"Right, right," said Kate. "And what's his name?"

"Oh, right. Well, actually it's a woman. Her name is Emily."

Kate had the look of someone who had been playing a game she had been winning, but had just found the score brought back to an equal footing. Her smile was unfriendly and, as she walked round the kitchen island away from Jack, he found himself thinking that he didn't recognise this person. Was this the individual he was really going to spend the rest of his life with? But another voice inside his head calmed him down. *C'mon Jack, one argument does not end a relationship. Get a sense of perspective on this.*

Jack realised that he needed to offer an olive branch and, looking at her directly, said, "Kate?" to which she stopped and turned round.

"Look I'm sorry if I was a bit grumpy and suspicious earlier," he offered. "I didn't mean to be. It's just that I've got a lot on my plate right now with work and the wedding and everything."

"Oh Jack, you silly thing," she said, coming to him and putting her head on his chest. "It's fine. Why don't we have dinner on Thursday, before you go?"

Later that evening, Jack walked out of the house, leaving behind a relationship that he couldn't quite define. Had it lost its foundation of trust and openness, or was it just a small ripple in something otherwise solid?

As he walked the distance to his own house, he turned the event over in his mind again and again. All he knew was that he needed space—a moment to collect his thoughts and re-evaluate the future he had once envisioned with Kate.

CHAPTER FIVE
Emily

Emily entered Darius's office and saw Jack already standing there in silence. She could sense the tension in the air. Darius was sat at his desk, looking at papers and wearing a hard expression, and Jack looked nervous. Emily didn't want to test her boss's legendary temper; they had to impress him with their progress on the Svravipona case.

Darius finally looked up, and Jack cleared his throat to begin. "We've made some good first steps on the case, and we have some updates for you."

Darius gestured for them both to take a seat, and Jack launched into a detailed briefing on the progress they had made so far. Emily chimed in with additional information, and together they outlined their suspicions that Russian organised crime was indeed involved in the financial fraud they were investigating.

Darius listened intently, nodding occasionally and taking notes. When they finished, he leaned back in his chair and rubbed his chin thoughtfully.

"Interesting," he said. "You've certainly made some progress. But we need results, and we need them soon."

"We understand," Emily replied. "That's why we're planning

to go to Bermuda to interview some people and investigate the office there."

Darius's face darkened. "Bermuda? Are you sure? It's a long way to go to get results. What about the time frame?"

"We know the pressure to get this done," Jack said calmly. "But we believe that this is the best course of action. We need to follow every lead, and this could be the key to cracking the case."

Darius leaned forward and stared hard at Emily. "Fine. It's your call, of course, but I support your decision. There's nothing quite like getting boots on the ground and seeing what the files in a remote office may offer up. But have you considered sending some juniors from your team?"

"Well, we did consider that but, given how broad the search will be and that we're not quite sure what we're going to turn up, then we thought it would be quicker and more effective for us to go."

Jack added, "I'll be honest, Darius, this whole case reminds me of the one we dealt with in Pretoria, do you remember? The one where all of the useful records were still on paper in that strange trucking depot."

Darius smiled. "Oh yes. Goodness me, I'd forgotten all about that. The De Villiers case, wasn't it?"

Jack nodded and they both shook their heads smiling in the memory. The atmosphere in the office had warmed considerably and they both looked ready to get up.

"Well, all good. Just don't let all this travel interfere with your wedding plans, what?" guffawed Darius. "I don't want an angry fiancée on my hands!"

Jack's face fell, and Emily's heart froze. She had no idea that Jack was even engaged, let alone getting married.

"No, sir," Jack replied coldly, his voice barely above a whisper. "You have my assurance that this will not interfere with my wedding plans."

Darius nodded, with a momentary look of confusion as to why his humour had not landed. It was rapidly replaced by a stern expression. "Good. Good. Given everything that's going on right now, it will be difficult to have two of my partners away," he said with more of an edge to his voice. "Let's be clear that this is an urgent business trip, not a holiday."

Even knowing how difficult Darius could be, Jack found this comment particularly insulting, and hissed back, "We know, we know. Rest assured we would only go if needed, and we'll be completely focused whilst out there."

Darius nodded and, at that, they filed out of the office. Emily's mind was racing; Jack was engaged? Fine, so he was engaged. So what? Did it matter? Her brain said it was none of her business, but if that was the case, why was her heart thumping? What on earth was going on?

She hurried down the hallway, her mind giddy with confused thoughts battering her from every side.

A few moments later, Jack made his way to Emily's office. As he approached her door, it was open, and he could see Emily sat at her desk. He hesitated for a moment, then gently knocked and stepped inside.

"Hey, everything okay?" he asked, mild concern etched on his face.

"Yes, sure," she said half-heartedly.

"It's just that you left Darius' office pretty quickly. Was it something I said?" He tried to smile but failed to turn his question into the jokey comment he intended.

"No, it's all fine. I'm just thinking through the plan for Bermuda. We'll need to hit the ground running when we get there."

"Yep, sure. Well, I'll let you get on," he said, with one hand on the door to her office.

"Jack?" Emily looked up staring directly at him.

"Yes?" he replied expectedly.

"I know we've only been working together for a few days but, err, well, I had no idea that you were getting married..."

The silence hung between them. Every instinct of Emily's had been not to raise it, not to put herself in a position of asking him, but she couldn't stop herself. She needed to see how he responded.

Both guilt and embarrassment flickered across Jack's face, but then his expression hardened. "My personal life is absolutely none of your concern. What I do outside of work is not your business."

"Of course, I fully understand," Emily replied, looking hurt. "I just felt like a fool for not knowing when Darius raised it."

"I agree I could have mentioned it," Jack said, still adopting a formal tone. "But it has no bearing on my work, and it doesn't change the fact that we have a job to do. We need to focus on the case and getting results, no matter what."

Despite his words, his face was flushed and he looked like a small boy caught stealing sweets but trying his best to brave it out. Emily just stared at him, speechless, as he sighed and walked away.

As she watched him head down the corridor, she couldn't help but wonder if there was more going on between them than just a professional relationship. They were both far more on edge with each other than the situation deserved, and he was right: why was it any of her concern whether he was attached or not? A surge of conflicting emotions swept over her. *Oh no, am I falling hard for this guy?* she thought and then, angry with herself, she got up, slammed her office door and got on with some work.

*

Emily was deep in her paperwork when her computer's email alert chimed, announcing a new message. She glanced up in response and could see that Sarah, Jack's always impeccably dressed personal assistant, was approaching her office with a gleam in her eye.

Sarah knocked and then quickly settled into the chair on the other side of Emily's cluttered workspace, a mischievous grin playing on her lips. "Emily Taylor, I don't feel that we've really spoken."

Emily sat back in her chair and cooly appraised the figure opposite, unsure whether she was facing friend or foe. Then, standing up and offering her hand, she said, "I agree. Good to meet you, Sarah Benton."

Smiling, Sarah shook her hand then sat back. "So, how's your first week in the lion's den been?"

"Well, I've survived so far. It's been a whirlwind of paperwork, contracts, paperwork, meetings, more paperwork, and desperate runs for coffee. Pretty much what I expected."

Sarah chuckled. "Ah, the glamorous life of a lawyer. You're fitting in nicely."

Emily tilted her head, curiosity piqued. "Speaking of fitting in… Is it just me, or is there some sort of underlying tension between the partners and other staff here?"

Sarah leaned in conspiratorially. "Ah, you've noticed, have you?"

Emily nodded. "I mean, I've been catching some not-so-subtle comments and sly remarks."

Sarah looked uncharacteristically serious. "You've got a good radar there, Ms Taylor. I love this firm, but there's still a lot of healing to be done after all the scandals. I'm sure everything will be fine, but there's still a lot of distrust."

"What a shame. You don't need to tell me if you don't want to, but have all the 'bad apples' been kicked out?"

Sarah paused and surveyed Emily with a penetrating stare. "Yes. Finally. But it took way too long. And, if I'm being honest with you, the firm could have supported the junior staff who raised the whole thing far more than they did. We lost a lot of good people who just got fed up."

"What a shame."

Sarah nodded. "This is why you joining has created such a stir; having someone like you here as part of the leadership will hopefully mean that we have a voice, someone to look out for us, and those things will never happen again."

"That's a lot to live up to."

Sarah smirked. "Well, your reputation precedes you."

Emily shrugged modestly. "Look, if there's anything I can do, I will. I'm certainly not going to tolerate any patriarchal crap from anyone and, whilst I don't want to be the poster girl for everyone's gripes, I'm not going to stand around if there's any form of discrimination."

"Wow, this has got a bit heavy. Apologies, I didn't mean to turn this into a feminist rally. I just wanted you to know how great it is that you're here."

"No, I know. Right, let's talk about something more interesting. How do I get in on all the juicy gossip?"

Sarah chuckled. "Now you're talking. What do you want to know? This place is rife with news about almost everyone."

Emily asked about a few of the individuals that she had met during her brief time at the firm and Sarah told her harmless gossip about their comings and goings.

"And what about your boss? The tight-lipped Mr Jack Braun?"

Immediately, the mood in the room cooled. "I can't say anything, Emily, except that Jack has been one of the most incredible positive figures in my life."

Not giving up, Emily leaned forward. "Honestly, I can't quite figure him out. He's charming, no doubt about it, but there's an air of mystery around him. Sometimes, it feels like he's flirting, and other times, he's almost obnoxious."

Sarah winked and put her fingers to her lips, gesturing that her lips were sealed.

"Oh you're a fat lot of good when it comes to the real gossip," Emily said, laughing. "Well, I suppose I'll just have to work him out for myself. But if I find out he's a serial killer and he murders me, I will blame you!"

Laughing, Sarah stood up. "Right, I'd better get on. Are you coming to the associate drinks this evening?"

"No, I didn't know anything was going on."

"Oh, you should come. Once a month, Darius takes everyone out for a drink. It used to just be for the annoyingly fresh-faced associates, but now anyone goes along. We rent a space at a local wine bar; it's pretty good fun."

"Ah, damn. I would normally come but I have something else on tonight. I agreed to meet up with some friends that I haven't seen for while."

"Never mind. Maybe next time."

"Absolutely. Hey, y'know I've really enjoyed our chat. Do stop by more often."

As Sarah walked away, Emily couldn't help but smile. Her first week at the firm had been a whirlwind of work and intrigue, but with allies like Sarah by her side, she felt like she was beginning to find her footing in this complex firm, where dry wit, amusing wordplay, and the occasional after-hours shenanigans were all part of the game.

*

That evening, Emily stepped into a cool and trendy cocktail bar in Hoxton, looking forward to seeing her friends, Chloe and Beatrice. The bar was dimly lit, with exposed brick walls and vintage furniture scattered around. There was a small bohemian crowd of artists and hipster software developers buzzing around the tables, giving the whole place a lively and achingly cool vibe.

She spotted her friends sitting at a corner table under a graffitied wall that read, *"Let's Adore and Endure Each Other"*. Chloe, with her edgy purple hair and tattooed arms, waved excitedly as Emily approached. Beatrice, in contrast, looked a little frazzled, with her hair pulled back into a messy bun and dark circles under her eyes.

"Em, it's so good to see you!" Chloe exclaimed, giving her friend a tight hug.

"Hi Em," Beatrice said quietly as she too stood up to hug Emily.

As they all sat down, Emily smiled. "It's so great to be back in London and see you guys in person!"

"So, how's it all going with your new job?" Beatrice asked.

"Bea!" cried out Chloe. "We haven't even ordered drinks yet!"

"I'll get them," said Emily, and she returned from the bar with a selection of cocktails from the happy hour menu.

Emily smiled, settling into her seat. "But to answer your question, it's good, thanks. Busy, but good. I'm working on a big case right now."

Chloe raised an eyebrow. "Ooh, juicy. What's it about?"

Emily hesitated for a moment, remembering the confidentiality of the case. "I can't say too much, but it's a bit of a mess. Involves a powerful businesswoman and possibly some embezzlement."

"Sounds good. Great to hear you're back into things so quickly" said Beatrice, with Chloe quickly adding, "We knew you would. You're so fab at work and it's the best place for you right…What I mean is…"

Chloe was lost for words and, catching a hard stare from Beatrice, swallowed and tried again. "What I meant to say is that it's great to have you back in London, no matter what the reason. Cheers!"

All three clinked glasses and quietly sipped their cocktails, deep in thought.

Emily broke the silence. "But enough about my boring job. What about you two? How's your work, Chloe?"

"It's good. I just finished a project for this tech startup, and it was really fun, but it's freelance, so I always feel a bit nervous about where my next pay check is coming from," Chloe replied with a laugh. "But overall, I'm really happy with how I'm balancing work right now."

"And dare we ask about the love life?" asked Emily.

Chloe smiled then excitedly told them about moving in with her girlfriend. As Emily and Beatrice expressed their surprise, given that Chloe had only met her partner a few months earlier, she explained, "I know it seems fast, but when you know, you know…you know? We just clicked. Plus, I've been renting this tiny studio apartment for ages, and I'm ready to move on to something bigger and better, you know what I mean?"

Emily caught Beatrice's eye and they exchanged a brief look of concern.

"Look I know you guys think I keep rushing into these relationships, but this time it is definitely different. Kat is an amazing woman and I love her lots and lots and lots," said Chloe excitedly.

Emily reached out and put her hand on Chloe's. "We get it. We just want to make sure you're okay. But we're thrilled for you, aren't we Bea?" As Bea nodded, she lifted her glass, saying, "Here's to Chloe and her new life with Kat!"

"Thanks, you two. Let me go and get some more drinks." Chloe left them to go to the bar.

Turning to Emily, Beatrice said, "I love her to bits, but I think she's going to get hurt again. I met Kat and her for a drink, and Chloe is way more into Kat than the other way round. But what can you do?"

"I agree; there is absolutely nothing we can do. We both love her and want to protect her like sisters, but she needs to make her own life choices. It's not our place to tell her what to do."

"No, I know. We just need to be there with the tissues if it all goes wrong."

"Exactly," agreed Emily and then, looking directly at Beatrice, asked, "How's everything with you? You always seem so put-together."

Beatrice laughed, taking a sip of her drink. "Put-together? You should see the state of my house and my hair most days," she said, her eyes twinkling. "But honestly, things have been pretty tough lately. Simon's been traveling a lot for work, and the boys have been driving me up the wall. I love them to bits, but they have so much energy, and it's hard to keep up with them."

Emily nodded sympathetically. "I don't know how you do it.

I can barely handle looking after myself, let alone three kids and a husband!"

"It's not easy, but it's worth it. I love my family more than anything, and I wouldn't trade them for the world."

Emily smiled at her friend, feeling a twinge of envy at how content she seemed with her life. "I'm so glad you're happy. You deserve it."

Beatrice's smile faltered for a moment. "Are you really okay, Em?" she asked, her voice soft.

Suddenly, Chloe appeared with a tray full of cocktail glasses of various obscene colours.

"What are we talking about?" she asked.

Beatrice looked earnest as if to signal to Chloe that this was not a trivial conversation and added, "I was just asking this reprobate how she really is."

Emily hesitated, taking a sip of her drink. "Oh, I don't know," she admitted finally. "My job has started well, but everything else...I'll be honest, I just feel like I'm constantly pushing back the clouds, never really able to relax in case they smother me."

The girls exchanged a glance, and Beatrice reached out to squeeze Emily's hand. "You know we're here for you," she said firmly. "Whatever you need, we've got your back."

"It's so brilliant that your back at work and doing what you love."

Beatrice smiled. "And how's the office? Any interesting men?"

"Bea!" exclaimed Chloe.

Emily smiled. "It's okay. No, there isn't. There definitely isn't. I am sure, err, that, uhm, there..."

"Whoah. Whoah. Back right up. Okay, what's going on?" challenged Chloe, smiling.

Emily sighed deeply, and said firmly, "I do not want, and am not looking for, some kind of tawdry office romance."

The other two stopped for a moment, then in unison burst out laughing. Through drunken cackles of laughter, Emily couldn't help laughing too and asking "What?"

"Oh you," said Beatrice just stifling her giggles. "You haven't changed a bit. Whenever you're hiding something, you go into this official-sounding voice like you're addressing a judge."

"Err, your honour, I can testify that I do not want, and am not looking for, love of any kind," added Chloe impersonating an official-sounding Emily.

Beatrice took a sip of her drink and with a pretend innocent expression, asked, "So, who is he?"

"Who?"

"Whoever it is at your new work that's got you all shook up?"

Emily rolled her eyes. "Well, if you must know the only half-interesting guy is this stuck-up, cold, know-it-all, Mr Darcy-wannabe, who whilst actually quite dishy, turns out to be engaged."

"And, of course, you've fallen for him," said Chloe, laughing.

"No. No, I haven't. In fact, I find him quite annoying. Actually!"

"*Ooooh!*" said the other two.

After the laughter subsided and they all took a moment, Beatrice spoke with tenderness. "Look Em, all joking aside, just be careful. You've just come back to work after a tough time. You're going to have all kinds of emotions flying round right now, and the last thing you need is a crush on a fellow lawyer who's unattainable 'cos he's getting married."

Emily sipped her drink and, blushing slightly, added, "I know. I really do. I'm not looking for anything and this guy is *so* annoying sometimes, but I just find him attractive on a—I don't know—like, on a subconscious level."

"Bea's right," said Chloe. "Just 'cos he's a big slab of hunkiness—not that I would know by the way—but just because he's like some kind of Greek God, doesn't mean you should fall for him."

"Thanks. Honestly, with friends like you two, who needs enemies," said Emily, smiling and keen to move the conversation on.

Beatrice added, laughing, "At your age, you need to preserve your energy and focus on the available talent. Not almost-married men."

"Yep, you need to get yourself online and start hunting down hotties on there!" joked Chloe.

Whilst they all chuckled away, Emily raised her eyebrows in mock annoyance. She tried to respond, but every time she said something the other two burst out laughing.

Eventually the laughter subsided, and Emily decided to share more with her friends. "Actually, for your information, I went on a date this week."

Both Beatrice and Chloe froze and turned towards her with surprise in their eyes.

"What?" said Beatrice.

"Who?" added Chloe.

"A surgeon, no less," said Emily, enjoying the looks on her friend's faces.

"And?" asked Chloe.

"Well, Anjay and I went for a nice meal."

"Yes…?" said Beatrice.

"And we had a nice chat."

"Go on…" said Chloe.

"And…He then proceeded to tell me all about how he is still in love with his ex-wife," said Emily and then took a sip of her drink.

Her two friends groaned with disapproval.

"Sorry, old girl. Bad luck," said Beatrice.

Emily smiled sadly back.

"Bloody men. I'm glad I'm not in that game," said Chloe, and added, "The thing is, you are so flipping awesome that you need someone way, way above average for you. You need someone who keeps you on your toes. Maybe even someone who can give you a run for your money in the boardroom, as well as the bedroom."

They all laughed, and Beatrice then chimed in. "I do agree

though. You've talked more passionately about this Jack guy than anyone else. He's definitely not the one, but maybe he's your type and you need to find someone just like him."

"Does he have a brother?" asked Chloe earnestly.

Emily rolled her eyes. "Stop. Please. I wasn't even considering Jack in that way. He is obnoxious and rude."

Chloe raised an eyebrow. "Well, maybe you just need to get to know him better, and see if he has a friend you might be interested in?"

Beatrice nodded in agreement. "Yeah, maybe he's not so bad after all. Think of him as a friend who could introduce you to other 'Jacks'. And let's be real, they wouldn't be worse than Mr 'I'm not over my ex-wife yet'."

Emily smiled. "Thanks, but no. Trust me, Jack is not the type to have any type of relationship with. In fact, I'm actually going to be on a short business trip with him soon and I have absolutely no doubt he'll turn out to be one of those guys who look great on the outside, but have nothing to offer in here." At this she tapped her heart.

Chloe and Beatrice exchanged glances and, after a pause, Chloe said in an exaggerated tone of indifference, "A business trip? Where might that be to?"

"Um…er…Bermuda," whispered Emily, barely audible over the noise in the bar.

Both Chloe and Beatrice burst out laughing again, and even Emily smiled.

Chloe put on her best Emily impression. "No, no, you don't understand girls, it's just a business trip to a romantic Caribbean island with a dishy successful lawyer. There's *nothing* in it!"

At this, Emily's two friends collapsed in giggles. Emily just shook her head and, laughing, took a sip of her cocktail.

CHAPTER SIX
Jack

When Jack got to his office the next morning, he noticed that Sarah had something on her mind. She smiled and wished him a good morning, but he could sense that something was wrong, so much so that it stopped him from just breezing past her as he normally did.

"What's wrong?"

Sarah looked almost lost for words. "I, err, I don't know how to…"

"Come in. Sit down." Jack entered his office and poured a sparkling water for them both as he gestured for her to sit on the sofa in the corner of his office. "Are you okay?" he added.

Now that Jack saw Sarah more clearly, he could see that she was upset and, more than that, she looked tired, like she hadn't slept. In all the time they had worked together, even when working all night on client deadlines, he had never seen her look less than immaculate. His mind was racing. What was going on?

Sarah took a few sips of the water. "I don't know how to say this. I'm really worried. I haven't slept at all."

"Do you want something stronger?"

Sarah shook her head. "No, no I'm okay." Sighing, she

continued. "You know I love my job and I love this firm and I love working with you and I don't want to lose that…"

"It's okay. It's okay." Jack could see her eyes welling up with tears, and he could feel an impatient anger building inside him. He pushed it down and gently urged her to continue.

"I went to the associate drinks last night. There were lots of us there, maybe a hundred. Everyone was drinking and having a great time. Darius was there, hosting the whole thing and keeping everyone entertained. You know what he's like. He was on top form, with lots of stories and anecdotes. Then, as the night went on, there was only a dozen of us left, so Darius suggested we go to his members club for dinner, so a few of us went and, I'll be honest, by this time I had enjoyed a few more drinks than I should have. I was tipsy though; not drunk, just slightly merry. We had dinner, which was great fun, and then as people left there was only Darius, Seamus and I left, so Seamus suggested we share a cab as he was going back to Fulham and my flat is roughly on the way."

Jack held his breath as he listened. He just sat there, hoping that his fears were wrong.

"Well. We got a cab together…" Sarah stopped, and Jack could see her eyes welling up. He moved to sit nearer her and gently said, "It's okay."

Sarah took several deep breaths then continued. "It had been a really great evening and I think I was still on a bit of a high from it and so we were still laughing and joking when we were in the cab. But then…Oh, Jack…even now I keep thinking it can't be true, then…Well, Seamus put one hand on my knee and the other round my shoulder."

Gesturing with her arms, Sarah acted out the movements. "He pulled me towards him and before I knew what was happening he was kissing me and then, oh Jack, I'm so embarrassed…"

Jack couldn't contain his anger. "Look at me You have nothing, I repeat, nothing, to be embarrassed about." He then softened his tone. "Here, have a sip of water. If you're able, can you go on?"

Sarah took a sip of the water before speaking. "Then he, well, err, he put his hand down my top and tried to force his tongue into my mouth and it was…Well, it was just so…I froze. I don't know how long, but I couldn't believe what was happening. Then I pushed him away with all my strength and he stopped. He then moved back to his side of the cab. I was speechless and just stared at him. He had this wolfish grin on his face and he sort of half turned to me and said 'Sarah, you're just too gorgeous'."

Sarah stopped to take another sip of water. "It was as if he thought that this made it okay. I could feel myself then getting upset but, before I could respond, the taxi driver shouted back asking if I was all right. When I looked back at Seamus he had fully turned towards the window and was now ignoring me. I was sat there confused, not knowing what to do, and I just stopped, I was trying to process what was going on. Before I knew it, the taxi driver pulled over telling me that we'd arrived at my flat. As I got out, Seamus didn't even turn round or say anything. I shut the door slowly and watched the taxi speed away."

"I understand. Are you going to be okay?"

"Not really, no. I couldn't sleep. What's going to happen? Am I going to lose my job?"

Jack's heart sank whilst his anger rose. "You are *not* going to lose your job! You've done nothing wrong. This is not your problem, it's his. I am going to fix this."

"Oh no. I don't want you to ruin your relationship with Seamus just because of me."

"Sarah, how long have you and I known each other? I am right beside you on this, you have my full support. I'll be honest, I don't know how this is going to play out, but Seamus' behaviour last night was not acceptable."

Sarah took a large gulp of the water and sighed. She looked slightly relieved and her features softened. As they both sat there in silence, Jack contemplated how to handle the situation.

"Okay, so here's what we're going to do. You're going to get a meeting with HR and put on record everything you've told me, and I'm going to speak to Darius."

"Are you sure that's wise?"

"Darius needs to know about Seamus' actions, and I want to give him the chance to do the right thing."

Sarah considered for a moment. "And what's the 'right thing'?"

"I'll be honest, I don't know. What would you like to happen?"

"I don't know either. I really don't. I just don't want it to affect my job."

Jack looked straight at her. "Sarah Benton, I swear on my life that I will do everything I can to make sure this has no impact on your job and career."

Sarah nodded in thanks.

"Right. You go to HR, and after that I suggest you take the rest of the day off. I'll speak with Darius as soon as he gets in."

As they both got up, Jack added "I will fix this, Sarah. I promise."

*

It was lunchtime before Jack got a call to tell him that Darius had arrived at the office. Jack made his way down the corridor, his pulse racing as he went over and over again in his mind how he was going to handle the conversation. Darius' PA, Annabel, smiled politely as he neared. She stood up, knocked and opened the office door for him, announcing him to the large figure stood at the window looking out over the London skyline.

"Take a seat, Jack."

Jack did as he was told and cleared his throat but, before he could say anything, Darius turned, fixed his gaze and spoke quietly but firmly. "I know why you're here."

"Then you know that I can't let this one lie."

"Look, Seamus came to see me at my house first thing. He knows he's been a bit of a naughty boy, Jack."

"Don't do that."

"Do what?"

"Belittle it. Treat it like something trivial that no one should take seriously."

"Was that what I was doing?" Darius shot back angrily.

Jack noticed that Darius was sweating heavily. Had he drunk so much last night that he had a hangover? That was unlike the man he knew. Or was he unwell? Jack needed to know that the man in front of him, the figure who had been like a father to him, would deliver on his promises to stamp out the unacceptable behaviour in the firm. Jack believed in him, and he needed to see action.

But Jack could see this was going to be hard on Darius, and on the firm. Losing a partner like Seamus would mean losing a significant amount of their fee income and profit for the year. Jack was no innocent; he knew that this was a consideration. But they had to make good on their promises. The alternative was accepting this type of behaviour, and if that happened there were many, including Jack, who would leave. He wanted no part of a firm that tolerated that.

"Seriously, Darius. He sexually assaulted her last night."

"Hmm. That's not how Seamus presented it."

Jack explained in detail what Sarah had told him, and as he spoke he could see Darius' frown deepen.

"Look, we were all drunk, and Seamus explained it as crossed wires, mixed signals. But…"

Jack leaned forward in his seat. "But nothing!" His features hardened in disbelief. "You, of all people should know that, even if there were 'crossed wires', he shouldn't have acted on it. As a senior partner, Seamus needs to act as a leader here. The junior staff all look on you and the rest of us senior partners as their heroes. When they look at us in adoration, it certainly is NOT an open invitation for sexual harassment."

"Don't lecture me. You're right; of course, you're right. It is not acceptable. It's just this couldn't have come at a worse time.

I'm just…I'm just not sure the business will survive this."

They both stared at each other, unable to fully come to terms with the discussion they were having. Darius wiped his brow and took a large gulp of water from a glass on his desk. Jack rubbed his eyes in tiredness.

"We need to make this right."

"I know."

"Today. Now."

Darius nodded. "I agree. I'll suspend him immediately and we'll get HR to run an investigation. But he won't go down without a fight. You know Seamus. How do we manage this to protect our firm, our people and our clients from the predictable mudslinging he'll bring?"

"I don't know. But I do know something; we could do to show we're taking this seriously and this won't be like before. But you might not like it."

"What?"

"We get Emily Taylor to run point on the whole thing. She can oversee the HR investigation and our external employment lawyers on behalf of the company. Everyone knows that she won't leave any stone unturned."

Darius got up and stood looking out the window, considering Jack's advice.

Eventually he nodded "Okay. Bring her in."

As Jack went out to find Emily, Darius rubbed his temples. He loved this firm and he loved leading it, but over the past few years it felt like they had lurched from one catastrophe to another. He and his old business partner had started he firm to specifically set a higher bar than the other law firms he had worked for. The scandals over recent years had hit him so hard and, just as he thought it was over, here he was, dragged back into the whole sordid mess again.

He could just about see the faded reflection of his father in the office window. Right, Darius, he told himself. That's it—no more wallowing. You've faced worse, now buck up your ideas and get back on your feet. He pulled out his handkerchief and blew his nose.

Darius turned as Jack re-entered the room, followed by Emily.

The three of them stood looking at each other before Jack spoke. "I've given Emily a very brief outline of the situation. Emily, as I mentioned there was an issue last night and we need to agree how to handle this going forwards."

Emily could read the room and, even with the scant details provided by Jack, could fill in the details. "Look, I'm not HR and I can't advise on that aspect at all. But, if I understand you both, you're looking for someone to independently make sure that this is addressed in the right way. Apart from doing the right thing, you want to also ensure that this doesn't undo all of the good work you've done over the past year to root out the toxic sexism in this company and make it a place where women actually want to work. Correct?"

They both nodded quietly.

Emily continued. "You might not like this, Jack, but I think you should leave. You've done the right thing but you're too close to the situation and you need to distance yourself."

"What? But…"

Emily held up her hand to silence him. "I know. I know. You're worried about Sarah, and you're worried about the firm. But that's not what we're talking about here and, for your own sake, I don't think you should be included in this discussion."

A hurt-looking Jack turned to Darius who stared back. "Emily's right, Jack. You need to step back from this, given you raised it, and it concerns Sarah. Seamus could use that against us and say this was a witch-hunt against him from a fellow partner."

Knowing there was no point arguing, Jack turned and left the office.

*

The office seemed eerily quiet for an early Wednesday afternoon.

As Jack walked back to his office, there were only a handful of people scattered across the large open-plan area, all with their heads down at their desks, not talking. With no Sarah to speak to, he sat down heavily at his desk and chewed over the encounter with Darius and, of course, Emily.

Why did he feel betrayed? He just felt that, after doing the right thing, they had dismissed him like a schoolboy so that the grown-ups could really solve the problem. Had he been too emotional in how he had handled Darius and the situation?

And then there was Emily. The way she had handled the situation had been impressive. He hated himself for thinking it, but she had looked stunning as she took control of the situation. *Come on, Jack, pull yourself together.*

Was he also just a bit envious that Emily was becoming a trusted lieutenant of Darius? He knew that it wasn't a zero-sum game, but he was very protective of his relationship with Darius and the thought of being usurped by Emily niggled away at him.

Steady Jack, he told himself. *You're reading too much into this.*

Regardless, feeling the weight of the world on his shoulders, he got up and paced around his office, glancing occasionally at the cold, lifeless screen of his computer. He just didn't have the motivation to tackle work; his mind kept drifting, unable to escape the gaping hole in his chest. He decided to phone Kate, hoping for some comfort, some support. Her phone rang several times, but there was no answer and it went to voicemail, her cheerful tone mocking his inner turmoil. "Hey, it's Kate. Leave a message."

He tried again, and again, but it was always the same result—voicemail. The knot in his stomach tightened. The more he failed to reach her, the more he needed to see her, to connect with her. He dialled the number for her workplace, his fingers trembling.

"Hello, Williams Media, how may I help you?" The receptionist's voice was pleasant, but Jack's heart was anything but.

"I'm trying to reach Kate Lawson. It's Jack Braun." He

struggled to keep his voice steady.

"I'm sorry, Mr Braun. Kate called in sick today. Would you like to leave a message?"

Jack thanked her and hung up, his mind racing. Sick? She hadn't let him know. Was she okay? He had to see her, needed to confirm that she was all right.

He grabbed his coat and left the office, quickly jumping into a black cab. She only lived in Fulham so it wouldn't take long, but as he made the way to her house, each mile felt like an eternity. The anxiety and dread gnawed at him. He just hoped that she was okay. His mind raked over all their recent conversations; had he not been supportive enough? Was she going through things at work that she didn't share? Were these things making her sick? *What a terrible fiancé I am,* he thought.

As the taxi pulled up near her house, he noticed Kate's electric bicycle chained up outside. A mild relief washed over him—she rarely went anywhere without it during the day, so at least she was probably in. She probably had some minor ailment and was just resting.

Not wanting to wake her if she was asleep, Jack let himself into the house, the familiar scent of her perfume offering another flicker of comfort. "Kate?" he whispered softly, hoping she'd answer.

There was silence, but the faint sound of creaking floorboards drew his attention upward. Quickly scanning the small rooms downstairs to make sure she wasn't there, he softly climbed the stairs, his heart pounding in his chest.

He reached the bedroom door, the wood seeming heavier than usual. He gently pushed it open, expecting to see Kate sleeping, her face peaceful in the afternoon sun.

But what he saw shattered him. Kate was there, naked and entangled with another man. Time seemed to halt. His mind couldn't comprehend the betrayal before his eyes.

Kate turned, her eyes widening in horror and mumbled, "Jack…"

The man scrambled to cover himself, shame written all over his face.

Jack stood there, frozen, unable to form words. The pain, the anger, the betrayal—it all surged within him, a tempest threatening to consume him. He felt as if the walls were closing in, with no air to breathe.

Without a word, he turned and fled from the room, from the house, from the life that had crumbled around him.

He walked and walked, without a destination, just trying to make sense of the broken pieces of his life. He instinctively blamed himself; maybe he hadn't been the most caring partner, and maybe he could get irritated by things. Had he pushed Kate away? Had he pushed her into the arms of this man? *But no,* he thought. All relationships have ups and downs; that doesn't make it right to cheat on the other person.

Jack cycled through all of these thoughts for some time and, by the time he came to his senses, he realised he had walked back into the centre of London, with the Houses of Parliament ahead of him. He looked at his phone: thirteen missed calls from Kate. He couldn't face this right now. He needed to go home and straighten himself out. But when he felt in his pocket, he realised his keys were in his briefcase on his office desk.

*

Some time later, he found himself back at the office, the one place that offered some semblance of normality. It was now dark outside and, with just his desk lamp on, the gloom of his office echoed the emptiness within him. He tried to work, to lose himself in the mundane details of law, but the images, the betrayal, kept flashing before his eyes. The keyboard felt foreign under his touch. Time dragged on like an eternity as he grappled with the ruins of his life.

He had no one. Darius, Kate… they were all gone; even Sarah was back at home with her partner. He was alone, abandoned in a world that had turned cold and indifferent. And in that solitude, he faced the shattering truth—the person he thought he knew, the woman he loved, had become a stranger. A stranger who had broken his heart, leaving him to navigate the wreckage all alone.

He should go, he thought. He packed up his things and walked to the lift, the faint hum of the air conditioner the only sound to accompany him.

As the lift doors opened, he saw a group of five people laughing and joking in the lift. Ignoring them, he got in and realised too late that the lift was actually heading upwards, not to the ground floor. They reached the top floor, and the doors opened to loud dance music from a rooftop bar that Jack had only been to on work events. "Excuse me, mate," said one of the group behind him, and he found himself stepping out of the lift to let them pass.

By all accounts, Jack should have stepped back into the lift. But as the doors closed behind him, he just stood and breathed in all of the activity and energy in front of him. He slowly moved to the edge of the building and looked out, the city sprawled beneath him like a galaxy of twinkling lights. He needed this, a refuge from the storm inside his heart. The night air was crisp, and the noise and the possibility of a drink felt like a welcome distraction.

He found a stool at the bar and ordered a double malt. Before he knew it, the scotch was burning a trail of warmth down his throat. Lost in his thoughts, he was roused by the laughter of two young women who had appeared beside him. Their energy was infectious, and a world away from where his mind had been.

"Is this seat taken?" one of them said, with a playful glint in her eye and a captivating smile.

"No, it's all yours," Jack replied, managing a smile in return.

Introductions followed, and soon he was chatting with them—Bronwyn and Laura. The conversation flowed effortlessly, a delightful reprieve from the sombre thoughts that had been haunting him.

As the evening unfolded, laughter flowed freely, becoming a soothing balm to Jack's wounded soul. For a few hours, he managed to escape the clutches of heartbreak, finding a momentary respite in their delightful banter. Both Bronwyn and Laura were just starting new jobs and their lively spirit proved contagious, brightening the heaviness that weighed on him.

"So, what brings you to this rooftop oasis tonight?" Laura asked, her eyes sparkling with curiosity.

"I just needed a break from the world, I guess," Jack confessed, swirling the whisky in his glass.

"Ah, we all have those days. Here's to escapism," Bronwyn chimed in, raising her glass.

As the night wore on, they shared stories and laughter. Jack discovered that Bronwyn was also a lawyer, but they agreed to keep the shop talk at bay.

"So, no lawyering tonight," she said with a wink. "We're in a lawyer-free zone."

"Agreed," Jack replied, clinking his glass with hers.

Bronwyn was a force of nature, unapologetically herself. The easy banter between them, clearly facilitated by their numerous drinks, was exactly what he needed. Despite their age difference—she was easily in her mid-twenties—they connected, finding common ground in their sense of humour and love for adventure.

The hours passed by in a blur of laughter and shared tales, fuelled by cocktails and whisky. But, as the night progressed, Laura excused herself, leaving Jack alone with Bronwyn.

"Looks like it's just you and me now," she grinned.

"Seems that way," Jack smiled, appreciating her vivacity.

An hour later, as the bar prepared to close, reality encroached upon their bubble of camaraderie. They both knew the night was winding down, but neither wanted it to end.

"I'm staying at a hotel nearby," Bronwyn mentioned quietly, gauging his reaction.

Jack hesitated, grappling with the maelstrom of emotions inside him. But something about Bronwyn's honesty and openness made him feel at ease.

"I'd like that," he finally replied, surprising himself.

Outside, the city lights still gleamed, a reminder that life continued despite the whirlwind in his heart. Bronwyn's hotel was just a short walk away, the brisk night air rejuvenating.

As they approached the privacy of her hotel room, Jack could feel the animal appetite building in him and could sense it from Bronwyn too. Both having drunk far more than they should have, they pawed at each other's clothes as soon as the door had clicked shut. As the night unfolded, they were two souls finding solace in each other. And in that London hotel room, Jack found a flicker of light guiding him through the darkness that had clouded his heart.

*

Jack woke to find the early morning light shining through gaps in the heavy curtains. Confused, he moved to look round the room, but was immediately hit by a wall of pain coming from his head. He gently raised his migrained head to see that he was in a hotel room, and rapidly became aware that he was not alone, with a figure laying beside him. He lifted the duvet to find a naked woman asleep, and suddenly the memories flooded back to him. Bronwyn, the girl from last night. Panicked, but not sure why and whether he should be, he slipped out of the bed quietly and grabbed his clothes from where they were strewn across the floor.

Fully dressed, he debated whether to wake the sleeping figure, but decided that the best thing was just to remove himself from the situation. A few minutes later, he was walking through the lobby and out into the City's early morning streets. He spotted an open convenience store and dove in to grab water and paracetamol.

Standing outside gulping the water, he was overwhelmed by embarrassment. *Oh Jack, what have you done?* he thought desperately. He decided he needed to get home as soon as possible. He would call in sick (a rare occurrence) and could work from there, if needed. A taxi and an hour later, and he was back in his apartment.

Grabbing a shower and some breakfast, he sat on a stool in his designer kitchen, looking out over the city and considering his situation. Had he just had what he was pretty sure was a one-night stand? He started to shake his head, but his still aggressive migraine stopped him. Bronwyn had been a beautiful, engaging woman, but she was almost ten years younger than him. She would no doubt be waking up with the same regrets that he had. And through this hangover-induced cloud, his mind flashed back to Kate and his stomach turned. He may have had doubts, but he still loved her, and to think of her in the arms of another brought tears to his eyes. He felt like such a mess.

He texted Sarah to let her know that he was not well and received a reply almost instantly: "Really? I hope you're okay. I can't remember the last time you were ill." He replied, writing that he just had stomach pains from something he'd eaten or drunk to which he received various heart-based emojis.

The morning passed in a cycle of water, thinking, coffee, thinking, sleep, and more thinking. By lunchtime, Jack reached his limit of self-pity and started working out how to rebuild his life. He needed to move on from Kate, focus on work, build up his relationship with Darius and then, and only when his life was back to stability, would he consider anything 'emotional'. Having agreed this with himself, he almost subconsciously picked up his phone and started checking his work emails.

He stopped breathing as he read the first one. It was from Emily Taylor, with the subject line: "Bermuda this Sunday?"

CHAPTER SEVEN
Emily

Emily walked briskly through the corridors of the law firm, heading towards Jack's office. She had important matters to discuss regarding the case they were working on, and she needed his insights. However, as she arrived at his office, it was empty. Perplexed, she approached Sarah, who was sat at her desk nearby.

"Hey Sarah, do you know where Jack is?" Emily asked, her brows furrowed.

Sarah hesitated for a moment, her usual cheerfulness replaced with a sombre air. "He's not in at the moment."

Emily raised an eyebrow, sensing something unusual in Sarah's demeanour. "Is he in a meeting?"

Sarah looked down for a moment before responding. "Not exactly. He's...He's not here."

Emily suddenly twigged that Sarah was still reeling from the encounter with Seamus. She just wanted to reach out and hold Sarah's hand and tell her it would be okay, but couldn't quite work out how to articulate her compassion.

Eventually, Emily said, "I just wanted you to know that I'm overseeing the investigation regarding Seamus."

Sarah stared back at her impassively.

"I will make sure that justice is done."

Sarah was still quiet and looked down at her desk. Emily felt like Sarah just wanted her gone, so she switched the conversation.

"All right then. Well, if Jack's not here then I'll email him. We need to discuss the details of the Russian case, especially about our plans for that visit to Bermuda."

Sarah shifted uncomfortably. "Sure. I'm sure he'll get back to you soon."

With that, Emily went back to her own office, firing up her laptop. As requested, her assistant had got her all the details for flights to Bermuda over the next few days. Emily composed a detailed email, outlining the urgent matters with the Svravipona case, proposing that they leave that Sunday and emphasising the necessity to get out to Bermuda, given the urgency.

As she delved into her work, Darius' secretary, Annabel, interrupted her focus. Emily wasn't expecting a meeting with her boss, but she followed Annabel to his office.

"Good morning. You wanted to see me?" Emily inquired as she entered his office.

Darius looked up from his desk, a thoughtful expression on his face. "Yes. Please have a seat."

She settled into the chair across from him, curiosity piqued by the unusual summons.

"I wanted to update you about Seamus. I've exited him due to his misconduct. I couldn't do anything else," Darius began. "But I wanted to extend my gratitude to you for your role in handling this matter. The HR team said you were a big help."

Emily nodded, appreciating his acknowledgment. "I was happy to be of assistance. If I may, I think you've done the right thing on getting ahead of this one. This had the potential of undoing all the good work over the past year."

"I agree. Having you on board and guiding this… Well, I couldn't have asked for more. I'm determined to get this firm back on an even keel. Thank you."

"You are very welcome," Emily replied, a sense of validation warming her. It was rare for Darius to express praise so openly.

He leaned forward, clasping his hands on his desk. "How are things going with the Svravipona case?"

"They're going well; we are making steady progress and our plan is to get out to the office in Bermuda this weekend," Emily replied.

"I'll just be repeating myself if I tell you again about the critical nature of the case. I have high hopes that you and Jack will find the smoking gun in those offices in Bermuda."

"Thank you."

Darius nodded. "With this whole Seamus matter, I'm hoping we'll score a win with this case. Who knows, we could do with a bit of luck to get the firm back on track."

"I hope you don't mind me saying this: there will be short-term pain in losing a high fee earner like Seamus, but in the long run it was the only option if you want the kind of firm that everyone feels valued in. If you had let Seamus get away with the kind of outdated sexist behaviour he was accused of, then I would have been one of the first to leave. Now that you've shown that you're serious about improving things, you will only increase the loyalty that we all have to you and to the firm."

Darius looked slightly uncomfortable with the emotion but nodded gravely.

"Sorry. I think I must have spent too long in New York," said Emily, smiling.

"Thank you. That means a lot. It really does. Now, I presume you have arrangements to make for your trip?" Darius said, dismissing her.

As Emily left his office, she mulled over the conversation. With Jack out of the office, she felt the weight of responsibility for the case and, if she was being honest, she loved it. It took her back to her previous life; but the small voice at the back of her head wondered if it was too soon.

Returning to her desk, she ignored her inner doubts and

started organising the upcoming tasks and responsibilities. She knew she needed to balance both the present cases and the impending trip, making sure no loose ends were left whilst she was away.

In the end, while the uncertainty of Jack's absence still lingered, she knew she had a job to do and a responsibility to the firm and its clients. She would handle it with the precision and dedication that had always guided her in her work.

Emily sat at her desk, contemplating the conversation with Darius. She knew she had to communicate the plan to Jack, ensuring they were on the same page. She finished the email she had been composing and changed the subject line to: *"Bermuda this Sunday?"*

Despite the unexpected endorsement from Darius, she anticipated a challenging discussion given Jack's recent behaviour. Well, she would deal with that later; first a coffee then a chat with her PA to organise flights. However, no sooner had she stood up than her phone rang—it was Jack.

Taking a deep breath, she answered the phone.

"Emily?"

His voice sounded different. It didn't have the same confidence she expected. He *must* be ill.

"Jack, did you see my email? We'll need to fly out on Sunday; I'm going to get the PAs to arrange the details," Emily informed him, trying to maintain a professional tone.

Jack sighed audibly. "Fine. I'll see you there."

"Is everything all right? You sound... off," she inquired, sensing the tension in his voice.

"I'm not well."

"Oh, are you okay? Is there anything I can do to help?"

"No. We'll talk when we see each other," Jack snapped with frustration.

Emily took a moment, attempting to keep her composure. "Jack, we need to be a team on this. If something is bothering you, we should discuss it now."

"Look, I said we'll talk about it later. I don't have the energy for this right now," Jack retorted.

Emily felt a mix of frustration and hurt. She had been working diligently, handling the recent crisis and juggling their workload while he had been absent. She couldn't fathom why he was taking his stress out on her.

"You know what, Jack? This attitude isn't helping. We're supposed to be a team, working together. If you have a problem, let's address it now, instead of brushing it off," Emily said, her voice rising with her own frustration.

"Fine, you want to know? It's your constant need to control everything. I'm used to leading my own cases, and I find your approach stifling," Jack shot back, his words laced with bitterness.

"I'm just trying to make sure things run smoothly. We have a responsibility to our clients," Emily retorted, trying to keep her voice calm, but her patience waning.

"My point, exactly. I do not need you to keep reminding me of that."

Emily refused to answer this, and let the silence grow between them.

"Look, I have a lot on my plate. I don't need your judgment on top of it," Jack replied, his voice softer, tinged with exhaustion.

Emily felt lost. She wanted to support him, but she also needed to stand her ground.

"Jack, we're a team, in and out of the office. If something is bothering you, we should be able to talk about it."

Emily paused. All she could hear from the other end of the phone was Jack making some sort of huffing noise. *He's clearly not in a good way,* she thought.

"Okay, Jack. We'll talk about this when we're together at the airport. I'll get my PA to organise the trip with Sarah."

With a formal tone he replied, "Thank you. Let's just get through this trip." And without adding anything more, he hung up.

"Charming," Emily said looking at the phone with distaste.

As she got up from her desk to grab a coffee, Emily reflected on their conversation. Jack had a great reputation and everyone she had spoken to was extremely complimentary about him and the support he gave to others; but for whatever reason that was not the Jack she dealt with. He may be handsome and intelligent and all those things, but in Emily's view, he needed to change his attitude and start showing her the respect he would show anyone else in her position.

*

As the late setting sun turned the tall buildings a pinkish hue, Emily strode along the bustling city streets, her mind wandering across her complicated feelings about Jack. He had been close to rude with her ever since they were both assigned the same case. He had been overly formal, dismissive and didn't seem to respect her as a lawyer.

But... But... she couldn't deny that she still found him attractive. And everyone else said what a great guy he was. For whatever reason, he had managed to get under her skin. Was this just part of her coming back to work like Chloe and Beatrice had warned? Had she just fallen for the first reasonably attractive guy that she'd met?

And, of course, he was engaged. Fact. So she needed to get a grip and close this whole thing down. So, she had a small crush on a co-worker. *So what?* she told herself. She needed to refocus her energy on work and get her act together.

Yes, working with him had been thrilling—exhausting but thrilling—and it had been exactly what she needed to get her life back on track. But that was it: just work.

Pleased with her new resolution, she turned into a quieter residential street. As she did so, a car sped past and thoughts flared up in her mind about the accident. Suddenly, she was overwhelmed by the memory of the sound of screeching tires, the smell of gasoline, and the crushing pain that followed. She immediately felt the weight of grief, and of loss, land on her like a physical weight on her chest.

She slowed her pace as memories of the car accident flooded her mind. She remembered the night clearly—the sound of the rain pounding on the roof of the car, the blinding headlights of the other vehicle, the quiet before the almighty roar. She remembered how the impact had thrown her from the car, how she had hit her head and blacked out.

When she woke up in the hospital, she was completely disoriented and desperate to know what had happened. It was only when the doctors told her that she had been in a coma for almost a week that she started to piece together the events. And then, and she would never forget this, her parents rushed into the hospital room to see her but the expressions on their faces were all wrong. Not pure joy to see her awake, but happiness tinged with fear and apprehension. They knew they would be the ones that had to tell her. Tell her the awful news that James, her boyfriend—my oh my, that word just didn't do their relationship justice, anyway her 'boyfriend' since university and the first person she had every truly loved—had died in the crash.

Unable to process this, she remembered that she had just kept shaking her head as if to dislodge the truth, but slowly like a sickness the truth had infected her. She was devastated. She had loved James more than anything, or thought she did, and now he was gone. Like a dream that evaporates on waking. Gone.

It had taken her a long time to even slightly come to terms with the loss, just to accept it as something true. She had spent months in therapy, trying to work through her grief and guilt, and she had tucked herself away at her parents' place back in the UK, unable and willing to face a world so cruel that it could just erase James and leave everything so irreparable. Even now, over two years later, the pain was still there, always lurking beneath the surface.

She stopped dead in the street, her breathing rapid and out of control. She sat on a nearby garden wall and focused on the exercises her therapist had taught her. She counted the cars in the street and the number of lampposts, anything to push away the dark, heavy thoughts. As she sat taking deep breaths, a cat walked along the road and, stopping in front of her, cocked its head as if to ask whether she wanted to feed or pet it. This made her smile and, before she knew it, she was back on her feet and walking the last few streets to her house.

The sun had set by now, and the sky was a deep shade of purple. She turned and looked back down the street, watching as the last of the daylight disappeared. Finally, she turned into her street, her thoughts still fractured and sharp with the jagged edges of the past.

Emily began to feel the slight chill of the night air settling in, so she quickened her pace, eager to reach the warmth and comfort of her house. When she finally reached her front door, she fumbled with her keys, trying to get the door open as quickly as possible. Inside, she flicked on the lights and kicked off her shoes, still feeling a bit disoriented from her walk. She tried to shake off the uneasy feeling that had been growing inside her. Looking at the clock on the oven, Emily realised that she had been walking for almost two hours, lost in her own thoughts.

She changed into loungewear and, listening to the radio, fixed herself a salad that she ate whilst balancing a book in front of her. She then poured herself a glass of wine from the fridge and opened the back door to her small garden. Sitting in a garden chair, wrapped in her favourite tartan rug, letting the night air cool her down, she watched the dark navy clouds edged by the city's lights traverse the night sky. Emily thought about how much she loved this little house, this city, with all its quirks and its highs and lows. She smiled, feeling a sense of contentment wash over her.

As she let her thoughts wander, they inevitably ended up on James. They had met when they sat beside each other in the university library two days in a row. He had made some corny joke about him liking the seat because of its view, and she expressed mock outrage that he was referring to her, and in the resulting flirtation they had agreed to go out for a drink. James had been studying Geography with the aim of saving the planet and he used to gently mock Emily's Law and Economics as her gateway into the world of grubby capitalism.

Initially they both got jobs in London, but when Emily was offered the once-in-several-lifetimes' opportunity to work in New York, James quit his job and followed her. What followed was almost ten years of Emily travelling around the US and the world, building a formidable career and reputation, whilst James worked quietly at an NGO in Manhattan that looked at climate change.

Emily worked seven days a week and often survived on little sleep. She knew that James had made sacrifices and she went out of her way to make sure that, when they were together, she did everything she could to put him first, which wasn't always easy. In many ways, she was only able to throw as much as she did at her career because James took care of the rest of her life. He was her rock; until one day he wasn't.

When James was quite insistent that they go away one weekend upstate, Emily started to wonder if he had an ulterior motive. They drove up to the Catskills, where James had booked them into a picture postcard log cabin in the woods, overlooking a stunning lake. As he prepared dinner, Emily became convinced that, after being together for a decade, he was going to propose and she felt a frisson of excitement. She may be a staunch feminist, but she was still a diehard romantic. So she went along with his preparations of the dinner on the veranda overlooking the shore.

As they finished dinner and sat in silence drinking wine and taking in the view, Emily could feel her heartbeat accelerating as she considered that James, who had always shunned conventions such as marriage, was about to propose. He turned to her and she could see his nerves coming through and his eyes slightly watering. *Oh bless*, she thought, wanting to hug him but knowing that this would probably be the wrong thing to do.

James cleared his throat. "Emily," he said, clearly unsure of how to articulate his thoughts. "Emily, there's something I need to say to you."

"Yes?" she replied, trying to make this as easy as possible for him.

"I wanted to tell you…I mean, I want to say…Look, there's no easy way to say this, but…"

"Yes?" said Emily, leaning forward.

"…I've been having an affair."

And there, in that split second, Emily's whole world shifted. Crumbling at the base. She couldn't fully accept what she heard. She knew she should be angry, but quietly she said, "What?"

"I'm really sorry, but I've been seeing someone else," he said, and having dropped that on her, he had the audacity to look relaxed, like he had done what was needed and now that he had declared this, he was fine.

Emily's anger now broke and she launched into a vicious rant at him, demanding details and reasons. Whist taken aback, James answered each question calmly, trying to pacify her as much as he could; something which, seen by Emily as a cynical attempt to control the situation, made her even angrier.

As her anger started to subside, James quietly said, "There is one more thing."

Emily stood up and stared at him with a Medusa expression. She had handled enough divorce cases to know where this might be going.

"Sam…Sam, who is y'know, *her*. Well, Sam is pregnant."

Emily sat down, crumpling into her seat. Even guessing that he was going to say this didn't help. The irony was unbelievable: one of the greatest divorce lawyers had just been told that her boyfriend was having a baby with another woman. And she couldn't help it, her mind immediately jumped into the little girl inside her asking, "Why didn't he want to have a baby with ME?"

She told herself she wouldn't cry. She insisted on it. So with dry eyes, she stood up and said, "I want to go."

"Want to go? Where?" asked James.

"Home. Now."

James looked around him. "But we're in the middle of nowhere. We can't."

"We can. And we are. If you think I am staying here tonight, with you, then you are sorely mistaken," said Emily.

"But I've had half a bottle of wine," protested James.

"I don't care. Let's go," said Emily and at this she walked into the cabin and started gathering her things.

And so, an hour later with all of their things re-packed and darkness all around them, they drove off, leaving the cabin behind them.

They were only five miles from the main highway when James took a blind bend just slightly too fast and a truck coming the other direction clipped the side of their car, flipping it over at speed.

The postmortem of James' body confirmed that he was over the legal alcohol limit and no fault was placed on the truck driver, but it hung like a cloud over the funeral back in the UK. His family, who had never really taken to Emily, were distant and she felt that they were suspicious of events around his death.

The chill in the air brought Emily back out of her thoughts and she took a moment to collect herself. She still felt a hole inside her where James and that life used to be. She still hadn't resolved her feelings about him, the accident, his affair and that there might be a baby out there with his genes. She looked up at the sky, its utter black emptiness matching her feelings. Would she ever be whole again?

She went back inside, the warmth enveloping her. As she turned off the light and headed to bed, she stopped in the silence and, for a moment, she felt a sense of something; not quite peace, but the beginnings of something like contentment. She couldn't help but wonder what tomorrow would bring. And what she would say when she saw Jack at the airport.

CHAPTER EIGHT

Jack

Jack stood inside the airport entrance, checking his watch as he waited for Emily. He hadn't slept well since finding out about Kate, but was trying to refocus all of his thoughts on the case and this trip to Bermuda. And of course, Emily.

Since she came into his life, it had been turned upside down and, whilst none of it was due to her, he couldn't help associating her with all of this upheaval. There was something about Emily that he couldn't put his finger on. Sure, she had been—he corrected himself—*was*, one of the most successful lawyers in her field, but it wasn't that, or not just that. Just her presence kept him on edge, but in a good way. He felt a buzz by just being in her presence. He'd never met anyone like her before; she was both intriguing and frustrating in equal parts. If anyone else had treated him like she had done, especially in front of Darius, then he would have considered them an enemy and done everything in his power to get them out of his life, but she was…

His phone bleeped. It was Emily texting to say that traffic had been bad and she was running late.

He grabbed a coffee from a nearby stand and sat watching all the people rushing in and out of the airport, their luggage trailing behind them. Where were they all going? How many of them were in love? How many were happy?

Jack shook his head. What was happening to him? One bad week and he'd been turned from a first-rate lawyer into a third-rate philosopher. He needed to snap out of this.

Finally, he saw Emily approaching. She looked stunning in a well-cut suit and confident demeanour.

"Well, good morning, Mr Braun," she said smiling. "I hope you're feeling better."

Jack faltered, slightly pushed on to the back foot by her confidence, "I'm fine. Thank you." He continued his defensive formality, adding, "Let's get through security."

As they walked through the crowded terminal, Jack glided through the security checkpoint with ease, while Emily seemed increasingly annoyed as she took off her shoes and belt.

"Ma'am, you can't take that water bottle through," a security guard told Emily, pointing at the bottle in her hand.

"What? Oh, right. Sorry," Emily said, handing the bottle over.

Making their way through the metal detector, Jack breezed through without a beep. Emily, on the other hand, set off the alarm and was pulled aside for a more thorough screening. She blushed with embarrassment as the security officer patted her down, feeling exposed in front of the other passengers.

As they proceeded to wait for their hand luggage to get through the screening machine, Jack teased her with a gentle smile. "Do you always get through security this easily?"

Emily rolled her eyes. "Only when I'm around you."

"Whose bag is this?" shouted one of the security staff.

"Mine," sighed Emily holding up her hand. She turned to Jack. "You had better go on. I'll catch you up."

Jack checked she was okay, then walked off to leave Emily to deal with the extra screening of her case.

When Emily finally arrived at the business lounge, Jack was already seated, sipping a glass of malt whisky. Emily plopped down beside him, looking tired and fed up.

"Smooth as always, I see," she said, rolling her eyes.

Jack wasn't sure how to respond and so just gave her an awkward smile back.

Emily leaned back in her chair, looking exhausted. "I swear, traveling with you is like traveling with James Bond. Everything always goes perfectly for you."

Jack chuckled. "Years of experience. You just need to know the system."

Emily bristled at this. "You're right of course. In my last role, I became too used to the corporate jet rather than having to navigate busy airports and crowds of people like this."

Jack's smile faded ever so slightly. "Here," he said, offering her the menu. "What can I order for you?"

Emily's mood lifted. "Well okay. Now we're talking."

Food and drink on its way, Emily tried to push the stress of the airport security out of her mind. "Jack, there's something I want out in the open with you. We seem to have got off on the wrong foot and I'm not sure why. Our call on Friday was a particularly low point. If we're going to work together…"

Jack held up his hands in mock surrender. "I couldn't agree more. I apologise. I really do. I've had quite a lot on my plate over the past few weeks, and it came to a head on Friday. Let's draw a line under it and start again. Truce?"

Jack held out his hand. Emily shook it, and he couldn't help noticing how slender and smooth her hands were. They felt amazing. He caught himself and his pulse increased slightly in embarrassment.

Emily opened her tablet and started typing. "Right, so we know that Sergey set up the Bermuda office three years ago, and our suspicion is that he used this to embezzle funds out of their company. What are we looking for when we get out there?"

Jack took a sip of his whisky and leant back in his chair. "Well, first things first, we need to gather all relevant paperwork together and secure the hard drives. We then need to go through everything that links back to Sergey. That means going through his financial records, talking to his associates, and finding out where he's been moving his money."

Emily nodded, looking thoughtful. "And we also need to figure out where he's hiding the money. I doubt he's just got it sitting in a bank account somewhere."

"Exactly," Jack agreed. "So we'll need to get creative in our investigation. We may even need some unconventional methods to get the information we need."

Emily raised an eyebrow. "Unconventional methods? What do you mean?"

"I mean, we might need to get our hands dirty. You know, talk to some unsavoury characters, throw some money around…"

Emily looked alarmed.

Jack waved his hand dismissively. "Don't worry. We're just brainstorming here. We'll figure out the best approach when we have more information."

Emily nodded, still looking sceptical. "Okay, well, let's just focus on gathering that information for now. We need to be methodical and thorough in our investigation."

"Agreed. And we also need to work together effectively. If we want to crack this, we need to pull together and work as a team."

Emily smiled, a determined look in her eyes. "Absolutely. I'm ready to do whatever it takes to get this job done."

Jack smirked in reply. "That's what I like to hear. Now, let's order another round and get to work."

*

Jack had been staring at the ceiling of his pod for what felt like hours. Despite being in the comfortable confines of a business class bed, he found himself restless and unable to sleep. He tossed and turned, unable to find a comfortable position, until he finally gave up and decided to get up and stretch his legs.

As he returned to his seat after walking around the cabin, he couldn't help but glance over at Emily, who was sound asleep in the pod opposite his. Her face was peaceful and relaxed, and she looked more beautiful than ever. As he sat back down, Jack couldn't help but feel a sense of awe and wonder as he gazed at her.

The pale glow from the overhead reading light cast a soft radiance on her delicate features. Her eyes, usually bright and lively, were now peacefully closed, revealing long lashes that gently touched her cheeks. Her lips, slightly parted, carried a subtle smile that hinted at dreams of happiness.

As Jack admired her, he couldn't help but reflect on the path that had brought him here. He thought about the twists and turns, the ups and downs, that had led him to this moment. It had only been days since Kate betrayed him but had it resolved something that was already broken; was it even, a good thing? He still couldn't process what had happened fully and true to form, he had put it in a little box deep, deep down in his mind, but he knew at some point it would resurface. But for now, looking at this beautiful woman whom he had both been attracted to and disliked immensely, he felt a deep bond. He knew she had a complicated past like him and he wondered whether they were actually very similar, possibly even suited to each other. It seemed as if fate had intervened, weaving their lives together in unexpected ways.

He traced his memory back to their first encounter, when they had crossed paths in the lift of the London office. From that moment on, his life had encountered a series of challenges and revelations. Through it all, Emily had just been this constant presence, which, if he was honest to himself, he had welcomed, even when he had found her deeply annoying.

Lost in his thoughts, Jack marvelled at the beauty that Emily emanated, not just in her physical appearance but also in her spirit. She had an energy about her, an infectious spirit that lit the room, even when it sometimes conflicted with his usual, more traditional style. Seeing her in this tranquil state, he was starting to realise how different she was and just how fortunate he was to have her with him on this trip.

A gentle turbulence jolted the plane, causing Emily to stir in her sleep. Her eyes fluttered open, revealing surprise and warmth as she met Jack's gaze. A shy smile danced across her lips, mirroring the unspoken connection between them.

"Oh. Good morning," Jack whispered, his voice tinged with a slight embarrassment at being caught staring at her.

Emily blinked, the sleep dissipating from her eyes. "Morning," she replied, her voice tinged with a hint of sleepiness. "Are we there?"

Jack regaining his composure replied, "No, not yet. I, err, heard something and just looked over."

She also blushed, her cheeks taking on a rosy hue. "Oh, okay." She yawned, turned over and closed her eyes once more.

As the plane continued its journey to Bermuda, Jack could feel a blurring of work and personal life. What was going on? This just wasn't like him; he felt so adrift right now.

He knew that they would be working closely together on this case, and he needed to keep their relationship professional. He also realised that he was in no fit state emotionally to think about anything more than that with a work colleague. In fact, far from considering her attractive, he should be focusing on making sure that they would be able to put their normal differences aside and work as a team.

But as he subtly looked back at Emily, he was suddenly struck by a different kind of emotion. He felt a warmth in his chest and tears welled up in his eyes. He was overwhelmed by the sight of her, so still and serene in her slumber, and he felt a sudden surge of emotion.

He wiped his eyes and looked around the cabin, suddenly self-conscious. He needed to get a grip and quickly. With his typical discipline, he promised himself that by the time the plane landed, the 'old' Jack would be back in control.

Bermuda in the summer was hot, humid and prone to hurricanes, but as they walked out of the airport, the sun and the obvious good-natured spirit of the people around them was infectious.

Driving straight to the offices from the airport, they arrived in Hamilton, Bermuda mid-morning. The office building exuded a unique blend of tropical charm and professional functionality. Nestled up against the island's lush greenery at the edge of the commercial district, it stood as a testament to the growing business landscape. The single storey building was a mix of lodge and office with a design that complemented the surrounding natural beauty. Large glass windows adorned the front, allowing ample natural light to flood the interior, and offering a glimpse of the work within.

As Jack and Emily stepped through the entrance, they were greeted by a small but well-appointed lobby. The reception desk, adorned with local artwork and tropical flowers, provided a welcoming atmosphere, and the air-conditioned space provided respite from the island's warmth.

The inside of the actual office was far less impressive. They set themselves up in one of the dishevelled offices at the rear of the building, having walked through the open plan area with boxes of paper surrounding most of the desks; and only four staff left where there were signs of ten times that number of people having worked there. It was clear that this was a company on the brink of closure, and they had arrived just in time if they wanted access to the information and files there.

One of the few staff, a middle-aged man called Aaron, agreed to help them find what they were looking for, and in no time he was bringing boxes of paper to the desks they had commandeered.

As they both worked through the documents, Jack's phone kept ringing. It was Kate. Jack couldn't help it, but his frustration was building up. He stood up and stretched his back and shoulders.

"Sorry about that," he apologised, sliding his phone onto the desk. "I've turned off my phone. No more distractions. Let's get to it."

Emily nodded in acknowledgment. They returned their attention to the stacks of files spread out before them, determined to uncover any hidden evidence of wrongdoing. This was tiring, manual work that they would never dream of doing themselves back in London, but here without their teams they just needed to roll up their sleeves and get on with it.

The company's outdated bookkeeping system presented a daunting challenge. Jack sympathised with Emily's exasperation as they painstakingly sifted through paper after paper, ledger after ledger.

Emily let out a deep sigh, lowered her head into her hands, and started massaging her temples.

"I know it's frustrating, but we have to keep at it," Jack encouraged, hoping to boost Emily's spirits.

"I *know*," replied Emily through gritted teeth, "but that doesn't mean I have to enjoy it."

Stay cool, thought Jack. *Just let her vent*. And he went out of the office into the town to find them some coffee.

On his return, a grateful Emily looked up and said, "Thank you. And sorry; I didn't mean to take it out on you."

A smiling Jack returned to the desk he was using and both of them continued with the arduous task of reading through the files.

*

Hours passed, the sun casting a warm glow that filtered through the office windows. Just as they were about to call it a day, Emily's eyes widened with excitement. She had stumbled upon an invoice for a storage unit that hadn't been mentioned anywhere else.

Jack's heart raced with anticipation as he met Emily's gaze. "This could be the key," he whispered, feeling a renewed surge of energy.

After going through the details and discussing whether they should investigate it straight away, they agreed to check it out immediately. With a newfound resolve, they gathered their belongings, found a taxi, and quickly made their way to the storage unit. As they got out of the cab, they found themselves in an industrial area with decrepit warehouses and newer prefabricated units separated by pot-holed dirt tracks. They located the unit they were looking for and the nondescript building loomed before them. As they approached the small hut that served as its reception, they hoped that within those walls, crucial evidence awaited their discovery.

After some negotiation and a small bribe to the security guard, they were in front of the now unlocked storage unit. As they stepped inside, Jack marvelled at the towering stacks of boxes and crates that filled the space. It was a daunting sight, but he felt a glimmer of hope.

Side by side, they started going through the seemingly endless collection of papers. They didn't need to go far before they started to find exactly what they were looking for. It was clear that the boxes contained well-documented financial records of shell companies and the various wire transfers between them, including some unknown Russian bank accounts.

Emily's eyes widened in triumph, relief and satisfaction washing over her. "We've found it. This is the breakthrough we needed."

Jack couldn't contain his excitement. He pulled Emily into a celebratory embrace, their smiles mirroring their shared triumph, shortly followed by a small awkwardness as they stepped apart.

They decided that they would take a couple of the boxes with them in the taxi back to the hotel and leave the rest for pick-up in the morning.

As they exited the storage unit, Jack felt a rush of gratitude for their partnership. Together, they had persevered and although this was only the start, it was great progress. Sharing this with someone like Emily made it all the sweeter.

Emily's smile illuminated her face as they walked side by side. Jack's admiration for her grew with each step. He couldn't get enough of her dedication, intelligence, and unwavering focus. He drank it in.

"This is such a significant step forward," Jack said. "I have no doubt that this will really help us crack this case. But this is just the beginning; there's a lot of documents to get through here."

She turned to him, nodding. "I agree. It's a good start but we've got our work cut out for us."

As they entered the lobby of the hotel, both with arms full of boxes and papers, there was an awkward moment where they looked at each other. Jack was tired and wasn't sure whether to ask Emily if she wanted to grab dinner, but then after a tiny beat of a pause, Emily smiled and said, "We do make a great team, Jack Braun."

And before he could catch his breath to reply, she was gone.

*

The next day, Jack could feel the jet lag punch him in the gut. He skipped breakfast and didn't see Emily in the lobby so decided to walk to the office. As soon as he entered the office, he could feel the tension building up inside him. He had barely slept the night before, and his phone was showing multiple missed calls from Kate, which had him feeling even more agitated. When he saw Emily at her desk, typing away on her computer looking serene, something rattled him and despite his best intentions he couldn't hold back his frustrations.

"Emily," he barked as he approached her. "Did you arrange for the rest of the boxes we found last night to be transported here?"

Emily flinched at his harsh tone but quickly recovered,

ignoring it. "No, I'm just trying to find a company that will do it now. I've spoken with my assistant and we're trying to find a company that we can trust, but so far none of them have opened yet."

"Come on Emily. That's a five-minute job. We need to crack on. The longer we drag our feet, the more risk that someone gets hold of those papers and moves them."

Emily stared at him, surprised by his outburst. "Hey, buddy," she said keeping her anger in check, "Just cool your jets there. I'm not some grad that you bark orders at when you feel a bit crap. If you wanted faster progress, maybe you should have turned up an hour ago when I first got here."

Jack felt like he had been slapped. He couldn't remember the last time someone had pushed back on his temper like this. He tried to calm himself down. He knew that he was being unfair, but he couldn't help it. The stress of the case, combined with his personal life, was starting to take its toll.

"I'm sorry," he said, more calmly this time. "I just want to make sure we get those files."

Emily nodded again, now avoiding eye contact. Jack knew that he had hurt her, and he felt guilty. He walked back to his desk, feeling defeated. He needed to find a way to keep his personal feelings out of the case, but he wasn't sure how. He was just about to say something to try and mend the situation when his phone went off; it was Kate again.

He had to finally speak to her, if only to stop the tirade of calls and texts. He stepped into one of the empty office meeting rooms to take the call. Even though he had closed the door, he was conscious that the thin walls meant that Emily could possibly overhear some of the conversation from where she was working at the desk. He slumped into one of the chairs, his hand clutching the phone, his mind a swirl of emotions. He hesitated and then pressed the green button, ready to confront the painful reality.

"Hello?" Kate's voice was a mix of nervousness and hope.

"Hello Kate."

"Oh, Jack. I was hoping you'd answer."

"What do you want?" Jack said, struggling to keep his voice steady.

There was a pause, a pregnant silence on the line.

"Jack, it's not what you think," Kate finally said, her voice almost a whisper.

"What do you mean it's not what I think?" Jack's voice edged towards frustration. "I saw you. I saw you with Jeremy. I saw what happened."

"I... I messed up. It was a foolish mistake," she stammered, her remorse apparent.

"A foolish mistake?" Jack's voice rose with incredulity and anger. "It was a betrayal of everything we had."

"I never meant to hurt you," she pleaded, her voice cracking.

"But you did hurt me. You hurt us."

"I'm so sorry. I don't know what came over me."

"You've shattered the trust we had. There is no coming back from this."

"We can work through this. We can fix this," she implored, her voice desperate for reassurance.

Jack sighed deeply, his heart heavy. "I thought we had something special. But I can't be in a relationship where I'm not valued and respected."

"I do value you. I love you," she said, tears aucible in her voice.

"Love isn't just about saying it. It's about actions and choices. And your actions have shown me a different reality,' Jack said, his words calm and measured.

Kate fell silent, the weight of his words sinking in.

He continued, "I deserve a relationship built on trust and respect."

"I, I, I understand. Forgive me, Jack."

"Goodbye Kate. Don't contact me again," Jack replied, and ended the call.

Standing up, he felt a strange combination of relief and sorrow. As he walked back into the room, he saw Emily typing up notes on the laptop. He could see from her expression that she had heard at least some of his conversation with Kate.

"I'm sorry you had to hear that," Jack said, taking a seat across from her.

"It's okay," Emily said, trying to hide her discomfort.

"I don't want my personal situation to affect our work," Jack said.

"It's not a problem," Emily said, not meeting his gaze.

Jack sat back at his desk, thoroughly depressed. His engagement was over, work was going badly and, worst of all, he had been mean and rude to Emily. My word, he was such an idiot. He felt like crawling into a hole somewhere and waiting till everything blew over. *C'mon Jack,* he thought. *Pull yourself together.*

Memories of his father came back to him, and he thought about another time and place when he had felt equally useless. He had just been bowled out for a duck again, and his teammates were shouting various insults in his direction. As he walked back towards the benches at the edge of the school cricket pitch, he saw his father standing there beckoning him over.

"Dad, you made it," the thirteen-year-old Jack said, looking up.

"Of course. I wouldn't miss it for the world. But what was that?" his father gestured back to the crease.

Jack was silent.

"Well?" his father continued.

"Their bowler is faster than ours and they didn't put me in the right place in the running order and…"

Jack stopped as his father held up his hand. "Jack, did you do your best?" to which Jack vigorously nodded.

"No, Jack. Did you really do your best?" and after a pause Jack slowly shook his head.

"I, err…" Jack began.

"Now, I know you tried hard but we both know you didn't give it your absolute best. In which case, there is only one person you should be mad at…"

"Myself?" added Jack.

"Exactly," said his father.

Jack remembered the long walk back to his teammates, feeling sick as he realised that the only person to blame was himself. He promised himself there and then that nothing less than his best was good enough; you must always give your best. This had stayed with him his whole life and was now a defining aspect of who he was. He would have loved to show his father that he had made good on that promise, but his father passed away less than a year later.

As Jack came back to his surroundings, he rubbed his eyes gently. *C'mon Jack, pull yourself together; you've faced worse than this and still given your best.*

*

Both Jack and Emily worked in silence for the rest of the day, buried in their own piles of paperwork. As evening drew in, they left the office for the hotel; they were professional with each other but said little.

Jack made his way outside whilst the sun was beginning its descent over the horizon, casting a warm, golden glow across the beach. He sat on a weathered wooden bench, his face one of both contemplation and confusion. The crash of the waves provided a soothing soundtrack to his troubled thoughts. He dialled Nate's number and put the phone to his ear.

"Hey, Nate," Jack greeted, his voice tinged with fatigue.

"Jack! What's up, matey?"

Jack took a deep breath, struggling to find the right words. "Kate and I... We're done. I ended it."

There was a moment of silence on the other end. 'Oh, Jack. I'm so sorry to hear that. Are you okay?"

"Yeah, I guess. It's just... it had to be done."

"Do you want to talk about it?"

"I don't know. I just... I don't know if I ever really knew her." Jack paused, almost unable to muster the next few words. "Nate, it turned out she was seeing someone else..."

"What!?! Oh, man. That is terrible. Now I *really* hate her. What a bitch. Oh Jack, are you okay? Are you on your own out there?"

Jack ran his hand through his hair. "No, there's someone else with me. You know, I actually mentioned her before: Emily Taylor."

Nate couldn't hide the chuckle down the phone. "Y'know, the temptation to take the mick right now is very high. If you didn't sound so down, I would be seriously ripping into you..."

"We're just colleagues." Jack couldn't help smiling. "Although, she is something else, buddy."

"You dog. Bermuda. Beautiful, successful woman. What's the problem, old chap?"

"See. This is why you're my best friend. You're like a guaranteed pick-me-up."

Nate laughed. "No problem; where do I send my bill? But seriously mate, what's she like? Emily?"

"She's driven, passionate about what she does. And she's kind. The way she treats people, it's something else." Jack hesitated, pondering how to put it into words. "She's smart, brilliant even. Strong-willed. But she can be so stubborn and frustrating at times. It's like arguing with a whirlwind. I've never met someone so infuriating."

Nate chuckled on the other end, sensing the complexity of the situation. "Well, that's love for you, my friend. It's messy, it's confusing, but it's beautiful too."

"Whoa, steady. I'm not in *love* with her. Yeah, she's the most unusual woman I've ever worked with, but well...it's confusing. Oh mate, I thought I had my life sorted out with Kate, but now my whole world has been turned upside down..." Jack confessed.

As Jack spoke with Nate, Emily approached the beach. She could see the outline of Jack on the bench and decided to check on him and ask if wanted to join her for dinner. Only when she got closer did she notice that he was on the phone, so she slowed her steps, not wanting to intrude. However, she couldn't help but overhear parts of the conversation.

"...she's so annoying sometimes. I've never met someone so infuriating," Jack said, and Emily froze, wondering who he was talking about.

Jack continued "She is just so obstinate. And direct to the point of being rude. I guess being in the States for so long has meant that she's lost all inhibitions about being direct…"

Emily quietly turned to leave, tears welling up in her eyes. Yes, she was tough, but she was also a woman and one who was on some level attracted to this man. To hear him so clearly describe her as infuriating was too much for her still-fragile ego. She didn't want or need Jack Braun's respect, but she thought they had connected over the past few days and his words were a savage blow.

She left the beach and made her way to the restroom to dry her eyes. She was out of earshot when Jack continued his conversation.

"But you know what, mate? Despite all that, I find her… I find her so very attractive. She's exactly the kind of woman I'd like to be with…" he confessed. "What the hell should I do?"

"Follow your heart, man. If she's the one you want, go for it. Life's too short for regrets."

"Thanks, old chap. I needed to hear that, take care." And with that, he hung up the phone. He remained still, just staring out at the sea and trying to get his jumbled thoughts into some sort of order.

Maybe he should say something to Emily. But not tonight, not whilst he was tired and emotional. Right now, he just needed to get some sleep.

The hotel phone rang loudly in the cool night air, waking Jack from his slumber.

"Hello?" said Jack groggily.

"Hello sir, it is the front desk. The manager wondered if you could come downstairs to meet with him."

"What?" replied Jack, now annoyed at being woken. "Why on earth…?"

He looked at the alarm clock beside the bed; it showed 01:35.

"I am very sorry, sir, but there is a delicate matter that the manager was hoping to discuss with you."

Reluctantly, Jack put on some clothes and headed down to the reception desk. He was greeted by a small, wiry man in a three-piece suit who took him to one side.

"I am so sorry, Mr Braun, but I was not sure what I should do," said the manager in a thick Bermudan accent.

"How do you mean?" Jack looked round for a clue.

"If you would follow me to the beach-side bar, please sir."

Jack followed the manager through the beautifully decorated lobby and the low-lit pathway through the well manicured gardens to the beach bar, which consisted of around thirty tables, a bar and a small, raised dancefloor, all partly covered by the sand from the adjoining beach.

Jack shook his head. The dance floor only had one occupant and it was Emily, staggering around with an empty cocktail glass in one hand, the other hand pointing at the slightly terrified DJ whilst she hurled abuse at him. Jack turned to the manager and indicated that he would resolve the situation.

"Hello Emily," Jack said as he approached her.

"Ah Jack!" she shouted in reply "Good. Good. I'm glad you're here. This idiot is refusing to play any more music, but I just want to dance. I JUST WANT TO DANCE, JACK!" she shouted.

"But Emily, it's really late and all these people want to go home." He gestured around at all the staff.

"Its not late; it's EARLY!" She stamped her feet in a mock tantrum "It's only…it's only…" Emily tried and failed to read the time on her watch. "Never mind that; it's definitely still early."

"C'mon Em. Let's get you some water and to bed." He gently steered her back towards the hotel.

"THANK YOU EVERYONE! SEE YOU TOMORROW!" she shouted and gave a defiant bow to the bar's last remaining occupants before giving in and following Jack.

Jack almost smiled, but then he remembered how bad this looked and found himself getting annoyed with Emily.

"What happened to you?"

"Jack, Jack-o, Jack-ee, I cannot lie. I was a bit upset and then I did find the cocktails very yummy and before I knew it I was dancing and dancing and then they stopped the music. Very bad of them, if you ask me."

"Okay, right, here we go," said Jack as they approached the door to her room. "Give me your key" he said.

"What key?" slurred Emily.

"Your room key."

As Emily started to fall asleep on his shoulder, he gently rocked her. "Emily, where is your room key?" But she didn't or couldn't answer.

"Christ," Jack muttered to himself and reluctantly walked Emily down the corridor to his own room.

Opening the door with one hand, he led Emily to the sofa in his bedroom. "You sit there and I'll get you some water."

Whilst Emily drank deeply from the ice-cold water from the fridge, Jack closed all the blinds and turned off all the lights apart from her bedside lamp.

"Right, so are you going to be okay?"

Emily sat despondently like a sack of potatoes at the end of the bed, looking up at Jack, who stared back. Her eyes started to well up and despite her best efforts, she couldn't stop sobbing.

Jack stood there, not knowing quite what to do.

"Why is life so cruel?" she sobbed.

Jack remained silent, staring fixedly at the carpet.

"Everything is just so hard. I just feel like I have to fight just to stay upright."

"I don't know. I just don't know," said Jack quietly as he was hit by a deep wave of sympathy.

The alcohol still coursing through her veins, her mood turned in an instant. "Oh it's fine for you. In your little middle-class bubble, with your fiancée and friends and… AND EVERYTHING!"

Jack exhaled deeply, pulled back the covers of his bed, gently guided Emily over to it and laid her back on the pillow. Having tucked her up in bed, he moved to the door, and, turning as he opened it, said, "You know nothing of my life, Emily Taylor. Now get some sleep."

CHAPTER NINE
Emily

Emily woke up with a throbbing headache and a sour taste in her mouth. She groaned as she opened her eyes and saw the bright Bermuda sun shining through the slatted window. She had a vague recollection of the night before, drinking too much at the hotel bar with some of the locals and other guests. And there had been dancing; way too much dancing. She forced herself to stop thinking about the night before; prodding every memory was like a tongue exploring an extremely painful abscess.

She slowly realised that the noise that had woken her was the phone beside her bed. She groaned, reaching out her hand to grab the receiver and put it to her crumpled face.

"Hello?" she whimpered.

"Hello?" said the female voice at the other end of the line.

"Hello?" repeated Emily.

"Who is this?" demanded the voice.

"Emily. Who is *this*?"

"I'm sorry, I must have the wrong room. What room number is this? I was looking for Jack Braun."

"Oh, you've got the…" and Emily stopped. She didn't recognise the room. Yes, it was similar to hers but a different shape and, as she slowly and painfully raised herself up, she spotted an expensive suitcase that she recognised as Jack's. Panicked, she slammed down the phone.

She sprang out of the bed as if it was a trap, staring around the room for an explanation, and immediately the pain in her head intensified. She then looked down and was relieved that she was wearing her outfit from last night. As the events of the previous evening unfolded in her memory, she started to think through what she should do. She needed to get back to her own room and get herself cleaned up. As she left the room, she almost sobbed, *What have I done?*

*

An hour later, Emily stumbled into the office, feeling terrible, and collapsed into her chair. Sipping her strong black coffee, she looked up to see Jack walking in, looking sharp as always.

"You look terrible," he remarked. "We have a lot to do today…"

Emily bristled at the comment. "Thanks for your concern, Jack. I'm aware of that. I'll be fine. Just give me a moment."

Jack's pupils dilated. "No, you're not 'fine'. You're acting like a bloody amateur. You're a senior member of this law firm. A stunt like last night was the kind of thing I see new graduates do."

Emily glared at him. "Excuse me? What I do in my personal time is my own business."

"No. No, it isn't. Apart from the fact that I had to come and rescue you from yourself, this is a small community and our work is sensitive enough as it is. Get your act together or get out."

Emily was seething with anger. "You know what? You're a sanctimonious prick. You think you're so much better than everyone else, but you're not. You're just as flawed and human as the rest of us."

Jack's face turned red with anger. "How dare you speak to me like that? You're lucky to even be on this case, and you're throwing it all away because of your reckless behaviour."

Emily stood up, her own face flushed with fury. "I'm done with this. I'm sick of your condescending attitude and your holier-than-thou demeanour. If you think you can do this without me, go ahead and try."

"Well maybe I will," retorted Jack.

"Oh and by the way, your fiancée?"

At the mention of Kate, Jack bristled.

"Well, she said hi when I picked up the phone in your room this morning…"

Jack's face fell and he visibly shrank as he processed what had been said. Stuttering, he mumbled, "W-w-what?"

"Your problem, matey boy, not mine." Emily stood up and lifted her bag. As she pulled her things together to leave, Jack stood watching, speechless. Suddenly they both turned at the sound of the office door opening. There stood in the frame was a small, slim figure with a standard-issue wheeled case beside her.

"Well, good morning everyone. I presume you're the Harrison & Associates team?"

After a moment's pause, Emily replied, "Yes, and you are?"

"I'm Bronwyn. Bronwyn Hart. I've been sent by Darius. He said you needed help, so I'm here to help you with…" As the newcomer's gaze fell on Jack, she stopped and then rapidly recovered. "Oh. Well, hello Jack…"

All colour left Jack's face and his body felt like stone. Bronwyn. The last time he had seen her had been when he had left her sleeping in the hotel room in London after a night of drinking in a rooftop bar. What on earth was she doing here?

"You two know each other?" asked Emily.

Jack was unable to respond as he felt his whole world crashing in on him. His brain went into over-drive. What should he say? What was she going to say? How could he get out of this situation?

"Oh, Jack and I met on my first day. He was sooooo supportive," Bronwyn drawled in her upper-class Home Counties accent, smirking at Jack as if they shared an inside joke.

Jack wanted to throw up. He had to get a grip, but how?

Emily looked at Jack with both annoyance and disbelief. Did Jack know this junior was coming out? She couldn't believe that Darius had sent them someone so inexperienced.

"What the hell...?" Jack muttered under his breath and ran his hand through his hair.

Bronwyn didn't seem to pick up on any hostility towards her as she began to unpack her things at the desk next to theirs.

"So, I'll need you to brief me on what's going on, so I can understand what to do," she said, her voice high-pitched with a grating uplift that turned every statement into a question.

"Actually, we're fine," Emily said, still feeling the effects of her hangover. "There's nothing urgent so why don't you start reading the main case files to get up to speed?"

"Oh, I read those on the plane. Maybe I could help with some of the Russian accounts; it seems like you haven't quite got round to those yet?" she said, gesturing to the pile on Emily's desk.

Emily and Jack exchanged glances. Jack could feel his stomach churn. "They were on a list to look at today. We'll let you know when they need your support," he said.

Bronwyn didn't seem to take the hint. "I'm fluent in Russian. Daddy was like an oligarch, or something." She waved her hand dismissively. "That was one of the reasons Darius thought it was a good idea to send me."

Emily looked away and rolled her eyes.

As the day went on, Bronwyn's behaviour only became more irritating. She constantly interrupted Emily and Jack, asking questions that, whilst on the surface were acceptable, always held some barbed nugget or put-down. Emily, who was slowly recovering from her hangover, was especially irritated with her and found herself snapping at Bronwyn several times throughout the day.

For his part, Jack ensured he stayed as far away from Bronwyn as possible, moving his work into a side office, and ensuring he was never around when Emily stepped out of the office. He was still unsure in his mind how to deal with the situation.

As they were wrapping up for the day, Bronwyn announced that she was going to check in to the hotel and then join them for dinner.

"Actually, we were thinking of just doing our own thing this evening," Jack said firmly.

But Bronwyn was persistent. She went up to Jack and touched his arm, saying, "Oh come on. I know how sociable you are."

Emily could see that Jack was about to lose his temper, so she interjected and suggested that they all meet for a light meal. She hoped that maybe, if they got to know Bronwyn better, they could find some common ground.

As they sat down in the restaurant, Bronwyn launched into a long and rambling anecdote about her time travelling round Asia with her friend, Tasmin. Despite numerous attempts by Emily to open up the conversation, or involve Jack, Bronwyn continued on and was only stopped mid-flow by the waiter appearing and asking for their order.

"Right. So, I've looked at the menu and read the reviews," said Bronwyn. "So if you're both okay, I'll just order for all of us."

Jack raised his eyebrows, but before he could say anything, Emily jumped in. "Thank you, Bronwyn, that's really kind of you, but I've actually not had someone order my food for me since I was, oh, about eleven."

"Oh, right. It's just that, I thought you'd all want to benefit from my research."

Jack and Emily glanced at each other before Emily replied slowly, "That's not really appropriate."

Looking put-out, Bronwyn ordered for herself and started scrolling through her mobile.

Emily sighed. With the last vestiges of her hangover still clinging on, all she wanted to do was have a salad, a warm bath, and an early night. How had she ended up babysitting a petulant Gen Z and an almost equally petulant, mid-thirties man?

Emily looked at Jack. He looked positively grey as though this situation, as if Bronwyn herself, was making him ill. At least his anger at Emily's behaviour last night seemed to have been completely displaced by his displeasure with this young woman. *Thank goodness for small mercies*, thought Emily.

Just as she was considering this and thought that Jack wouldn't be able to hold his tongue for much longer, he stood up, pushed his chair violently back, threw down his napkin and stormed out of the restaurant. Emily looked round at both Jack's half-eaten main course and a look of shock on Bronwyn's face.

Slightly embarrassed, Emily knew that the working relationship between the three of them was going to be even more strained after this disastrous dinner.

Bronwyn remained shocked and they both finished their meal in silence. As they walked back to their rooms, Bronwyn eventually tried to make small talk, but Emily could tell that she was annoyed with Jack, and by extension Emily, for leaving the restaurant so abruptly.

When she finally made it back to her room, Emily collapsed onto her bed, exhausted and frustrated.

"Oh my word, what a day," she muttered to herself.

*

The next day saw a rejuvenated Emily, fresh from an early morning swim, get to the office shortly followed by Jack.

"How are you feeling?" he asked genuinely, and a little sheepishly.

"Much better thanks. I even managed to get some fresh air this morning."

Jack smiled. "Me too. I managed a 10K along the beach. It's

really cleared my mind."

"Any sign of…?" asked Emily, but before she could finish her question, Bronwyn appeared holding three coffees.

"Good morning," she said in a sickly-sweet voice. "I bought us coffee."

Thanking her, Emily took one and moved to her desk.

"After all, I had lots of time whilst I waited for the two of you to arrive and open the office," continued Bronwyn. "I see things are already running on Caribbean time."

Both Jack and Emily's face fell. It was only just after 8am and the accusation was pretty unfair.

As they sat down to work through all of the records and paperwork, Bronwyn started to talk continuously about the case and the work she was doing. Both Jack and Emily tried not to pay much attention and focus on their work, but Bronwyn's constant chatter was a major distraction.

"Excuse me, Bronwyn," Emily finally interrupted. "Could you please work quietly for a bit? We need to get some work done."

Bronwyn looked a bit hurt but nodded and started typing on her computer. However, after a few minutes, she couldn't resist the urge to start talking again.

"I can't believe we're working on a case with links to the Russian mafia," Bronwyn exclaimed. "It's like something from the movies."

Jack rolled his eyes and glanced at Emily, who looked equally irritated. But before they could say anything, Bronwyn's phone rang. She answered it with a loud greeting and Jack gave her a look that strongly suggested that she should take the call elsewhere, but it failed to have any impact on Bronwyn.

"Yes. Yes. Yes, of course," Bronwyn said, her voice rising. "What? No, I don't want to hear that. No. NO. NO!"

She slammed the phone down on the desk and glared at Jack and Emily.

"What's wrong?" Emily asked cautiously, not really wanting

an answer.

"It's nothing," Bronwyn muttered, her eyes brimming with tears. "Just some stupid family drama. It's none of your business."

She turned back to her computer and started typing furiously, but Emily could see that she was still upset.

"Listen," she said, trying to sound sympathetic. "If you need to talk to someone, we're here for you."

Bronwyn looked up, her eyes red and puffy.

"Really?" she said, her voice barely above a whisper. "You mean that?"

Jack's expression was blank, but Emily smiled encouragingly. "Of course. We're all in this together, right?"

Bronwyn nodded and, for a moment, the tension in the room seemed to dissipate.

But just as they started to get back to work, Bronwyn's phone rang again. This time, she answered it with a smile, and the conversation quickly turned to her personal life. Jack and Emily exchanged an exasperated look and tried to tune her out.

As the day wore on, Bronwyn's chatter became more and more irritating. She interrupted them constantly and talked over them, completely ignoring any attempt at conversation. By the end of the day, Jack and Emily were both ready to pull their hair out.

"Thank goodness that's over," Jack muttered as they packed up their things that evening.

Emily nodded, but then glanced over at Bronwyn, who was still typing away at her computer.

"We can't just leave her here," Emily said quietly. "It's getting dark out, and she shouldn't travel on her own."

Jack exhaled heavily but nodded in agreement. Together, they walked over to Bronwyn's desk.

"Hey," Jack said, trying to sound friendly. "We're calling it a day. Are you coming back to the hotel?"

"Well, I guess I can keep working back there. Okay."

She quickly gathered her things and they all jumped in one

of the many taxis outside in the busy street. The ride back to the hotel only took five minutes, but Bronwyn still managed to cram in another anecdote about her and her friends.

Once back in reception, Bronwyn scurried away to her room. "Thank goodness," Jack muttered again, but Emily just stared after her.

"We can't keep ignoring her," she said. "It's only making her worse. She's here to help us, whether we like it or not. We need to figure out a way to work with her."

Jack shrugged, but Emily knew that he agreed with her. They couldn't let their annoyance with Bronwyn get in the way of the case. They just had to figure out how to manage her better.

*

The next morning, Emily watched as Jack pulled a flipchart into the middle of the office and indicated for Emily and Bronwyn to gather round.

"Okay, so it's Friday and we've done a week here. Let's review where we're at and what we've got left to do."

As he listed out the main items with the others both contributing, it became clear that their work, and the case itself, was coming together.

Emily summed it up. "My view? We're almost done in terms of what we can achieve here. What we're still missing is…"

Suddenly the door burst open and in stormed a broad, wild-eyed man with a thick beard. Scanning the room, his eyes narrowed on the trio. "Who are you? What are you doing here in my office?" the man demanded in a thick Russian accent, his tone menacing.

Jack stepped forward, his hand held out in a calming gesture. "We're lawyers from the London office of Harrison & Co. We're here on official business."

The man sneered. "Business? What business?" He looked at Bronwyn, then at Emily. "You two look like children. Why are you all here in my office?"

Emily bristled at his condescending tone. She stood up and faced the man. "We're here at the direct request of Mariya Svravipona."

The man laughed harshly. "That old hag? Are you her little doggies? Routing around in my affairs? You accuse me of fraud? This is something I did not do."

"We haven't accused you of anything, Mr…?" Jack replied.

The man stood still, calculating his options.

Jack doubled down. "Could it be that you are, in fact, Sergey Kuchovski? Ms Svravipona's business partner?"

At this, the man harrumphed and walked to the window to check the outside of the building.

"What do you know?" he growled as he turned round to eye them again.

Jack coldly stared into the man's eyes "We're investigating some financial irregularities. If you *are* Sergey Kuchovski, then I suggest you talk to us as openly as possible. I've been doing this job for over a decade now and there are only two ways this can go for you. The better option for you is to co-operate with us and arrange a way to settle things amicably."

The man ran a sweaty hand through his thinning dark hair.

"We want to help you…Sergey," Emily added softly.

Something clicked in Sergey's mind, and he went red and started shouting. "You want? You want? You child! What about what I want? Yes?" and at this he started striding around the office gesticulating wildly. "You say co-operate, but you don't know what that means. You say work with you, but you have no idea. You threaten me? ME? You have balls to say to me that I have two options? Bah!"

His accent getting even heavier, he walked right up to Jack and, prodding him in the chest, he yelled, "What you know about the Moscow office? And one in Kyiv? Or funds in Cyprus?"

Jack exchanged a subtle glance with Emily; this was what they had been looking for. "We know enough," he said cautiously.

Sergey slammed his fist on the table, causing Emily and Bronwyn to jump in their seats. "You offer me two options? I offer you one. You leave this alone. Or…"

"Or what, Sergey?" Jack said firmly. "We have a job to do."

Sergey sneered at Jack. "You Brits and your jobs," he spat. "You don't know who you're dealing with. I suggest you be careful. Very careful."

With that, Sergey turned and left the office, slamming the door behind him. Emily let out a sigh of relief, while Bronwyn looked pale and frightened.

Jack turned to Emily. "We need to step up our investigation. That man is dangerous, and he knows that we're on to him."

Emily nodded, feeling a sense of purpose wash over her. "We can't let him intimidate us. We have a job to do."

Bronwyn timidly spoke up. "Um, what can I do to help?"

Jack stared after Sergey before turning and saying, "Why don't you start by going through these files and start cross-referencing Moscow and Kyiv with Cyprus. Sergey may just have given us our best lead in days."

Bronwyn nodded and took the files from Jack, eager to prove her worth.

As they got back to work, Emily experienced a sense of excitement mixed with fear. This was a far cry from her Manhattan world of celebrity and powerful clients. But somehow this felt right, like she was using the law to right wrongs, even if the closer they got to the truth, the closer they were getting to danger.

*

Emily set off on her hike along the Railway Trail, a path that spanned the length of Bermuda's coastline. The Saturday morning sun shining down on her, she felt the warmth seeping into her skin. As she walked, she passed hidden caves, secluded coves, and powdery white sand beaches. The centuries-old forts and lighthouses dotted along the way added to the trail's charm.

It had been an intense week, so the three of them had agreed to take the day off to refresh before meeting back at the office the next morning. Bronwyn had declared that she was hitting the gym, and Emily had no idea what Jack was up to, but she was determined to get outside and try and detach herself from the stress of the past week.

With a lot on her mind, the peacefulness of the trail helped her gather her thoughts. She thought about how her life was slowly coming together again and how she hadn't trawled through her memories of James and the accident for several days. *Crikey!* She suddenly realised that she hadn't even cried this week. Did this mean she was moving on? She considered whether it was the excitement of this case or possibly—and she shuddered slightly as she considered this—Jack.

As she walked, she couldn't help but think about him and how he made her feel. They clearly had a connection that she couldn't deny, but she just didn't know whether it was little more than a complex working relationship. There were few people who had really got under her skin like Jack did.

Even just thinking about how much he annoyed her at times was making her pulse quicken. Yes, he could be deeply aggravating and cold and even rude, but he was also smart and kind and genuine. He was also, and she had kept trying to push this away, deeply gorgeous.

If she had met him outside of work, she would definitely be attracted to him. Not that she, Emily Taylor, would do anything about it. Not now her life was over, she thought sarcastically.

Hold on, was this the old Emily popping out of whatever hole in her mind she'd been hiding? Since when did she start mocking herself for not getting over James' death?

Enough, she told herself, and she focused on the wide sandy path in front of her as it wound its way along the beautiful coastline. As she continued her hike, Emily felt a sense of calm and tranquillity wash over her. The natural beauty of the trail was awe-inspiring, and she felt grateful to be able to experience it. She knew she would have to return to the real world soon, but for now she allowed herself to bask in the serenity of her surroundings. The fresh ocean breeze, the sound of the waves crashing against the rocks, and the sun shining above gave her a sense of peace she hadn't felt in a long time.

But before long, she once again started to turn over in her mind the conversation with Jack about her getting drunk. She felt so foolish and knew that he was right, even if his delivery was pretty insensitive. The 'old' Emily would never have done something so stupid and would have given hell to anyone else who had risked the reputation of the firm with such behaviour.

She tried to clear her thoughts. She didn't want to go down that road again; she had apologised and drawn a line under the stupid mistake. But again, it made her consider her feelings for Jack. She had treated him as a competitor from work and, whilst he had been snooty about her joining the team at first, he had been nothing but supportive since. Had she actually put up boundaries and created issues just to push him away and ensure he was an enemy and not getting close? What if all the hostility between them had actually been because she was pushing him away? *Oh my word*, she thought, *am I totally losing my judgment?*

She stopped and decided to walk down to the beach and the water's edge. As she made her way down the hill, she found herself in a small cove, where a narrow river gushed its way to the sea. Shaded from the bright mid-morning glare by rocks on either side, she sat on a large rock and watched the water flow down to meet the crashing waves of the Atlantic. The whole scene calmed Emily's thoughts, and she felt a deep connection between herself and the outside world.

Lost in her thoughts, Emily had no idea how long she had been sat there when she heard a voice behind her. "Beautiful, isn't it?"

Emily turned to see an older man standing on the other side of the river, dressed in hiking gear and carrying a backpack. He had a warm smile on his face, accentuated by a long, shaggy white beard juxtaposed against his dark skin.

"Yes, it is," Emily replied, returning the smile.

The man gestured to a rock. "Do you mind?" and when Emily shook her head, he sat and, like her, stared at the scene in front of them.

After a while he reached into his backpack and took out a drawing pad and pencils. As he started to sketch, he turned to face her. "We think of these beautiful scenes as permanent, but they are as temporary as we are. Just look at the sediment layers in this rock. A thousand years ago, this river would have been above us and a waterfall would take it crashing, violently into the sea but now look how gently it flows."

"Do you think nature always calm things down?" said Emily, as much to herself as to the man.

"Nature, or maybe just time itself. I think old age always rubs the corners off the most jagged of things." At this, he stroked his beard and laughed.

As he sketched the scene, they struck up a simple conversation, and they were comfortable talking about the scenery and the weather without feeling the need to ask too much from each other. The man shared some of his stories about growing up on the island. As they talked, Emily realised that she had been missing this kind of simple interaction with someone else.

Eventually, they said their goodbyes and Emily decided to head back to the hotel. As she walked, she was overwhelmed by a sense of wellbeing after the unexpected encounter. It was just good to connect with someone else, without the weight of expectation placed on it.

Nearing the end of the trail, Emily stopped and, as she looked out at the stunning scenery before her, she felt like she was healing. The scars, the pain, the fear, it was all receding and, whilst it was still hard to think about, she could now see what was unthinkable only weeks before: a way back to her old self. With a smile on her face, she walked towards her hotel.

*

As Emily walked back into the lobby of the hotel, she saw Bronwyn in a heated argument with the manager. Bronwyn was flailing her arms about, clearly agitated, and the manager looked exasperated.

"Excuse me," Emily interjected, approaching the two of them. "Is there something I can help with?"

Bronwyn turned to her, her expression softening. "Emily! Thank goodness you're here. This hotel is trying to tell me that they can't upgrade me to a better room. There are noises coming from the AC in my room and I want to move. They're telling me that's not possible, if you can believe that. "

The manager looked exasperated. "Ms Hart, I've explained to you that all our rooms are booked, and we're doing the best we can to accommodate everyone."

Bronwyn crossed her arms. "Well, I won't stay in my current room; it's too noisy and probably a death trap. I demand that you find me something better."

Emily rolled her eyes. Bronwyn was always such a drama queen. "Listen, let's just try to find a solution here. Maybe we can all sit down see what can be done?"

Reluctantly, Bronwyn agreed, and the three of them sat down in the hotel lounge to discuss the issue. After an intense discussion, facilitated by Emily, Bronwyn agreed to stay in her room if the manager personally checked that the AC unit was fixed and the manager offered a complimentary drink with their dinner.

Having sorted this issue, Emily begrudgingly agreed to then have dinner with Bronwyn, not wanting to come off as rude. They walked to the hotel's restaurant and Bronwyn immediately began to complain about the waiter, who wasn't serving her as quickly as she'd like. Emily tried to ignore it and make small talk, but Bronwyn kept interrupting her.

Emily decided that she needed to take a more forceful

approach with Bronwyn if she was going to survive the dinner.

"If I may, I'd like to offer you some advice."

At this, Bronwyn opened her mouth to start talking, but Emily intervened forcefully holding up her finger. "No, wait. Before you respond. I need to tell you a few hard truths for your benefit and if I could ask you not to interrupt me, I'd really appreciate that."

Bronwyn looked surprised and then slightly apprehensive.

"Bronwyn, you are a smart, beautiful, young woman with a successful career potentially ahead of you..."

Bronwyn beamed, clearly happy to hear this feedback.

"*But* you are currently lacking in empathy to an extent I've not seen in a long time. Your Emotional Intelligence is so low in comparison to your normal intelligence, you are actually a danger to yourself and others."

Bronwyn looked crestfallen and shifted uncomfortably in her seat.

"If you genuinely want to be successful, you need to start thinking about those around you and your impact on them. No more snide comments, no more talking over people, no more lectures. You need to respect people and listen as much as you speak."

Emily stopped, feeling better for getting a week's worth of annoyance out on the table. Bronwyn's expression was frozen, and Emily was worried she'd gone too far.

Eventually Bronwyn took a sip from her glass of wine, put the glass down and looked at Emily before she calmly said in an uncharacteristically quiet voice, "Thank you. And I mean that genuinely. That is the first piece of genuine feedback I've had since I started."

Emily smiled caringly at her and replied, "I hope you know that it comes from a place of wanting you to fully achieve your potential."

Bronwyn nodded, but before she could reply their food arrived.

As they ate their main courses in quiet appreciation of the food, both of them were thinking about the exchange Eventually Bronwyn broke the silence. "Look, I know I can be a bit much. If I'm honest, I've found this week very difficult. It's not easy trying to hold your own with two of the best lawyers around. I guess I may have gone a bit over the top in trying to show you how great I am." Bronwyn paused, and Emily could see her eyes moisten before she continued, "I'm sorry. I really am."

Emily felt terrible. "No, I'm sorry. I should have looked out for you much more and realised how daunting this situation was for you. Look, let's put it behind us. Here's to good colleagues." Emily raised her glass for Bronwyn to toast.

As they sat there, sipping their wine, Emily noticed that Bronwyn started to relax. She was a lot more thoughtful and even started to ask Emily about her life. They talked about their childhoods and their families, and Emily found herself opening up more than she ever thought she would.

Bronwyn revealed that she was sent to Bermuda by Darius as a way to prove herself in the company, and that she felt a huge amount of pressure to succeed. Emily could relate to that feeling, and they bonded over their shared experiences.

As the night wore on, Emily found herself enjoying Bronwyn's company. She never thought she would, but once Bronwyn had shed her armour, it turned out she had a dry sense of humour that Emily hadn't seen before, and they found themselves laughing along at their conversation.

Before they knew it, it was late and they had been talking for hours. They hugged goodbye almost like old friends, which surprised both of them even though it felt natural. Emily walked away feeling surprised at how much her opinion of Bronwyn had changed. She stepped out of the restaurant into the cool night air. The moon was full and bright, casting a soft glow on the beach. Emily decided to take a walk and clear her head.

As she strolled along the shore, she thought about the day's events and her mixed feelings towards Bronwyn. It was strange, she thought, how people could change; she had initially disliked Bronwyn but now that she knew why she acted like she did, she was actually good company. Perhaps it was the wine, or her walk earlier, but she felt philosophical about everything going on around her.

She walked a bit further, lost in thought, until she noticed a group of people gathered up ahead. Curious, she quickened her pace and soon saw that it was a beach party, with music and dancing and people laughing and having fun.

Emily hesitated for a moment, especially given her recent drunken evening, but then decided to join those sitting on the edge, enjoying the atmosphere. She ended up talking to a few of the other guests, enjoying the moment and forgetting about her worries for a little while.

As the party began to wind down and people started to head back to their hotels, Emily felt a sense of contentment wash over her. Things would be all right after all. She made her way back to her room, feeling a little bit lighter than before.

CHAPTER TEN
Jack

Jack sat on the balcony of his room with his laptop open in front of him. Fresh from a run and work-out in the hotel gym, he had showered and dressed and was now cooling off in the tropical wind that blew in from the sea. Even though nothing had changed since the morning, he felt better having had the time and space to contemplate everything that was going on. He still felt enormous pressure from the case and he dared not think too hard about his personal life, which he had mentally packed into a metaphorical box labelled 'train wreck'. With a deep breath and a straight head, he was able to convince himself that he'd been through worse, and he just needed to push on till things worked themselves out.

His phone bleeped. It was a text from Kate.

"I know you're sleeping with Emily Taylor. I phoned your room and she was there. I know I made a mistake but two wrongs don't make a right. Can we just talk? We can't just throw something this beautiful away. K xxx"

Jack deleted the text and blocked the number. He stood and lent on the balcony, looking out over the beach and occasionally shaking his head. After some time, he turned as a sound from his room woke him from his thoughts. His laptop had lit up with a familiar tone ringing from its speakers. As he expected, it was Darius.

"Hello Darius."

"Dumbfound it. Why the hell won't this blasted contraption work?"

"Darius?" Jack could hear his boss, but not see him; it looked as though the video was disabled.

"Hang on, Jack dear boy. I'm just trying to get this infernal device to…"

The window closed and the connection was lost. Jack smiled and sat back. As expected, within moments the laptop rang again and Jack answered.

"Ah, there you are, finally. Good afternoon."

Jack could now see Darius, who was clearly at home in his study. He was surrounded by bookshelves neatly populated with everything from law journals to business bestsellers. Jack couldn't help noticing that, even though it was a Saturday afternoon, Darius was still wearing a tie and tweed jacket. Jack had to admire his style.

"Hello. Everything okay?"

"Yes, yes," he replied, exasperated. "Just this sodding laptop and its inability to do anything I want it to. Remind me to sack the whole IT department when you get back."

Jack gently laughed and Darius smirked back before continuing. "So, how's it going out there?"

"Good. We've got a good amount of information and a couple of leads. We need to get through the rest of the information we secured from the lock-up and chase down the statements from the Russian bank accounts that we found yesterday. I think we're almost done here."

"So you think another couple of days will do it?"

"Yes. I think by Tuesday we should have everything we can get from here."

"Good. I've had our client on the phone asking how things were going, and I informed her that you and Emily were making good progress."

"Absolutely. There is one thing…"

"Go on."

Jack had contemplated whether he would tell Darius about Sergey or not. He didn't want to panic Darius and certainly didn't want him to insist on them coming back, but now that he was talking with him, he felt dutybound to mention it.

"We were visited by Sergey Kuchovski in the office. He was pretty upset and was throwing around all kind of threats."

Darius' expression became grave, and it was clear to see he was considering the risk that Sergey presented to Jack and the team. Darius was as competitive as Jack, more so in many ways, but he wouldn't risk the wellbeing of his employees for a case. He took a moment and was about to speak when Jack interrupted.

"Look, I know what you're going to say, but hear me out. I think Sergey is all talk. You know I've been threatened more times than I care to remember, and I could just tell that he was mouthing off. Whilst it wasn't great, I just don't think he's stupid enough to try anything."

Darius stroked his chin in thought. "And what does Emily think?"

"She agrees. In fact, she was more bullish than I was. I don't think this is her first walk round the garden either."

"All right, if you want to stay, then fine. What about our Security team? Do you want me to get them involved?"

"I honestly wouldn't. By the time they get up to speed on this, we'll be gone."

"Okay. But please be careful."

They then proceeded to discuss a few of the more technical aspects of the case and Darius asked how Bronwyn was getting on, which Jack answered positively without giving any indication of having met Bronwyn before.

Jack tensed up slightly, which continued as they discussed

how well Emily had slotted into the team, but as Darius then went back into talking about the case, he relaxed. He found talking with Darius soothing and it helped shape his thoughts on how to handle the remaining last few days of activity.

Before they both knew it, an hour had passed and Jack noticed that the sun was markedly lower in the sky.

"And what about you, dear boy? How are you doing?"

The question caught Jack off guard and he stuttered a positive, if muted, reply.

Darius was not convinced. "I can see you're not feeling your best right now. I don't know what's going on but given that the case is on track, I can only imagine it has something to do with your personal life."

If Jack hadn't felt so raw, he would have smiled. There was no point hiding anything from Darius; he was an expert on the human condition. In another life, he would have been an incredible psychiatrist.

"I've ended my engagement with Kate. We've....well, we've split up."

"Oh. Oh Jack, my boy, I'm so sorry to hear that."

He looked out over the beach and sea, his brow furrowed.

"Jack, how long have you and I known each other?"

"I don't know. Twelve, thirteen years?"

"Exactly. And how often have I given you advice on your personal life or interfered in your affairs?"

"Well, if I'm honest…never."

"Indeed. So let me break my rule and say one thing to you. You are a brilliant, young man with an incredible future ahead of you, but you are only human. We all go through ups and downs in our personal life, and this is what life is all about. The trick is to face the hard times with the same integrity and confidence as the good times."

Darius stopped, waiting for a reply from Jack but when none was forthcoming, he pressed on.

"Don't do anything rash, dear boy. But as someone who

knows you, I would strongly suggest you find some time when you get back, to get your thoughts together on what you are looking for from life."

Jack softly replied, "Thank you. I will."

"You're going to be fine, old chap. You really are. You just need to get through this."

Hanging up, Jack bit into his lip, something he hadn't done since he was a child.

*

It was another blisteringly bright morning in Bermuda and, despite being a Sunday, the office buzzed with energy as Jack, Emily, and Bronwyn worked diligently, their efforts nearing a conclusion. The office and its various desks were all cluttered with documents, charts, and laptops.

As Jack looked over at his two colleagues, he could only just see their heads above the stacks of files. The weight of the case had been heavy on all of their shoulders, but Emily especially had remained as determined as he was to uncover the truth and bring justice to their client, Mariya. As he looked back at the bank statements in front of him, he thought about his call with Darius and how lucky he was to have a father figure like him looking out for him. Suddenly, his thoughts were interrupted by an audible gasp from Emily's direction.

"Jack? JACK!"

He shot up and looked over at Emily, whose eyes were wide in disbelief.

"I think I've found it. Look."

As Jack joined her, she showed him how she had found a trail of evidence, a series of breadcrumbs leading her to the money they had been chasing. As she joined the documents together, it revealed Sergey's cunning tactics—a deliberate scheme to siphon off Mariya's assets for his own gain.

"This is it. These documents...they're the smoking gun we've been searching for!"

Jack leaned forward, his brows furrowing in concentration as he examined the papers Emily had discovered. His eyes widened as he realised the magnitude of their findings.

"My word. You've done it," Jack said, his voice full of astonishment and admiration. "He's been quietly selling off Mariya's assets at a profit and funnelling the funds into his own pocket through a series of bonds and loans to these new shell companies."

Emily nodded, her heart pounding with a mix of exhilaration and a deep sense of responsibility. "It's a pretty smart scheme. It's deliberately designed to make it difficult to trace the money, but these documents provide the crucial link we've been missing. Now we can expose Sergey's actions and bring him to justice."

A sense of relief washed over them both as they realised the significance of their discovery. Days of tireless investigation and late nights had finally paid off.

"This really is fantastic news," Jack said, and he uncharacteristically hugged her gently.

Emily's cheeks flushed and she was speechless. She didn't know whether it was because such praise from Jack was so rare, or because of the physical contact.

Regaining her composure, she offered an overly formal, "Thank you, Jack. But it's not just me. We're a team, and we've all done our bit."

Jack nodded, a small smile playing at the corners of his lips. "Of course, you're absolutely right, Emily. And we couldn't have done it without you too, Bronwyn."

Sat a small distance away, Bronwyn smiled politely but seemed wary of coming too close to the couple she saw in front of her.

"We need to share this breakthrough with both Darius and Mariya and let them know the end is within reach. There's still a lot to do, but this finally gives us the lead we needed."

Emily's eyes sparkled with anticipation. "Absolutely. Mariya will want to hear the news firsthand. If this is all we need then we should also start thinking about packing up everything for our departure. Can I suggest we see if we can bring our flights forward to tomorrow night and close down the office tomorrow morning? I also reckon we should celebrate our success tonight—dinner on me."

Keen not to leave the incriminating files in the office overnight, given Sergey knew about their work, they packed all of the papers into several boxes and gathering their belongings, they closed the office. Outside, they had to hail several cabs to accommodate everything, and they rode the short distance back to the hotel under the late afternoon sun.

They dropped the boxes in Jack's room and decided to have a pot of tea on the hotel veranda.

"So do you think the evidence we've found will provide Mariya with the means to reclaim her money?" asked Bronwyn.

"I think it will," said Jack. "Our findings provide clear evidence that can be used to indict Sergey and freeze the funds he stole. Yes, there's still a lot more to do, and I don't want us to celebrate success prematurely, but this could be the key to getting justice for Mariya and her company. I think we can be pretty proud of what we've done here."

Emily's eyes shone with a renewed sense of purpose. "You're right. This is just the beginning. Together, we can ensure that Sergey is held accountable for his actions."

"Yes, it's been a challenging journey, but we've managed to trace almost all the bank accounts where the stolen money has been hidden. Once we get the warrant to freeze them, we'll be one step closer to retrieving the funds."

Bronwyn chimed in, her voice also rich in enthusiasm. "I've been preparing the necessary legal documents and with this evidence we can file these papers tomorrow. Is it always like this? This is like TV or a movie!"

As they sat there, looking out over the hotel's grounds, all three fell silent. Deep in their thoughts, no one spoke and they all just basked in the knowledge that they had made real progress.

After finishing their cups, they agreed to meet in just over an hour for pre-dinner cocktails in the bar and all drifted off to their rooms.

*

The hotel bar was dimly lit, a sanctuary from both the last rays of the setting sun outside and the hustle and bustle of the restaurant. Jack entered wearing a smart lightweight suit with a crisp, open shirt. He scanned the room to find the others, and headed over to Bronwyn, who was sat alone at the bar itself. As he settled onto a stool beside her, Jack offered a polite nod and, signalling to the barman, he then turned to his colleague. "Everything good?"

She was wearing a tight-fitting red cocktail dress which accentuated her attractive figure. As she turned to face him, her lips curved into a playful smile. "All the better now that you're here."

Before he could answer, the waiter arrived looking at Jack expectantly. "I'll have a gin and tonic, please. Bronwyn?"

Bronwyn continued to sip the straw in her tall cocktail and gently shook her head.

As the barman headed off with Jack's order, he started to relax. Their work here in Bermuda had been successful, the tension had lifted, he was more at ease than he had been for a while.

"Everything okay?" he offered to fill the silence between them.

"Yes. Yes, it is," replied Bronwyn. "I feel that, even though this was a short assignment, it was a useful one for my career. International experience always looks good on one's resume."

Jack smiled to himself. It had been a while since he had spoken to anyone quite so blatantly ambitious, even in a law firm.

As he picked up the drink the barman had delivered, he

offered a toast. "Here's to the future."

"The future," Bronwyn replied as they clinked glasses.

"So, you never told me that you could speak Russian."

"I don't remember you asking," she said playfully.

Jack paused, sensing danger in the direction of the conversation.

But it was too late. Bronwyn leaned closer, her voice lowered. "You know, it's funny, we've hardly spoken about what happened back in London. When I woke up the next morning, you were gone."

Jack's throat tightened, and he took a deep sip of his drink, his discomfort evident. "Bronwyn, I don't think we should—"

But she wasn't finished. She laughed lightly, her tone teasing. "Relax. I'm just messing with you. Oh my word, you're blushing!"

Jack's unease turned into defensiveness, and he retorted, "Look, we had both drunk a lot. People can get carried away."

Bronwyn leaned back, eyebrows raised, her tone sardonic. "You're right, Jack. People *can* get carried away. I'm just glad that no one knows what happened given you're now my boss…"

Jack felt the world fall away from him. Heat rose to his face and his shock turned quickly to anger. "Listen here," he said keeping his voice painfully quiet to avoid shouting, "we both know we crossed a line that night. We didn't know what we were doing or who the other person was. It was a mistake."

Bronwyn's eyes flashed with irritation as she leaned in, her voice sharp. "A mistake? Speak for yourself. I knew exactly what I was doing. Did you think I didn't know who you were?"

The tension in the bar thickened as their confrontation escalated. Jack felt trapped, his heart was racing. "Firstly, this isn't the time or the place for this conversation. Secondly, if you ever…"

"Hi guys."

They both froze as Emily appeared between them, smiling generously. But as she looked from one of them to the other, her smile slightly faltered. "Err, what's going on?"

"Nothing. Nothing," said Jack after just a beat too long. "We were just discussing the firm."

"Oh. Okay."

Regaining her composure, Bronwyn added, "Yes, Jack was just telling me what an amazing career I could have at Harrison & Associates. Weren't you, Jack?"

Jack nodded and took a long gulp of his drink.

"Should we go into dinner? I'll have a drink with food," suggested Emily.

They agreed and all made their way to the restaurant. Jack held back and lent towards Bronwyn whispering, "That matter is *not* closed. I will not be blackmailed by you, or anyone."

Bronwyn just smiled and stroking his arm, said "Oh come on, you just need to relax." And without another word, she walked off towards Emily.

*

As Jack sat down for their last dinner in the elegant hotel restaurant, his encounter with Bronwyn still simmered beneath the surface, leaving him in a sour mood. He felt as though his personal life was lurching from one crisis to another, and he was especially challenged by the thought that his judgment had been so lacking. His mind was everything to him and the thought that he had made a series of wrong decisions was deeply unsettling. As he brooded, Emily and Bronwyn sat on the other side of the table and seemed to be getting on like old friends.

Bronwyn stole a glance in his direction, and he knew that she could see the impact of what she had said on him. She and Emily chatted away, but her attempts to bring Jack into the conversation fell on stony ground. Even Emily could feel something was amiss but didn't know what, and she proceeded to keep the conversation flowing to try and ease the atmosphere.

But, as the courses and wine flowed, Jack's mood started to ease. Emily, the mediator, was determined to make their last dinner together pleasant.

Whilst Jack was far quieter than usual, they engaged in polite conversation talking about the hotel, the beautiful island, the wonderful people, and their return back to London.

Keen to bring Jack out of himself, Emily asked him, "Will you miss this paradise?"

Jack looked up. "I'm looking forward to being back in the head office. The sun and sand have been great, but I miss the hustle and bustle of London."

Emily chuckled. "I think I'll miss this weather. Wet and grey London isn't quite the same."

Eventually their conversation turned to the recent issues within their law firm. Bronwyn was clear on her views. "It's about time, don't you think? There's no place for such behaviour in a modern company."

"It's fine to say that, Bronwyn," said Jack, emphasising her name. "But changing behaviours which have been tolerated, even rewarded, in the past is not easy. I've always called out any discrimination, and I welcome the recent purge of bad apples, but we shouldn't underestimate how hard this has been on Darius and others."

Bronwyn just smiled and took a sip from her glass, whilst Emily looked at both of them in turn with an expression of mild confusion.

As the evening wore on, the conversation dried up and Jack could tell that he wasn't the only one who felt weary.

"Shall we call it a night?" he asked, standing up before anyone could disagree.

They made their way through the lobby and Emily bid them good night, heading towards the elevators that would take her to her room. As she left, a slightly swaying Bronwyn turned to Jack and started stroking his shoulder. "What about you? Are you calling it a night, or could I tempt you with a nightcap back in my room?"

Jack firmly removed Bronwyn's hand. "I don't think so. I

think what you need is to get a good night's sleep."

Offended, Bronwyn pushed Jack away and said loudly, "Oh, I get it, now that it doesn't suit you, you don't want to sleep with me, is that it?"

"Bronwyn…"

"No, forget it. I thought you were a fun guy, but all you wanted was to screw me once and then forget me!"

Bronwyn saw Jack's face go a pallid grey with a startled expression falling over it. He was looking at something over Bronwyn's shoulder and she instinctively turned to see what it was. Emily was standing there, frozen, and for a moment they all stood looking at each other.

"I, err, I left my purse in the…"

Jack moved forward. "Emily, I…"

Emily rubbed her temples as if trying to wake up and, after staring at both of them, took a deep breath and marched off back to her room.

"Probably for the best," muttered Bronwyn and also moved to go.

Jack finally came to. "No, Bronwyn, *not* for the best," he hissed. But she was gone and Jack was alone.

He felt giddy and placed a hand on the nearby wall to steady himself. Emitting a deep moan, he could feel his eyes moisten. All he could think about is how Emily would now see him. He didn't know how he felt about her, but the thought of her thinking of him as some cheap Lothario pained him. A deep pain that he didn't understand. What was going on? Why was his life falling to pieces bit by bit?

He didn't know how long he stayed there, just holding on to the hotel for dear life, but when he finally had enough energy, he shuffled his way to his room.

CHAPTER ELEVEN
Emily

Emily ran back to her room and slammed the door behind her. She slid down the back of it and crumpled on to the floor. Oh, what a fool she'd been. How could she not have known? Had they laughed at her behind her back? She scoured her memory for any comments they had exchanged, any side-glances between them, anything. She had been so stupid.

And then, predictability, the darkness returned. She should have known she wasn't ready to return to a work environment. She wasn't strong enough to deal with others. She should have stayed with her parents and just kept herself to herself.

Lifting herself into the bathroom, she rummaged around in her bag finding the blister-pack of pills she was looking for. She had already taken her prescribed amount that morning, but she didn't care. She would do anything to stop this dark cloud enveloping her. The self-doubt was killing her. She took two pills and then, fully clothed, got into bed, tucking the sheets under her chin, just wishing for it all to go away. The darkness was a relief as it washed over her.

Waking later than usual, Emily couldn't face going down to the restaurant for breakfast, so ordered something from the room service menu and jumped in the shower. She ate in silence, staring at the wall and, when finished, started doing the exercises—both physical and mental—that her counsellor had taught her. By the time she left the room, she felt ready to take on whatever the day would present.

As she entered the office, both Jack and Bronwyn looked up from behind their piles of papers. She ignored their looks of concern and sat at her desk, continuing to get the papers ready for transport ahead of their exit. The silence was almost unbearable, so Emily decided to take control of the situation. She got up and stood between the other two. "Right, are we clear what we need to do to complete the forms and leave the office ahead of tonight's flight?"

They went through everything that needed to be done and agreed that it was all possible before they needed to take a cab to the airport.

Emily sat back at her desk and, after a few moments, Jack tentatively crept over to her desk and leaned in towards her.

"Emily, are you okay?" he whispered.

"I'm fine."

"Should we talk about…?"

"Not now."

"But…"

She looked angrily direct at him. "Not now. And not here."

Jack's face fell, and a guilty expression flitted across his face. He stood and uncharacteristically didn't seem to know where to go or what to do. Eventually he just walked out of the main door and, when Emily looked over at Bronwyn, they both caught each other staring after Jack.

There was no time for this nonsense, she thought. They had

a deadline and they needed to make it. Regardless of everything else.

*

Emily and Bronwyn continued working, and after a while they couldn't help but notice Jack's absence. Despite everything between them, they exchanged concerned glances, their brows furrowing with worry. It was unusual for him to disappear for so long, especially considering it was their last day in the office and they had important tasks to complete. Emily immediately felt guilty about being short with him and raked over her words to check how abrupt she had been with him. No, she had been right to establish a clear boundary between work and their personal lives. She tried calling him, but it went unanswered.

"I hope he's all right," Emily murmured, her voice tinged with worry.

Bronwyn nodded in agreement, her lips forming a thin line. "It's not like him to just disappear like this."

Deciding to proceed with their work, they settled into their respective desks. Bronwyn delved into finalising the injunctions they needed to submit, while Emily focused on the legal documentation that needed to be signed by their client when they got back to London.

As another hour passed, the two of them continued with their own work with the absence of Jack hanging over them. Questions lingered in their minds, and their concern deepened with each passing minute. They exchanged occasional glances, silently communicating their shared worry. Despite the uncertainty, Emily and Bronwyn persevered, determined to complete their tasks. The weight of their impending departure added an urgency to their work, and they diligently pushed forward, meticulously ensuring that every detail was addressed.

As the clock ticked towards noon, they both looked up as the doors to the office flew open, crashing against the wall. They were shocked to see three large men enter rather than Jack.

The shortest and oldest of the three strode into the room and squared up to Emily. "You got two minutes to get the hell outta here before you burn." At this, he gestured to the other two who held up jerry cans and started tipping petrol all over the office.

"What? What the hell are you doing?" asked Emily, shocked.

As the man turned and smiled, Emily was dismayed to see Bronwyn run out of the door, leaving her to fend for herself. "Bronwyn?" shouted Emily, but her colleague had gone.

"You should go back to your country and not interfere in things that do not concern you," spat the main in a thick Barmudan accent. When Emily froze, he screamed "Go!" in her face and grabbing her, he shook her violently.

Emily didn't know what to do. The physical violence brought memories of the car accident flooding back, and she found her body just wouldn't respond to anything she was thinking. She wanted to run, she was screaming at herself to run, but her body remained still. What looked like a defiant stand to the thug in front of her was actually emotional paralysis.

"You think you're tough, eh? You think I won't hurt pretty white girl?" The thug pulled out an old-fashioned razor blade from inside his jacket. Unfolding it, his eyes lit up and he smiled at Emily. "Now this is your last chance."

She was so terrified that the next few seconds were a blur. All she knew was that the man in front of her was suddenly thrown across the room with force and Jack's stern face swam into her view.

She didn't even respond as Jack sat her down on a nearby chair and then went over to the thug, who was just getting up, and punched him squarely on the jaw. The man fell backwards and lay still on the floor. The other two men, who had until now been occupied with covering the office with petrol, put down their fuel cans and started moving towards Jack, who assumed a classic boxing stance.

Just as it looked like Jack was going to be attacked on both sides by the men, the doors flew open and a loud voice yelled, "Freeze! Police!" Everyone turned to see three uniformed officers advance into the room with guns held high, followed by a very smug-looking Bronwyn.

Everyone in the room stopped and there was momentary silence before the police rapidly moved towards the men, handcuffed them, and marched them out of the building. One of the police officers remained and was talking on his radio at the office entrance.

Still in shock, all three of them collapsed in chairs around the office. As the adrenaline dissipated, they sat gathering their thoughts and breath. Emily was the first to break the silence.

"Jack, were you actually about to start a bit of boxing with those two thugs?"

Her comment hung in the air and, as the three of them realised the absurdity of their situation, they all burst out laughing, including Jack. The release of tension was palpable.

"Absolutely. I was going to give them what for," he said, putting up his fists in a mock boxing style.

"That was…Well, that was one of the strangest experiences ever," said Bronwyn. "Does this happen all the time?"

Jack and Emily laughed again.

"No, that definitely does not happen all the time. Unless this is a regular Harrison & Co activity, Jack?"

Jack looked up smiling. "No, I'm pleased to say that is the first time I have had to relive my university boxing days."

As they sat there contemplating the events of the day, they surveyed the mess left after the incident. Most of their paperwork was now covered in the foul-smelling petrol and needed to be re-done or photocopied to get it back into shape for submission.

Emily stood up and faced both of them. "Look, I know today has been downright crazy, but we can't let these criminals win. We need to go through all of this, salvage the paperwork we can and re-do the rest. Otherwise we won't be able to file it as we planned. We need to put aside everything else." She shot Jack a meaningful glance then continued, "Agreed?"

They both nodded, trying to ignore the shock of the day. At this point, a more senior-looking police officer came into the office and walked over to speak with them. He introduced himself as Sergeant Jones and explained that they were well aware of the three individuals who had tried to burn down the office: they were basically thugs for hire. They would try and find out who had hired them but didn't hold out much hope. They asked if the three lawyers could make themselves available for interview over the next few days.

"I'm terribly sorry, but we're planning to fly back to the UK," said Jack.

The policeman did not look impressed at this, and Emily quickly intervened. "Officer, if I stayed behind tomorrow, then would it be all right if my colleagues returned back to the UK? It's just that they have important work to do there."

"Yes, that is fine," said the officer. "You should stay at your hotel, Miss. This office is no longer a safe place."

"I'll also delay my flight and stay to support your investigation," said Jack, to Emily's surprise.

At this, they thanked the officer and got on with the large task of completing their work amongst the fumes of petrol. Emily caught Jack staring at her, and they exchanged a meaningful glance. She was still angry with him, but the tension in the air had been punctured by both the adrenalin of the attack and the release of humour when they realised they were safe. The events of the day had created a greater distance between the anger she had felt last night and her feelings right now. She knew she still needed time to process everything that had happened, but for now she was just glad they were all okay. *Later*, she told herself, as she compartmentalised her feelings in order to get on with the job in hand, as she had done so many times before.

*

As the afternoon sun slowly headed down towards the horizon, Emily and Jack sat on two chairs on the hotel lawn, staring out to sea. After completing everything they could in the office, including filing all the paperwork needed to start getting Mariya's money back, they had said goodbye to the office for the last time. Returning to the hotel, they had also seen Bronwyn off in a taxi to the airport and were both just taking a moment to reflect on everything that had happened.

Jack looked directly at Emily and they both shifted uncomfortably; there was still so much unresolved between them.

"You were incredible today," she said quietly, not looking at him.

"It was nothing. Anyone would have done the same."

"Hmm, I'm not so sure," replied Emily, who couldn't help but notice Jack's tension rebuilding. "Do you think it was Sergey?"

"Yes, probably. Typical move from someone who's worried about a paper trail. I'm just annoyed at myself. I knew we'd rattled him, but I didn't think he'd be so brazen as to send round heavies in the middle of the day to burn the office down. I should have…"

"What?" she asked gently.

Jack's shoulders drooped slightly. "I don't know. I'm just… Oh, I don't know. I just saw red when I thought he might hurt you," he admitted, his voice tinged with vulnerability. "And Bronwyn, of course," he added immediately, triggering his cheeks to gently flush.

She couldn't look at him. She couldn't straighten out her own feelings and still felt conflicted about the whole situation.

He ran a hand through his hair. "Emily, I'm so, so sorry."

"About what?" she said, although really she knew.

"The whole Bronwyn thing. It was a real mess."

Emily froze as a shiver darted down her spine.

"Look, I was in a really bad place, having found out that my fiancée was cheating on me. I stupidly went out and got drunk, and the next thing I know we'd spent the night together," he confessed, his voice heavy with regret.

"Jack, it's really none of my business…"

"But I want it to be. I like you. I really like you. And this, well, this type of thing just isn't me. I know we don't know each other that well and I don't want you to think I'm that kind of guy…"

The words hung in the air. She felt her heart beating faster and just didn't know how to react to his words. She still couldn't shake that sense of betrayal from finding out that the people she had worked so closely with actually had a history she wasn't aware of. But part of her, a small but growing part, was also thrilled that Jack actually felt something for her; that the two of them might actually have similar feelings for each other.

He stared at the floor, unable to meet her gaze. "It was a mistake, Emily. It really was."

"A mistake? But…I mean, I just, I mean…how could you not tell me?"

After staring at the ground for what felt like an age, he finally responded, his voice wavering. "It wasn't me. It *isn't* me. I don't make such foolish, impulsive mistakes. I didn't want you to know because I'm just so embarrassed. I didn't want anyone to know."

"But Jack, I don't trust anyone anymore and I was just getting close to trusting you and then this."

He winced. "I'm sorry. I never meant for this to happen, and I never wanted to hurt you."

"And what about Kate, your fiancée? How does she fit into all of this?"

Jack couldn't meet her eyes as he admitted, "It's definitely over between Kate and I." He added quietly, "In truth, it's been over for a while."

A small wave of sympathy mixed with her anger as she pressed further. "What about Bronwyn? Where does she figure in your overly complicated love life?"

He looked up at her, his expression pained. "I think we both knew it was a mistake. She was just venting at me last night."

Emily still felt betrayal as she processed his confession. She couldn't help but ask one more question. "So, what now? What does this mean for us, for work, for everything?"

Jack's tone was heavy. "I don't know. I understand that you're upset. I would be too. All I can do is promise that I'll be open from now on and that you *can* trust me."

The tension between them was palpable as Emily contemplated the newfound complexities of their relationship.

As the sun dipped below the horizon, casting a golden glow over the island, they sat side by side, silently appreciating the beauty before them, neither wanting to break it by speaking. The moment was too fragile and Emily found her heart swelling inside her, coupled with her familiar insecurities; what was she doing here, sitting beside a man she was attracted to in this perfect, romantic setting? She could feel her pulse racing and panicked, she needed to just get away. Slightly shaking, she mumbled a goodnight to Jack before hurrying off back to her room. Jack gazed after her, looking utterly confused as to what had just happened.

Without another word, Emily hurried along the corridor, her mind racing as she grappled with the shocking revelation and the emotional aftermath.

*

Emily sat on the edge of her bed and put her head in her hands. "For goodness' sake, what *am* I doing?" she said out loud.

Slowly, mustering all her energy, she got up. As she opened the balcony door, she felt the cool evening air wash over her soothing her skin which was burning up. She sat and reflected on the day's events. The conversation she had with Jack lingered in her mind, stirring various emotions within her. She felt conflicted about her own feelings, torn between being angry with Jack for his dishonesty and behaviour, and thrilled that they were getting closer.

As she replayed their discussions, a bittersweet ache settled in her heart. Emily admired Jack's formal nature and his integrity, but a part of her couldn't deny the flicker of disappointment that ignited within her when she thought about him having a one-night stand with someone like Bronwyn. It was just so tawdry and didn't fit with her picture of who Jack was, or who she wanted him to be.

She found her fingers absently tracing patterns on the surface of the balcony table. Emily questioned her own feelings, wondering if it was merely a product of the intense circumstances they found themselves in, or if there was something deeper at play. After all, it was only a few weeks ago that she had started to come out of her shell and re-emerge into society. She wrestled with the conflicting complexities of her own emotions.

Closing her eyes, she allowed herself a moment of vulnerability. She acknowledged the attraction she felt towards Jack, the undeniable bond that had grown between them. It was a flame that flickered in the depths of her soul, even if she tried to conceal it behind a veil of friendship and professionalism.

With a sigh, she admitted to herself that these emotions were both beautiful and terrifying. Beautiful because they reminded her of the capacity to feel deeply and form relationships that transcended the ordinary. Terrifying because they threatened to disrupt the delicate balance she had established, and plunge both of their lives into uncharted territories.

Emily knew she had a choice to make. She could push her feelings aside, bury them deep within and prioritise the friendship they had built. Or she could acknowledge the truth within her, allowing herself to explore what lay beyond the boundaries of familiarity. Would she, could she, tell Jack how she felt? Was that even fair on him? Would she just be ruining an embryonic friendship or was there a chance that he actually felt the same?

As the moon cast a soft glow through the curtains, Emily resolved to tread carefully, navigating the uncharted waters of her heart with caution. She knew that the path ahead was strewn with uncertainty, and that decisions would have consequences. But she also realised that denying her own truth would only lead to a lifetime of regret.

The night wrapped its soothing embrace around her as she drifted into a peaceful sleep, her mind was bustling with thoughts of friendship, love, work and the delicate dance between the three.

CHAPTER TWELVE

Jack

As the old yellow taxi pulled up outside the police station, Emily jumped out and Jack paid the driver. Emily looked down the street at the dusty, colonial buildings with their wooden-slatted windows and solid wooden doors. The police station itself was unremarkable, and from the outside could have been anything: a bank, an office, a school.

As they stood at the reception desk, an older, white-haired officer took down their details on a long form in front of them. He asked them to wait on the hard wooden benches for the officer that was dealing with the case. As they sat in silence, there was an unspoken thawing between the two of them that had begun at breakfast when they had chatted over porridge and toast. Jack had been left slightly disappointed by Emily's sudden exit the night before, but had been pleased to find her smiling and chatty as usual this morning.

After ten minutes sitting in comfortable silence, the officer they recognised from the day before appeared and asked them to follow him into a small interrogation room.

"This is a bit intimidating, officer," said Emily with a smile, gesturing to the tape recorder and hooks on the table for handcuffs.

Sergeant Jones chuckled, showing a full set of bright white teeth. "Don't worry, they're not for you. Unless you give me any trouble," he said, laughing at his own joke.

As they sat, the officer set up the tape recorder and took out his notebook and pen. "So, before we talk about the men coming into the office, can you tell me a bit about why you are here?"

They explained in broad terms the work they were doing and what had led them to the office. They mentioned that they were investigating the theft of large sums of money on behalf of their client.

"And who is your client?"

Jack's expression hardened. "I'm afraid I can't disclose that."

Jones sucked his teeth. "Hmm, now that makes my job just that little bit harder. Not good. Not good."

Emily tried to soften the mood. "Sergeant Jones, we are happy to co-operate in any way we can. We wouldn't be here otherwise. But you can't ask us to disclose information that breaches our own confidentiality arrangements. What else would it be useful for you to know?"

The officer considered the situation carefully before speaking. "Okay, tell me about the actual incident?"

Jack couldn't help staring at Emily as she sat forward and then, in great detail, took the officer through what had happened, ending in him punching one of the men. His pulse raced as he stared and absorbed how powerful this incredible woman was. To Jack, she was one of the strongest people he had ever met. He still couldn't fully reconcile the celebrity lawyer that he had been aware of through the industry news with the Emily he now knew, but he could now see how she had survived events that would have kept others down. He had never been taken so much by someone he was also working so close to. There was an energy between them that he couldn't explain but, whenever his mind focused on it, his heart went crazy and he could feel electricity across his skin. He rapidly pushed away his feelings and tried to focus on her words.

"…and then just as you were coming in with your men, Sergeant, Jack knocked out the leader of the group and, well, you saw what happened next.'

Jones nodded and sucked on the end of his pencil. "You know, Ms Taylor, we don't tend to get much crime here. Oh sure, we get the usual drunks and petty thieves, but not much more than that. The main crime committed on the island is by high finance suits and their lawyers…" He took a moment to emphasise his words. "What worries me is not these three thugs, but the wider situation that made them want to burn an office building down, if you know what I am saying?"

Like guilty schoolchildren in a headmaster's study, they both looked down at their shoes.

The officer continued. "So, I am hoping that you are going to help me out today and promise me that when you get on your flight tomorrow, which we are happy for you to be on, that will be the end of whatever you are involved in and I won't see or hear anything more about this."

Jack looked up and directly at Jones. "You have my word, officer. We now have what we needed and neither our law firm, nor our client, have any further business in your jurisdiction."

"Then I am happy to thank you for your time and say goodbye," Jones said, standing up and indicating towards the door.

As they walked out of the station, Jack and Emily looked at each other. "Well that went just about as well as it could have done. Let's get back to the hotel and update Mariya."

*

Back at the hotel, they found themselves a quiet corner and dialled into the virtual meeting room, their laptops perched on a table, waiting for the video call with Mariya, their powerful

Russian client, to begin. Their diligent work in Bermuda had led them to this critical moment, where they would update her on their progress.

As the call connected, Mariya's stern face appeared on the screen, her presence commanding attention. The air was thick with anticipation as Jack and Emily prepared to deliver their report.

"Ms Svravipona, thank you for joining us. We wanted to update you regarding the progress of the case," Jack began, his voice steady and professional.

Mariya's piercing eyes bore into the screen, her voice carrying an air of authority. "I hope you have something substantial to report. My patience has worn thin."

Emily nodded, her focus unwavering. "Rest assured, we have made significant strides in freezing the funds associated with the illicit activities. The accounts have been successfully locked down, and the money is no longer accessible."

A flicker of satisfaction crossed Mariya's face, a rare expression amidst her steely demeanour. "That is indeed good news. The first step towards justice. But what about the individuals responsible for this betrayal? Have you made any progress in identifying them?"

Jack exchanged a glance with Emily before continuing. "We have reason to believe that the main perpetrator was indeed Sergey, and he may attempt to retrieve the frozen funds in London. We are devising a plan to lure him into a trap. If successful, it could lead to his capture and ensure he faces the consequences of his actions."

Mariya leaned forward, her eyes narrowing. "And what guarantees do I have that this plan will succeed? I have entrusted you with my faith, but faith alone is not enough."

Jack spoke with conviction. Learning the lesson from his first meeting with her, he was determined to reassure Mariya. "Ms Svravipona, we understand the gravity of this situation. We have carefully constructed the plan and taken precautions to mitigate risks. While we cannot guarantee absolute success, we will exert every effort to bring him to justice."

Mariya's expression softened slightly, her tone less harsh. "You both have impressed me thus far. Do not let me down. This is not just about money; it is about vindication. I want justice served."

Jack and Emily nodded in unison, their resolve unwavering. "We understand. We share your desire for justice, and we will do everything in our power to ensure that the guilty are held accountable."

As the call came to an end, Jack and Emily exchanged a brief moment of silent acknowledgment, the weight of their responsibility hanging heavy in the air.

"We still have our work cut out for us," Jack said, breaking the silence. "But I think we have a way to bring this case to a close."

Emily nodded, looking focused and determined. "We've come too far. We'll do whatever it takes to ensure we get Sergey."

Jack and Emily closed their laptops, ready to face the challenges that awaited them back in London. But then the realisation seemed to hit them both that they were nearing the end of their time working almost alone together in this golden paradise.

"What a case…" Jack said quietly, his voice tinged with a hint of melancholy. He looked down as if he was almost talking to himself.

Emily turned to face him, a soft smile gracing her lips. "Yes. Yes, it's been quite the journey."

Jack nodded, a flicker of something in his eyes. "I couldn't have asked for a better work colleague, Emily. You've been…I mean, you're…" He stumbled over his words. "It's been really good."

Emily's cheeks flushed, touched by Jack's words. "And you. Your resilience, your ability to think on your feet... It's been nothing short of remarkable. We make a great team."

"But now we must move forward," Emily said, her voice tinged with bittersweet determination. "London awaits…"

"Look, I know we have an early flight tomorrow, but given everything we've achieved, would you do me the honour of being my dinner guest this evening?" He had assumed the overly formal tone he adopted when lacking confidence.

Emily was thrilled but ensured that she kept her reaction muted, "Jack Braun, I would be happy to accept."

*

The sun began its descent on the horizon, casting a warm golden glow over the tranquil Caribbean sea. Jack and Emily sat at a beautifully laid dinner table, complete with crisp white tablecloth and candelabra. They were on a pontoon, afloat on the gentle waves, a short distance out from the beach of the hotel. They had only just got used to the unusual setting, but already their table was adorned with an array of delectable dishes. The air was infused with the aroma of freshly prepared seafood and the sound of soft waves lapping against the pontoon.

As they sat across from each other, a spark of anticipation filled the air. The setting was undeniably romantic, the essence of an idyllic evening. The waitstaff, dressed impeccably in smart uniforms, skilfully navigated their boats, delivering each course with grace and precision.

Emily's eyes sparkled with delight as a dish of succulent lobster was placed before her. "This is incredible. I can't believe you arranged all of this."

Jack smiled, his gaze locked with hers. "I wanted to create a memorable experience, something that would mark the end of our time in Bermuda and celebrate the journey we've been on together."

Their conversation flowed effortlessly as they savoured each bite, exchanging stories and sharing laughter. They delved into personal anecdotes, dreams, and aspirations, discovering new dimensions to each other. The world around them seemed to fade into the background, leaving only their relationship in focus.

In the midst of their laughter, a realisation flickered in their minds. It was a subtle shift, an acknowledgment that the bond they shared might transcend the boundaries of work colleagues or even friendship. As their gazes met, excitement and uncertainty swirled within them, leaving them momentarily breathless.

The night progressed, and the atmosphere grew more intimate. Soft whispers replaced boisterous laughter, and their voices carried a newfound tenderness. The subtle undercurrents of attraction lingered, though unspoken, as they navigated the uncharted waters of their evolving connection.

Jack couldn't help but wonder if he had set the stage for something more than just friendship. Did the romantic ambiance blur the lines between their roles as colleagues in a professional setting? And wasn't that what he wanted? He observed Emily, her beautiful eyes glistening under the moonlit sky, and a flicker of desire briefly clouded his mind.

As the evening drew to a close and the sun lowered itself in the sky, they found themselves becoming quieter, their words gently ebbing away. The realisation that their time together was nearing its end weighed upon them, blending with the uncertainty that now coloured their thoughts.

The waiting staff discreetly cleared away the remnants of the meal, their smiles hinting at the assumption that Jack and Emily were a honeymoon couple. A fleeting exchange of glances passed between the white jacketed waiters as they packed everything away.

A short trip across the gentle waves in one of the hotel's small boats, and Jack and Emily were back on the beach. The sea breeze carried with it a blend of emotions, both exhilarating and daunting. Uncertainty loomed, but amidst it all, an undeniable sense of possibility lingered in the air.

As they slowly walked along the sand, their footsteps

mirrored the cadence of their thoughts. Jack's hand brushed against Emily's, a subtle gesture that felt both soft and electric, sending his pulse racing. With a shared understanding, they began the walk back to their resort, the weight of unspoken words intermingling with the sound of the crashing waves.

Emily felt a sense of calm settle over her. The time had come to share the depths of her past with Jack, to reveal the haunting tragedy that had shaped her life in ways he could never truly comprehend. She looked over at him, his eyes offering warmth and understanding, and she inhaled deeply. The weight of her memories pressed upon her heart, but she knew that opening up to him would bring her solace and perhaps strengthen the bond that was forming between them.

She decided there and then that she had to share with him. She stopped and turned to him ensuring that no one else was around.

"Jack," Emily began, her voice soft and tremulous. "There's something I need to tell you. It's about what happened to me— something I'm not sure I'm over…"

"Emily, you don't need to say anything."

"No, I want to. I need you to hear this direct from me."

Jack listened intently, his focus never wavering from Emily's face. He knew she carried burdens, shadows that he could only catch glimpses of. He had read about the accident in the newspapers, but he would never dare to broach the subject unless Emily chose to share it with him.

They moved to some nearby sun loungers and sat opposite each other. Emily cleared her throat and took a moment, steadying herself as she began to recount the harrowing tale. Her voice quivered with emotion, and tears threatened to spill from her eyes.

"It happened back in the States," she whispered, her voice carrying the weight of grief and longing. "James and I, we were childhood sweethearts, growing up in the same small town. We had been together for some time, we…" Her voice faltered, memories resurfacing, as she continued, "We'd had a terrible argument. He had…" Emily swallowed to keep the tears back and with resolve continued. "He admitted he had cheated on me and I ended our relationship. I was angry; so, so angry. I insisted that we drove home and, as we made our way through the winding roads of the Catskills, we went round a tight bend and a truck suddenly appeared. James swerved to avoid it, but... we lost control. Our car tumbled over the edge of a cliff and flipped right over."

Jack reached out and took Emily's hand, gently holding it with a silent reassurance that he was there with her, supporting her through the retelling of this painful chapter of her life.

"By the time the emergency services found us, it was too late for James. He… He didn't make it."

Her voice broke, tears streaming down her face as she shared the profound loss she had endured. The weight of the tragedy had been etched upon her soul, a scar that had shaped her very being.

"When I woke up, over a week later, I was shattered," Emily whispered, her voice barely audible above the sound of the waves. "The news of James' death crashed over me like a relentless wave, threatening to consume me. I was left with the reality of my own physical and emotional healing. The thing is—and I've never told anyone this—I initially came back to consciousness in the car immediately after the accident. I was hung there upside down and woozy, but I remember James talking at me. We were trapped, hanging precariously in that overturned car," Emily continued, her voice trembling. "For hours, we clung to life, paralysed and alone. He just kept saying 'Please forgive me, Em. Please just forgive me,' and I think I did but I could hardly speak. After a while I passed out. And I just don't know if he heard me. To this day, I just don't know if he heard me. I hate the thought that he could have died in pain and all he wanted was my forgiveness and that he may not have heard it."

Emily swallowed, her breath hitching, before continuing. "I

had to undergo extensive rehabilitation to learn how to walk again, to reclaim my independence. But even as I regained my physical strength, the emptiness in my heart remained coupled with the guilt that he died begging for forgiveness It's... It's been unbearable."

Silence enveloped them, the weight of Emily's words hanging heavy in the air. Jack moved beside her, absorbing her story, feeling the depth of her pain and resilience. Without a word, he put his arm around her, holding her tightly against his chest, offering her comfort and understanding.

In that moment, as the tears mingled with the saltwater on Emily's cheeks, she felt a profound sense of release. She had bared her soul, shared the darkest corners of her past with Jack, and he had embraced her with unwavering compassion.

They sat on that moonlit beach, bound by a shared understanding, their hearts entwined in the tender embrace of vulnerability. The echoes of Emily's tragic tale resonated within them, forging a bond that went beyond the surface.

As the night air whispered around them, Jack whispered softly into Emily's ear, "Thank you for trusting me with your story. I'm here for you, every step of the way."

And in that fragile moment, as the waves gently lapped at the shore, they found peace in one another's arms, a glimmer of hope amidst the shadows of their pasts, as they navigated the uncharted territory of their budding relationship.

*

From the hotel, a band started up and the soft strains of music began to flow across the beach, casting a melodic spell over the night. They loosened their embrace and looked in each other's eyes, their hearts connected by the poignant conversation they had shared.

Jack's eyes met Emily's, a silent invitation passing between them. With a gentle but firm grip, he stood up and took her hand in his. Slowly, they began to sway then dance alone on the beach. The world around them seemed to fade away as they moved in synchrony, their steps measured and graceful. The warm Caribbean breeze brushed against their skin, caressing their faces as they twirled and swayed to the gentle music. The night was alive with the magic of possibility and, in that moment, Jack and Emily surrendered to the enchantment.

Time lost its meaning as they danced, their bodies moving as one. With each tender step, their link deepened, transcending the boundaries of friendship and venturing into uncharted territory. Their silhouettes blending with the darkness, they found their movements became more intimate, their bodies pressed together, hearts beating in unison.

Emily lifted her head and they stared at each other with a mix of vulnerability and desire. In that moment, the world held its breath, anticipation hanging heavy in the air. And with the gentlest of gestures, Jack leaned in, his lips brushing against Emily's.

It was a kiss full of tenderness, a delicate exploration of their newfound relationship. In that stolen moment, they discovered a depth of emotion that words could never capture. Their souls intertwined, and the universe seemed to hold its breath in reverence.

After the kiss, they remained locked in an embrace, their bodies pressed together, hearts beating as one. The music eventually ended leaving behind only the echo of their melodies, a backdrop to the intimate dance Jack and Emily shared. The night enveloped them, a tapestry of stars illuminating their path. They held each other in silence, savouring the sweetness of the moment, the vastness of their emotions. The world seemed to shrink, leaving only the two of them, entwined on that makeshift dancefloor.

In that moment, they had both found comfort and the promise of a love that defied the boundaries of time and circumstance. And, as the night deepened, they remained in each other's arms, cherishing the beauty of this newfound connection.

With both trepidation and anticipation, they bid each other goodnight. They walked away from the shore, their minds heavy with thoughts of what lay ahead and their hearts tethered by the allure of the unknown.

CHAPTER THIRTEEN
Emily

Monday morning arrived, ushering Emily back into the familiar walls of the London office. The previous week's events lingered in her heart, a bittersweet reminder of the moments shared with Jack under the moonlit sky. But as she stepped through the corridors, searching for him, she found herself met with a surprising chill in his demeanour. Jack passed her in the hallway, his eyes averted, his greeting cold and formal.

Doubts crept into Emily's mind. Had their intimate time together been nothing more than a fleeting dream? The memory felt hazy, like a fragile wisp slipping through her fingers. She hadn't seen him the next day, and they had taken different flights back to the UK, but she had hoped for something more than simply being ignored.

Resolute in her commitment to professionalism, Emily chastened herself for allowing her emotions to cloud her judgment. They had a crucial meeting scheduled for the afternoon with Darius and their client, Mariya. There was no room for personal distractions. Curiosity compelled her to inquire about Bronwyn's whereabouts, hoping to glean some clarity from her assistant. The news she received, however, failed to scratch that itch. Bronwyn had been dispatched to assist on another case in Dubai, leaving Emily to wonder if their encounter in Bermuda had been nothing more than a passing chapter in their lives.

With a sigh, Emily retreated to her office, determined to bury her focus in a summary of the work they had completed in Bermuda ready for the meeting later. Her gaze fixed on the screen before her, she was resolute to be the old Emily, the hardened no-nonsense New York lawyer. She fought against the temptation to steal glances out of the window, where her imagination painted pictures of a life intertwined with Jack's beyond the confines of the plush offices of Harrison & Associates.

The minutes turned into hours as Emily closed off various loose threads and summarised everything that had been done. Her desk phone rang; it was Annabel, Darius' PA, confirming the Mariya Svravipona meeting and that Darius wanted Emily to lead on the briefing. As Emily agreed to the request she smiled. She thought that something like this might happen, hence the pre-emptive work she had done all morning. She meticulously finished her preparations for the meeting, arranging her thoughts, and ensuring every detail was in order.

As the clock ticked closer to the appointed hour, Emily paced the office, annoyed with herself for being anxious. She had met with more senior, more famous, more important people than Mariya, so what was going on? Just as she was about to blame the accident and her recovery, she silenced her demons. It had nothing to do with the car crash. No, this was a new factor in her life. It was Jack.

Reminding herself she wasn't some lovesick teenager, she steeled herself, ready to slip on her armour and take whatever life threw at her.

*

The meeting room was tense as Jack, Emily, Darius, and Mariya gathered around the polished boardroom table. Mariya listened intently as Emily led the presentation on their progress on the case. They detailed the extensive efforts made to freeze the embezzled funds, and their coordination with Interpol to potentially apprehend Sergey if he attempted to access his ill-gotten wealth in person.

As they concluded their presentation, Mariya's expression turned to one of satisfaction. She commended Jack and Emily for their diligence and was looking forward to the final meeting scheduled for a few weeks later when the work was done. However, before leaving, she dropped a bombshell that left both of them stunned.

"Oh and congratulations on the two of you coming together in a—how can I say—personal relationship," Mariya remarked, her tone laced with amusement and authority. "Don't look so surprised. You didn't think I would be stupid enough to not keep track of your progress myself, did you? You would be wise not to underestimate my knowledge of your affairs."

Jack and Emily exchanged glances, their faces flushed with embarrassment. Mariya's words revealed a depth of cunning they hadn't anticipated, leaving them feeling exposed and vulnerable.

Emily sat there shocked. Whilst she was sure there was no malice in Mariya's actions, only self-interest, this was still a major blow to both Jack's and her own credibility.

As Mariya exited the room, the revelation settled heavily upon all three of them. Darius spoke first, in a voice far different from his usual friendly tone. He spoke slowly and quietly in a way that Emily found chilling. "What the hell were you both thinking? Even before we consider the ramifications of you engaging in some tawdry holiday romance, how naïve do you have to be to assume that you weren't being observed by our client or her representatives?"

"Darius..." started Emily.

But Darius interrupted her firmly, "Your actions are completely contrary to *everything* we've established over the past year. For God's sake, you're meant to be leaders of this business, leading by example. Not copping off with each other as soon as you're out of the office!"

Jack looked grey, flinching at every word that Darius threw at them.

"Where the hell was your professionalism? Even if you *did* find each other attractive, then surely you know not to let personal matters get in the way of your professional obligations."

Darius continued getting both louder and louder, and redder and redder in the face. "We have a clear rule here: no relationships between staff. It protects you, it protects me, and it protects all of our staff out there. But clearly, you both feel that this rule doesn't apply to either of you?"

Emily, defensive and wounded, retorted, "It's nothing to do with work. We didn't do anything to risk the case and as you heard, Mariya doesn't regard it as an issue for our work. Our personal lives should have no bearing on the work we've accomplished."

Darius was about to argue back when Jack who had sat silently, stood up and with a steely calmness, uttered only three words. "I understand."

He then walked out of the office, leaving a palpable void in his wake.

Once the echoes of his departure subsided, Emily, now composed, turned to Darius, seeking answers amidst the swirling chaos of emotions. "What the hell was that? What did Jack mean?"

Darius, wearied by the weight of the situation, let out a heavy sigh. He was still angry, but his voice also carried a tinge of sadness as he replied, " Jack has always been an enigma. He keeps his personal life to himself, revealing only what he deems necessary. I don't know quite what happened out in Bermuda and I'll be frank, I don't want to know, but I can guarantee that right now our boy, Jack, is working out how he can *fix it*. Whether I like it or not, he will aim to rebuild that wall between work and his personal life."

"But…"

"No, 'but' nothing. I know this may seem heavy-handed, but your actions have risked our firm. We cannot afford any more scandals and no matter how you view it, two senior partners romancing each other whilst on a business trip does not pass muster. I'm going to speak to HR about what to do and how best to handle this and we will get back to you. For now, I need you and him to close out this case but consider this a warning that I won't put up with any more shenanigans from either of you. I know I can trust Jack to do the right thing; can I trust you?"

Emily nodded sheepishly.

"Then off you go. And, on a personal note, I have to say I am extremely disappointed in you."

Emily dashed out of the office as quickly as she could gather together her things. Fighting back the emotions, she felt bruised by the events that had just happened. Darius' reaction left her in a turmoil—was she angry with Jack for just leaving the room like that, or was she concerned for his wellbeing.

Yet, amidst the uncertainty, a resolve took root. She needed to understand him more, not out of mere curiosity, but out of a genuine desire to connect with Jack on a deeper level. With newfound resolve, Emily realised she would not rest until she understood the enigma that was Jack—the first person to get past her defences and touch her heart in a long time; a man who had made her really *feel* again.

And so, as the office hummed with a lingering tension, Emily considered her next steps. She almost felt as though she could no longer trust her own judgement. And whilst she hated to admit it, she couldn't work this all out on her own. She needed a drink, and more importantly, she needed her friends.

*

That evening, Emily sat at a high table in the bustling West End bar, where the clinking of glasses and laughter filled the air. Her friends, Chloe and Beatrice, joined her, their faces glowing with excitement and curiosity. Chloe, unable to contain her enthusiasm, leaned in and exclaimed, "So, spill the beans! How was Bermuda? Tell us everything about the case and the romance. We need all the juicy details!"

Emily smiled, her eyes sparkling with intrigue and fond memories. "Bermuda was an incredible adventure. We made real progress on the case, and I realised how much I've missed the thrill of piecing together a case."

Beatrice, her voice tinged with mischief, leaned forward, her eyes gleaming with curiosity. "And? Did you find any love in paradise? Don't hold back!"

Emily's cheeks flushed slightly as she took a sip of her drink, savouring the moment. "Well, let's just say there was a hint of romance in the air. A fleeting interaction that caught me by surprise."

Chloe's eyebrows shot up, her excitement palpable. "Oh, for goodness' sake, don't be so coy! Who's the lucky person?"

A range of emotions danced within Emily as she recounted the tale. "It was Jack, my colleague. But... it's complicated. He just broke off with his fiancée. Oh, and he slept with one of our younger colleagues…"

The table fell silent. Chloe and Beatrice exchanged concerned glances before Beatrice spoke up, her voice laced with empathy. "Oh, that sounds a bit of a, err, complicated situation. How are you handling it?"

Emily stared almost blankly, "Honestly, it's been a whirlwind of emotions. Jack and I had a bond in Bermuda, at least I think we did, but since returning, things have been a bit complicated…"

Chloe's voice softened, with concern and protectiveness. "Look, you deserve someone who's fully committed. He needs to make a choice and be honest with you."

Emily nodded. "I know. You're right, of course, you're right, *but*, things are complicated. Honestly, I won't allow myself to be caught in the middle or settle for half-hearted affection, but I don't want to throw something away just because it's not simple."

Beatrice's mischievous side emerged, a playful grin spreading across her face. "Well, my dear, it's time to play a little hard to get. Let him realise what he's potentially losing. Show him your worth and let him come to you."

Chloe's eyes sparkled, her smile widening. "Absolutely! Focus on your own happiness and growth. Engage in activities you love, spend time with friends, and let him see the incredible person he risks losing."

Emily laughed, "Sure. Look, I really appreciate your advice, I do. But I'm not sure he's the kind of guy who will come running if he sees I'm having a great time elsewhere. I think I need to bring this to a head somehow. My head hurts just trying to work out what to do. Also—and I can't believe this, even as I say it—I've only been back in 'real life' for a few weeks. This is all very fast."

The three friends leaned in closer, forming a circle of support and empowerment. As the night unfolded, their conversation continued, a vibrant tapestry of ideas, dreams, and shared experiences. Emily absorbed their words, feeling uplifted and ready to embark on a journey of self-discovery. Armed with newfound strength and a touch of playful mystery, Emily knew she had the power to navigate the complexities of her emotions. With her friends by her side, she felt invincible, ready to embrace her own happiness while keeping an open heart.

The night carried on, with laughter, friendship, and a renewed sense of possibility. The bar buzzed with energy as Emily, Chloe, and Beatrice delved deeper into their conversation, exploring various scenarios and strategies to navigate the intricate web of emotions surrounding Emily's relationship with Jack.

Chloe, her eyes shining with energy and a number of glasses of Chardonnay, leaned forward. "You deserve someone fabulous. If it is this Jack guy, then you need him to bring his game. He needs to put his cards on the table."

Beatrice nodded, her voice firm yet compassionate. "Exactly,

Em. You can't wait around indefinitely, hoping he'll figure things out. Focus on yourself, and if he realises what he stands to lose, then maybe there's a chance."

Emily took a moment to contemplate their words. "You're both right. I'm not going to put my whole life on hold, just waiting for him. This needs to come to a conclusion. Here's to getting on with it!" And at this they all clinked their wine glasses and laughed.

"And remember, we're here for you every step of the way," said Chloe.

Beatrice playfully nudged Emily's arm. "Besides, who knows? Maybe this situation will lead to something unexpected and wonderful. Life has a funny way of surprising us."

Emily's lips curved into a hesitant smile, hope and caution in her eyes.

As the hours slipped by unnoticed, Emily's friends encouraged her to embrace her worth, reminding her of the incredible person she was. They reassured her that she deserved a love that was genuine, reciprocated, and free from complications.

Finally, as the night came to a close, the three friends stood outside the bar, bathed in the glow of the streetlights. Chloe squeezed Emily's hand; "Remember, you're a total catch. Don't settle for anything less than...than...*everything*!"

Beatrice chimed in. "And if this Jack can't step up, then that's his loss."

Emily nodded, and as her eyes moistened, she said, "Thank you, both of you. You two are the absolute best; you mean the world to me."

With hearts full of hope and the bonds of friendship fortified, Emily bid her friends farewell, feeling a renewed sense of purpose. As she walked away, she knew that, whatever the future held, she would face it with grace, resilience, and a steadfast belief in her own worth.

*

Emily's mobile buzzed in her pocket, and she instinctively brought it out to read the notification whilst she walked. She was surprised to read that it was from Anjay, who she hadn't heard from since their date a few weeks earlier. He was just wishing her well and seeing if she wanted to meet up. She wasn't sure whether she wanted to see him again, but regardless it was still reaffirming for her that there was indeed life outside of work and even more so, life outside of Jack Braun.

As Emily continued to leisurely stroll along London's vibrant Southbank, the gentle rhythm of her steps matched the cadence of her thoughts. The city's energetic pulse surrounded her, intermingling with the melodies of laughter and conversation that filled the air. She watched as couples walked hand in hand, their smiles radiant in the glow of streetlights, and groups of friends shared animated stories, their camaraderie palpable.

The sight of people immersed in each other sparked a poignant realisation within Emily. It was as if a dormant ember had been reignited within her, prompting a deeper longing for human companionship. The tragedy that had once cloaked her heart had started to dissipate, replaced by a yearning to embrace the warmth of shared moments and the potential for love.

As she observed the world around her, and despite her wishes, Emily's mind wandered to the meeting earlier with Darius and Jack. She hated the way it had made her feel like she was some junior member of staff who had been caught having an affair with a colleague. She was *Emily Taylor*, for goodness' sake, not some newbie who needed to be told off by the boss. Her old self lingered at the back of her mind like a nagging aunt—*you shouldn't risk your career for one man, especially one that suddenly ups and leaves you to take the blame, you need to prioritise yourself,* it told her. But that wasn't how she truly felt. Maybe it was the endless sessions of therapy after the accident, but she felt more able to consider her own emotions than ever before and she understood that she really felt something for this man, warts and all.

Whether she liked it or not, Jack had subtly woven his way into her life. Damn him. Emily resented that with each encounter, their relationship had grown stronger. It was as if they were dancing to an unspoken rhythm, their minds in sync, amid the complex backdrop of their work. But the tides of her emotions swirled with love and hate. Jack had walked away from the meeting, he had walked away from their embryonic relationship, and the weight of that reality cast shadows upon her burgeoning feelings. Doubts nestled within her mind. *God, the whole thing is just too annoying*, she thought. *Like an itch I can't scratch.*

Emily rose from her thoughts to find consolation in the bustling Thames riverside, and sought refuge on a bench overlooking the river and the buildings on the North bank. She was growing to love this city; she still missed Manhattan but there was something about the culture, the mood, the attitude of London that made it an incredible place to be. She had spent formative years here and whilst NY would almost certainly be the place she felt comfortable in, the connection she had with this town made it the right place to be right now.

She leaned back on the bench. *But what do I do about this whole Jack thing?* she wondered. As she saw it, she had two options: shut the whole relationship down, or reduce it to something formal or even non-existent. She knew she was capable of that. 'Old' Emily had made plenty of sacrifices in her time to serve her career and this would just be another one. *Or*, she sighed, *or I try and make a go of this.* She looked up into the sky, the city's twinkling lights mirroring the constellation of thoughts swirling across her mind.

She smiled. Who was she kidding? She knew what she was going to do. If she'd learnt nothing else from the past few years, it was that life was too short. She'd had money, she'd had success, what she wanted now was to love and the emotions she had already experienced with this mildly infuriating man showed her that more than anyone else she'd met, he could be the 'one'. With this revelation, her heart felt simultaneously daunted and exhilarated, like a bird poised to take flight from its cage.

As she rose from the bench, an air of renewed purpose enveloped her. Emily knew that the path she had chosen would be riddled with challenges, requiring her to confront her own vulnerabilities and navigate the complexities of relationships. As she continued her meandering journey along the Southbank, Emily carried with her the weight of possibility. The stars above twinkled in approval, as if the universe itself conspired to guide her towards a destiny intertwined with love. And as the vibrant city lights illuminated her path, Emily's mind buzzed with a kaleidoscope of thoughts, contemplating the steps she needed to take. She knew that pursuing her burgeoning feelings for Jack meant traversing delicate territory. She knew Jack carried as much baggage as she did, and she would need to find the route through to giving them the best chance of a relationship. If after doing all that, they weren't together, well then at least she had given it her all.

Later that night, back in the peace of her own house, Emily prepared for the day ahead. She carefully chose her attire, selecting an outfit that mirrored her newfound confidence—a delicate balance of elegance and self-assurance. The mirror reflected a woman on the cusp of an emotional journey, radiating strength and vulnerability in equal measure. Lying in bed, the moon casting a soft glow upon her, Emily's thoughts swirled with excitement and apprehension. Sleep did not come easy, her mind too consumed by the possibilities that awaited her on the morrow.

*

With the first light of dawn, Emily rose from her bed, full of willpower. The morning air greeted the new, or possibly more accurately the old, Emily with a gentle caress as she prepared for the day ahead. As she adorned herself with the trappings of confidence, she repeated a silent mantra, grounding herself in the belief that she deserved happiness and the chance to explore her relationship with Jack. How different she felt from only a few weeks earlier when she woke in tears, still rebuilding her damaged psyche.

Stepping out into the world, Emily felt a renewed energy coursing through her veins. The city hummed with life, mirroring the exhilaration within her heart. Every step she took brought her closer to the moment of truth, where she would confront Jack and lay bare the depths of her emotions. The sun climbed higher in the sky, casting a warm glow over the city's bustling streets. Emily's pace quickened, her heart pounding in synchrony with her footsteps. She felt the weight of anticipation settle upon her shoulders, yet she carried it with grace, knowing that this pivotal moment held the potential to alter the course of her life.

Arriving at their familiar meeting spot, the entrance to their shared workspace, Emily stopped, taking a moment to gather her thoughts and steady her nerves. She drew in a deep breath, summoning the courage to face the uncertainties that lay ahead. With a resolute step forward, Emily pushed open the door and entered the realm where her connection with Jack had begun. Leaving the elevator, the office buzzed with activity, yet her focus remained unwavering, fixed on the imminent conversation that would shape their future.

After dropping off her things in her office, she immediately walked towards Jack's office, her heart thumping in her chest, a symphony of emotions and possibilities. She caught a glimpse of him, engrossed in his work, unaware of her presence. Her steps faltered for a moment, nervousness and excitement intertwining within her. Summoning her resolve, Emily approached Jack, her voice as steady as she could make it. "Jack, we need to talk," she began, her voice carrying the weight of her unspoken desires and the hope that had taken root within her.

His gaze meeting hers. Jack nodded, his expression unreadable. "Yes," he replied, his voice tinged with a juxtaposition of anticipation and caution. "But not now. Let's meet for lunch, outside the office."

They both relaxed slightly with this postponement. Emily nodded and she wondered if he felt as she did about their discussion.

When lunchtime arrived, they found themselves strolling through the bustling streets of the City, making their way towards the nearest garden square. The sun filtered through the leafy canopy overhead, casting dappled shadows upon their path. Their footsteps falling with the weight of unspoken words, the tension between them palpable.

As they entered the tranquil sanctuary of the garden square, Emily's heart fluttered with nervous anticipation. She had rehearsed the words she wanted to say countless times in her mind, but now, in Jack's presence, they seemed to elude her.

They walked side by side, their steps steady and measured, mirroring the rhythm of their conversation. Emily was mustering the courage to lay bare her feelings.

"Jack," she began, her voice tinged with both vulnerability and determination. "I need you to know how I feel about you. Since the accident, you are the first person I've connected with on a deeper level. I've tried to fight it, tried to tell myself it's just friendship, but it's more than that. I care about you. More than I should."

Jack listened intently, his eyes fixed on the path before them. His silence fuelled Emily's desire to reveal the depth of her emotions, to bridge the gap between them.

"I know we both put our careers ahead of everything else and this could undermine that, but if there's something here...well, if there *is* a possibility of something between us then shouldn't we kindle that flame and not just extinguish it in the name of work?"

With no response, Emily continued, her voice trembling

slightly. "I know it's only been a few weeks, but the time we've spent together, here and in Bermuda, I feel a real connection between us."

A conflicted expression crossed Jack's face, his eyes searching hers for an answer. "Emily, I care about you too," he finally admitted, his voice soft with longing and resignation. "But things, well, they're…complicated."

Emily's frustration began to bubble within her, mingling with a hint of frustration. "So, you're willing to sacrifice your own happiness for the sake of what? Professionalism?" she retorted, disappointingly. "Is that how you view this, as just another situation to manage? Are you so afraid to take a leap, to follow your heart?"

Jack's silence spoke volumes, the weight of his conflicting emotions hanging heavy in the air. The argument folded back on itself, the questions lingering unanswered.

"I… I don't have a good reply," he admitted, his voice in turmoil. "I'm torn between doing what's right and what I feel when I'm with you. It's not easy for me either."

Emily's frustration gave way to a tinge of resignation. The circles they were walking mirrored the futility of their conversation. She halted, turning to face him directly, her eyes brimming with emotion.

"What do you want?" she said, sadly. "I can't keep walking this path with you if it only leads to confusion and heartache. I need clarity, and I deserve someone who can fully embrace their feelings for me."

Jack's expression softened, regret evident in his eyes. "I never meant to hurt you or lead you on. I care about you deeply, but I just need time. I need to do the right thing. By you, by Darius, by the firm, by everybody."

Disappointment slowly settled within Emily's heart. "I understand," she whispered, her voice barely audible. "But it doesn't mean I agree."

Jack reached out, his hand gently brushing against her arm.

"I'm sorry. Please just give me time."

Emily nodded, her eyes welling up with unshed tears. "I can see this is not the right time for you," she replied softly. "But I need to move forward and find my own happiness. If we're not going to try and be together then I don't think we should see each other at all."

She could see him bristle at this ultimatum. "Fine. If that's how you want it, then so be it. You deserve someone..." his voice softened, "...someone who can give you all that you want and deserve. I hope you find that person."

Their conversation hung in the air, the unspoken words echoing between them. It was a moment of realisation, of accepting the reality that, sometimes, timing and circumstances simply don't align.

As they walked back towards the office, their footsteps carried the weight of unspoken farewells. She couldn't help but feel a sense of loss, a void left by the fragments of a relationship that could never fully be realised. Yet, within that void, there was a glimmer of hope. Hope for a future where Emily *could* find someone who would reciprocate her feelings, someone who would walk hand in hand with her, embracing the love they shared.

They reached the office, their silence speaking volumes. Without even a final glance, Emily turned away, steeling herself for the next chapter of her life. She knew it wouldn't be easy, but she had to close the door on Jack for her own good. She needed the strength to move forward, to seek the happiness she deserved. She had been true to her heart and, even if that meant that she may have ended her feelings for Jack, she had followed her heart and been honest.

As she stepped into her office, Emily whispered under her breath, "Goodbye Jack Braun."

*

Emily sat at her desk, determined to close out the case in front of her regardless of the emotions swirling around. As she had done many times before, she sought sanctuary in her work, pushing aside the frustration and disappointment from her walk with Jack. The hours flew by, and making good progress, the afternoon gave way to evening and her mood started to lift.

At the sound of a knock on her open door, she raised her head and looked over to see Sarah, Jack's assistant, standing there.

"Excuse me Emily, do you have a minute?"

Emily smiled politely, "Of course, come in."

"I am really sorry to bother you, but Jack has had to leave early and I need a signature on the invoice for the Svravipona case," she said apologetically. "Normally, I would have left this till next week, but I'm being chased by the Finance team who want to send out the invoice tonight. Sorry"

Emily took the paper and quickly scanned it before signing. "No problem. There you go."

Sarah looking relieved took the document and went for the door, but at the last moment, turned to ask, "I hope you don't mind, but are you okay?"

"Yes of course," said Emily. "Why wouldn't I be?"

"Well, it's just that..." Sarah stopped. She looked down and shook her head gently.

"Sarah? Sarah, what is it?"

Staring hard at Emily, she continued, "Can I trust you? I feel like I can. But can I *really* trust you?"

Emily was taken aback but nodded. "Of course, you can. What is it? You know you can talk to me," she added and gently gestured for her to take a seat.

Sitting, Sarah looked straight at her. "I don't know what exactly is going on between you and Jack. I can guess, but I don't want to interfere. What I will say is that since he got back from Bermuda, well, he hasn't been the same."

Emily opened her mouth to speak, but uncharacteristically couldn't think of what to say.

Sarah continued, "I know he's split up from Kate, but it's not just that. There's something that is conflicting him, driving him to distraction, on his mind constantly, and the only thing I can think is that, well, that it's you."

Emily looked away from Sarah out at the view of the city. *What a mess*, she thought to herself. All she had wanted was a fresh start in a new job in a new city. But here she was stuck in the middle of...well, that was the problem—she didn't know what she was in the middle of. Was Jack saying *not now* or *never?* She just wasn't sure. Part of her was worried that she had cut him short too soon on their walk, but then she had to look after herself and she refused to be left in some romantic limbo whilst Jack made up his mind.

"I don't know, Sarah. It's just so complicated. I know you're only looking out for Jack, but he needs to work out what he really wants."

"I've known Jack for a long time now," she replied, "and he is one of the most incredible and kind people I've ever known, but the one person he often doesn't look after is himself. And that's what I think is happening here."

Emily could see Sarah's eyes moisten as she continued. "He won't say, but I think he has fallen for you in a big way. And I think his need to do the right thing by the firm and his career and whatever, is conflicting him so much that it's hurting him."

"But I shared with him my feelings today and he, well, he pushed me away," said Emily.

"Did he? Or was he just trying to navigate between the two of you and this place?" said Sarah gesturing around her.

Emily rubbed her eyes. "Oh, what the hell do I do?"

"I don't know," said Sarah, blowing her nose on her handkerchief. "I hope I did the right thing coming here. I just wanted you to know."

Emily stood up and walked towards Sarah. "Thank you. Genuinely thank you." And at this she offered her a loose hug.

Embracing then stepping back, Emily considered her words

carefully and then gently said, "Look, I didn't want to raise it before as I didn't want to intrude or I don't know, whatever, but are *you* okay? I mean after the whole Seamus thing?"

Sarah took a sharp intake of breath and there was a pause as she worked through how to respond.

Emily felt so awkward, she jumped in, "Oh crikey, I'm so sorry. I wasn't sure whether to bring it up. You know I'm here for you. We all are."

"No, no its fine," Sara responded. "You just caught me a bit off guard. Look, I'm okay. I really am. I almost feel embarrassed that the whole thing became so big it ran away from me..."

"You have nothing to be embarrassed about. Trust me. You did exactly the right thing."

"Thanks, I really appreciate that. I just want to draw a line under it and move on. Seamus is gone and I don't really want to ever think about it again."

Emily nodded and put her hand on Sarah's shoulder. "I'll never mention it again. But if you need anything, please, just reach out."

"Thanks, that means a lot. And please bear in mind what I said about Jack. He may appear tough on the outside, and he may push you away, but underneath he does really care." And at that, Sarah left the office.

Emily stood looking out of the office window her brow furrowed in thought. After several minutes, she sat back at her desk and lifted the phone. "Hi Annabel, is there any chance I could get five minutes with Darius before the end of the day?"

*

"You're sure?" said Darius, trying to hide his disappointment as much as possible.

"Yes. Absolutely," replied Emily. "My position here is no longer tenable. I appreciate everything you've done to welcome me here, but this is not the.... the *situation* I need right now."

"Because of..."

"I know what you're thinking. And yes, it *is* mainly because of Jack. But not because he's made it difficult or anything like that. It's just that in this delicate time in my recovery, I can't have this amount of complication."

Darius looked up. "You realise how this might look? The gossip version of this will be that a senior male partner made unwanted advances and forced the only senior female partner out of the business."

Emily bristled slightly at this. *Who cares what anyone thinks*, she thought to herself. But quickly calming down, she recognised the truth in what Darius was saying.

Considering her options, she suggested a small change to her resignation. "That's the last thing I want. Why don't I work my notice and we make sure that our comms and PR team message this in a way which is more linked to me finding a new role? I'm sure if we all hold the same line then this won't descend into mudslinging."

"Agreed," said Darius. "And look, on a personal note, I will miss having you around. You've done a great job on the Svravipona case and anyone that can keep up with Jack professionally is damn impressive."

"Thanks, Darius."

He continued, "Look, it's none of my business but I'm sat here worried about both you and Jack. I don't need to know the details, but is there anything I can do to help?"

Emily paused, then said with her voice trembling slightly. "I won't lie to you; it's been tough. Very tough."

He nodded, his eyes reflecting empathy. "I understand. Personal issues are always harder to manage than work ones. I, myself, have found the last year particularly hard personally."

She looked down, contemplating her words. "I'm so sorry about all of this," she said softly. "I'm completely embarrassed about the whole situation. I don't want you to think that I will just fall for anyone even remotely eligible because of what I've gone through."

"Emily, Emily, stop. That's the last thing on my mind. You are an experienced, uniquely talented lawyer with an incredible intellect and wisdom. The problem is: so is Jack. It's none of my business of course, but I should've realised that the two of you were bound to be drawn to each other. Apologies are absolutely unnecessary."

Relieved to hear his response, she relaxed and sat back in her chair.

Darius leaned forward, his voice gentle but steeped in wisdom. "I hope that you will continue to fully recover. I really do. I want nothing but the best for you. But I also want Jack to be okay as well. He is a man of integrity and that's not easy in situations like this. He has his own battles, his own past that shapes who he is."

Emily looked up, her eyes searching his face for understanding. "What do you mean?"

Darius exhaled deeply, his focus distant for a moment. "Let me share something with you in absolute confidence. Before I hired Jack, I did a thorough background check. It revealed a difficult upbringing, losing both parents and a stable home. Before he was finally adopted by his mother's former employer in Skye, who he now refers to as his uncle, he was passed around various foster families in some of the most impoverished neighbourhoods of Glasgow. He faced violence and adversity, and yet, he rose above it all. That's what makes him the man he is today."

Emily's heart swelled with compassion. "I had no idea," she whispered.

Darius nodded, a hint of a smile on his lips. "Jack's strength lies in his ability to do what's right, even when it's difficult. He may appear composed on the surface, but beneath it all, he carries the full weight of his past. Honour. Integrity. These aren't just concepts to Jack; they are the very foundation of his character. That's why he guards his emotions so closely."

Emily pondered his words, absorbing the depth of insight they held.

Darius lent forward. "Oh, you must prioritise yourself and your well-being. Love can be a complicated journey, but don't let it overshadow the incredible progress you've made. Focus on your work, continue to grow and thrive. Just look how far you've come since you rejoined the legal profession. And know this: the door to this firm will always be open to you."

Tears welled up in Emily's eyes. "Thank you. I needed to hear that. But you're right, I do need to prioritise my well-being and that's why I need to leave.", Emily stood and turned to leave.

As she left his office, she felt both sadness and relief. It was a difficult decision to make, but she knew it was the right one for her. She needed time and space to heal her heart and figure out her next steps. As she stepped out into the bustling office, she knew that her life was about to take a different path, one with uncertainty but also the possibility of new beginnings. And for now, that was enough.

CHAPTER FOURTEEN
Jack

The Sunday morning sun cast a soft, golden hue over the city of London, its rays gently filtering through the floor-to-ceiling windows of Jack's penthouse apartment. Nestled within a historic red-brick mansion, the grandeur of his residence was a testament to his achievements and the life he had meticulously built. However, as the first light of day kissed his face, Jack awoke with a sense of unease that seemed to permeate the air.

His body, covered in a thin layer of perspiration, betrayed the restlessness that had plagued his sleep. With a heavy sigh, he swung his legs over the edge of the bed, his thoughts already consumed by the conflicts that troubled his heart. The opulent surroundings offered little solace as Jack surveyed the room, a symphony of lavish furnishings and intricate designs. It was a sanctuary he had created, an oasis of luxury and comfort. Yet, in the midst of this splendour, his soul yearned for something more—an experience that transcended material possessions and societal expectations.

As he made his way to the balcony, Jack's mind was a tempest of emotions, swirling and colliding like waves crashing against the shore. Leaning against the railing, he gazed out at the panoramic view of London, his eyes drawn to the Thames and the various activities taking place on or beside it; the city was bustling with life.

The gentle breeze caressed his face, carrying with it whispers of uncertainty and longing. He ran his fingers through his hair, a gesture that had become a familiar reflex during moments of contemplation. What had he done? First of all, he had driven Kate into the arms of another, and now he had pushed away one of the most incredible women he had ever met.

It was as if the wind itself mirrored the internal conflict raging within him, torn between wanting to nurse the wounds inflicted by Kate and the intense bond he had formed with Emily. The memories of their time together in Bermuda, like fragments of a beautiful dream, danced through his mind. That beautiful evening they shared together; it tugged at his heartstrings with an irresistible force.

Yet, the pain he felt from Kate's betrayal bore down on him, casting a shadow of guilt over his burgeoning feelings. He had promised himself to another, holding steadfast to his principles of loyalty and honour and she had undermined all of that. She had treated him like a fool and at his core, a fire of anger burned unabated, threatening to consume his every thought.

And then there was work. He prided himself on always putting his career first and protecting the carefully carved reputation from any accusation of imperfection. But how could he maintain his position if he was in a relationship with another senior partner at the firm? It was unthinkable, and yet whenever he thought of Emily his heart lurched towards her.

But were the professional implications just an excuse? As the sun climbed higher, casting its warm glow upon the city, he considered the consequences of following the course his heart silently urged him to take, knowing full well the anxiety he had that he would be discarded again. Was that what it really came down to? Fear? The weight of his decisions rested heavily upon his shoulders, a burden that threatened to overwhelm him.

The idea of starting a new relationship so soon after Kate weighed heavily on him. The thought of the broken future they had envisioned filled him with guilt and uncertainty. How could he just dismiss the love he held for Kate and transfer it on to Emily?

As he contemplated his feelings, Jack's thoughts drifted to Sarah, his confidant, and the one person who always seemed to have the right words of wisdom. He reached for his phone, seeking the familiar voice that could guide him through this labyrinth of emotions.

With his assistant's face illuminating the screen, Jack felt a sense of relief and comfort wash over him. It was as if a lifeline had been thrown, offering him understanding and perspective. He could see that Sarah was in her gym gear and had a sheen to her skin that suggested she'd just been exercising.

"Hey, you got a sec?"

"Of course, what's up?"

"I'm really sorry to call you at the weekend. It's just..." Jack found he was lost for words.

"Hey. Relax. It's absolutely fine, you know that. What do you need?"

Jack stared at the image. This felt harder than he had expected. He was going to have to open up in a way that was going to be tough.

"I think I've made a mistake. I'm off my game and my judgment is all over the place."

"Go on. I'm here for you, Jack."

"Well, it's Emily."

At this, Sarah couldn't help smiling.

"No, no, it's just that..." he continued. "Well, I had the whole thing out with her and basically, well, I told her that I was choosing my career instead of a relationship with her. And, well, I've hardly slept all weekend. I think I got it wrong. Totally wrong."

Sarah gently shook her head and took a moment before

responding.

"Listen, I can't tell you how tempted I am to give you a hard time right now. If this wasn't so tragic, I'd be seriously making fun of you. Why? Because you're an idiot!"

Jack looked shocked but quickly regained his composure as she continued. "Emily Taylor is perfect for you. Yes, the timing is terrible. Yes, you've just come out of a—let's be honest—doomed engagement. And yes, you work together. *But* you're into her and – unbelievably – she's into you." Sarah snickered. "Look, this opportunity may never come around again and, if you want my advice, you'll grab it with both hands."

He let out a heavy sigh. "I know you're right, but I'm...well, I'm *just not sure*. If I'm being honest, and I would never say this to anyone else, but I'm scared of doing the wrong thing, scared of what this means for the firm, scared of messing Emily around, and I'm scared of what I'm like at the moment. I look in the mirror and I don't recognise this indecisive, vulnerable shadow looking back."

"C'mon, how long have we known each other? You are a brilliant human being, but you are not perfect. You are just going through a tough time, and you need to stop holding yourself up to impossible ideals. Think of this like a virus; until you get your strength back, you need to give yourself a break."

Jack took a moment to absorb her words, realising the truth in them. He knew he couldn't keep ignoring his feelings, pretending they didn't exist. He couldn't ignore the undeniable bond he had with Emily, even if it made him uncomfortable.

"Look, in full disclosure, I spoke with Emily yesterday," she told him. "She is really into you but feels like you pretty much shut that down when you went for that walk."

"What? Oh no, I didn't..." Jack looked downwards as his words trailed off.

"It's okay. I explained to her that you're going through a really tough time right now and that she needed to give you a chance to come round."

As Jack processed her words, a sense of clarity washed over him. He knew he couldn't avoid his feelings any longer. The truth had a way of demanding to be acknowledged, and he owed it to Emily to share all of his feelings completely with her.

"Thank you. Really. You are the best."

"I know," she smiled. "Now go get her…"

With a renewed purpose in his heart, Jack ended the conversation, feeling both apprehension and hope for the future. The road ahead was uncertain, but he knew he couldn't continue to live in a state of conflict. It was time to face his fears, be honest about his emotions, and trust that the path he chose would ultimately lead him to where he truly belonged.

As he put his phone down, he stared ahead, preparing himself to begin the difficult but necessary process of finding his way through the tangled web of love and uncertainty. The journey ahead would be challenging, but he knew that facing the truth was the only way to move forward and find the happiness he sought. He was resolute; he would speak to Emily and make a decision, one way or the other.

*

Jack walked towards Darius's office, his mind weighed down by a multitude of thoughts and emotions. As soon as he got into the office that morning, he had tried to find Emily but she wasn't in her office and Sarah didn't know where she was. He considered calling her mobile, but this was a conversation he wanted face to face. His nerves were on edge as he entered the room, which felt both familiar and daunting, with its polished wooden desk and shelves adorned with legal books. Darius looked up from his work, sensing the gravity of the situation from the expression on Jack's face.

"You asked to see me, Darius?"

"Jack, come on in. Have a seat. You look like you could use a moment."

"Thanks. I don't really want to bother you with…" Jack replied, sinking into the plush armchair across from his boss.

"Nonsense, you know I'm here for you," said Darius, his voice edged with concern.

"I know. I know."

"Well, I can tell that you're not quite yourself, old chap. Take your time, I'm here to listen."

Taking a deep breath, Jack gave as dispassionate account as he could of the past few weeks, from the break-off of his engagement with Kate to his realisation that he had feelings for Emily. He tactfully left out any mention of Bronwyn.

"You know my loyalty to you and the firm is beyond question, but I really feel for Emily and look, I know this is difficult, and I know that this is against our rule of no company relationships, but I can't just ignore my emotions."

Nodding, Darius acknowledged the weight of Jack's words. "No, I fully understand."

They stared at each other and Jack finally replied, "Thank you. Really, thank you. I can't tell you how much I appreciate your support. It means…"

"But Jack, there is something I need to tell you. You need to not react immediately but consider your response."

A look of confusion flickered over Jack and he froze waiting for Darius to continue.

"Well, last thing Friday, Emily and I had a very in-depth chat about her and the firm and despite my objections, she decided to resign."

"What!?!" exclaimed Jack, standing up.

Darius held up his hands, signalling for Jack to sit back down, but he remained standing.

"But she can't just quit. She's only been here for a few weeks!"

"She can and she has. I agree with her that she needs to look after her own mental health and if this job isn't helping her then it might be for the best."

Jack started pacing up and down in front of the desk.

"I'm sorry, but I disagree. We can't afford to lose her. She's an exceptional lawyer, and her dedication to her work is unparalleled. Regardless of my feelings, we must find a way to keep her."

Darius's expression grew pensive as he listened to Jack's plea, he had never seen his young protege this emotional. "Of course, you're right. Emily is a tremendous asset to the firm, and her departure would be a significant loss. But I can't have both of you working here constantly feeling conflicted about being in each others' presence. It just won't work."

And as if a lever in Jack had been pulled, he switched into the proactive, objective fixer that Darius knew him to be.

"Leave this with me. This has gone on too long now and we need to sort this. I'll handle this situation delicately and tactfully to a conclusion."

Darius was wary of Jack in this new mood, but felt dutybound to support him. "Speak to her. If you convince her to stay, then great, but I just want what's best for everyone."

And before he even had time to wrap up the conversation, Jack had left the room striding towards his office.

Darius sighed gently and turned back to the file he had been reviewing.

*

After a thoroughly unproductive morning, Jack decided to go home. He walked over to Sarah's desk and, before he could say anything, she whispered, "No, Jack, for the millionth time, she has not come in yet."

"I'm thinking of going home," he muttered.

"I think that's an excellent idea. Look, I'll hold the fort here and if she does come in, I'll text you. How about that?"

Jack nodded, grabbed his things and left the office.

Just over an hour later, unable to bear the restlessness any longer, he got off his couch and quietly got into his running gear. The city outside was in the sleepy lull between lunch and rush hour. The streets near his apartment were nearly empty with just the endless hum of the city to break the silence. He stepped out into the rich afternoon air, his feet carrying him on a familiar route through a couple of the central London parks and a few landmarks. But this afternoon was different; his thoughts consumed him, and he couldn't find his normal peace of mind in the familiar drumbeat of his run.

As he made his way through the city, his mind retraced the moments he had shared with Emily—their laughter, their late-night conversations, and the spark that seemed to ignite whenever they were together. But the reality of their circumstances still weighed heavily on him. He cherished his career and at Harrison's, and he knew that any romantic entanglement with a colleague could jeopardise everything he had worked so hard to achieve. He pushed these unwanted thoughts away. He had to be convinced that his current course was the right one. No, the only thing that should concern him now was how he was going to tell Emily he had changed his mind. What words would unlock the situation?

Each step he took seemed to amplify the concern he had on what to say. *This is ridiculous,* he thought. *I've built a career on words, they've never held anything but opportunity for me, so why should this be any different?*

The afternoon light began to creep towards the horizon, casting a soft reddish glow over the city's iconic landmarks. As the end of the working day drew near and the rush hour stirred into life, Jack formed the words in his mind. He considered the balance between coming on too strong and holding back, and found the right set of messages. He repeated them to himself over and over like a mantra, each time building the courage he needed to share them with Emily.

As he neared his apartment, he stopped to catch his breath, his heart pounding not only from the exertion of the run but also from the weight of his decision. He looked behind him over the city, its various surfaces reflecting the soft hues of dusk, and he knew that this was a major step forward in his life.

With a newfound sense of determination, Jack turned and made his way into his building. Climbing into the shower, the fatigue of the run finally caught up with him. But, as he closed his eyes, he felt a glimmer of hope that in taking this leap, he would find the life he now sought and, perhaps, discover a new sense of direction and purpose.

As he came out of his ensuite, his phone bleeped. He picked it up to see a text from Sarah. "No sign of Emily, but I pulled a few strings and here is her home address, where she'll no doubt be tonight…"

Jack inhaled deeply. *Okay,* he thought. *This is it.*

CHAPTER FIFTEEN
Emily

Emily walked down the street with bags of shopping weighing her down on either side. She didn't know how long she was going to stay in London, but having run out of food, she had popped to the nearest shop to pick up some things to keep her going, including wine and chocolate. Turning the corner into her street, she could see an animated figure walking up and down the road peering into the front garden of Emily's small Victorian house. As she got closer, the figure became a young, well-dressed woman and Emily wondered if she had got lost and was looking for someone to help her.

Emily approached the woman, and as she did their eyes met and the recognition in the other woman's eyes was clear to see. Her eyes were clouded with both anger and vulnerability. It took a moment for her to gain her voice. "Emily? Emily Taylor?"

Nodding, Emily felt a pang of fear. *Who was this woman and what did she want?*

"I'm Kate. Jack Braun's fiancée."

Emily's concern only increased. "Why are you here, Kate? And how did you know where I lived?"

Kate's face went red and her eyes welled up. "I'm so sorry. I followed you all the way home last week. I don't know what I'm doing. I just wanted to speak with you..."

At this she erupted in tears and buried her head in her hands.

With cautious steps, Emily approached Kate, her mind racing with questions. Instinct took over and she guided the woman towards her front door.

"You'd better come in," she said, and they entered the house. They moved into the kitchen, silent apart from Kate's sobs and wary of each other.

Emily coughed and managed a weak "Tea?", her eyes fixed on the other woman. Kate dried her eyes and regained her composure. Emily could sense the mix of emotions radiating from her, and she braced herself for what was to come.

Kate's voice trembled with anger and hurt as she spoke. "You took Jack from me," she whispered and then more forcefully added, "*You* are the reason he won't come back to me."

Emily's heart sank, considering that she may have been the one that had inadvertently led to Jack breaking off the engagement. She tried to remain composed, her voice steady as she responded. "I assure you, I didn't intend for any of this to happen. Jack and I have only really just met and it's a complicated situation; it's not as simple as it seems."

But Emily could see that Kate's anger was only getting worse. Her words grew sharper, fuelled by heartbreak, guilt and frustration. She lashed out, hurling insults at Emily, trying to find a measure of relief in blaming someone other than herself for the dissolution of her relationship.

"You think you're so special, don't you?" Kate sneered, her voice infused with bitterness. "But let me tell you something, Emily. Jack will get tired of you too, just like he did with me. You're nothing but a temporary distraction."

"I understand that you're hurt, Kate, but please try to see that I never intended to cause any harm. Jack's feelings are his own, and I can't control them."

Again, Kate crumpled into tears, "I just don't know what to do. I thought we were going to get married, have a future together. And now, it's all gone. Just gone."

"I understand how devastating this must be for you. I am so sorry."

"Sorry? Is that all you can say? Sorry?" sobbed Kate. "I just want him back. I thought we had something real, something lasting. Why did he have to go?"

The weight of Kate's words hung heavy in the air, each one a painful reminder of the complexities surrounding Jack's actions. Emily felt both sympathy and defensiveness. She knew she couldn't fully comprehend the depth of Kate's emotions, but she also knew that Jack probably had his reasons for ending the relationship. There were always two sides to these situations.

"But Kate, to be clear, I'm not with Jack. He hasn't left you for me. I've not even spoken to him since we were working together in Bermuda."

Kate rolled her eyes. "Oh come on, Emily. It's clear he's fallen for you hard and the uptight, old-fashioned, *gentleman* that he is means that he will do the *right thing* and excuse himself from a delicate emotional situation."

Emily didn't know how to respond. As Kate's anguish became more apparent, her words turned from accusations to pleas, a desperate attempt to make sense of the situation.

"Why won't he speak to me? Why won't he answer any of my calls? *Why?*" wailed Kate.

Emily's concern was wearing thin with this self-centred, overly emotional character. Taking a deep breath, Emily gathered her composure. She knew she needed to act, but didn't know what to do and how to exit Kate from her house.

"Kate, I'm truly sorry for your pain," she said, her voice sincere. "It is the last thing I wanted, but please know that it wasn't my intention to hurt you at all. But let's be honest, there's nothing I can do to help. You need to be with friends and family who care for you and will support you."

Emily's words hung in the air, and in a sudden movement, Kate stood up and strode out of the door. She had a strength of mind on her face and was out of sight quickly.

"Kate? Kate?" shouted Emily, but she had gone.

Emily was left standing alone in her kitchen, wondering what had just happened. Feeling jangled and a little upset, she picked up her phone and called a recent number, putting on her most upbeat voice. "Hi. How are you doing? Do you fancy dinner? Sure, how about takeaway food round at mine?"

CHAPTER SIXTEEN

Jack

Jack stood outside Emily's house, a bottle of expensive red wine clutched tightly in his hand. He paused, trying to steady his nerves before he knocked on the door. As Emily opened it, shock and curiosity flashed across her face.

"Jack?"

"Good evening. I wondered if I might have a word?"

"Oh, err. Um. Yes, of course. Come on in," she said, stepping aside to let him enter.

As he stepped into the open plan kitchen at the back of the house, he froze. There, sitting across from Emily's seat, was a man he didn't recognise. Jack's heart sank as he realised he had interrupted their dinner.

Emily stepped further into the room. "Jack, this is Anjay. Anjay, this is Jack, a colleague from work."

Anjay nodded politely, his eyes assessing Jack with a hint of curiosity. "Nice to meet you, Jack," he said, his tone friendly but guarded.

Jack forced a smile, his composure slipping slightly, especially at the way Emily had introduced him. "Likewise, Anjay. Sorry to intrude, Emily. I didn't realise you had company."

"It's okay. What did you need?" She looked up at him and he took a beat as he breathed in her beauty. Panicked, he realised the script he'd prepared didn't anticipate a third person being there. What was this anyway? A date? Or were they just friends? Jack ran his fingers through his hair.

"Right, yes. Well, err. I'm wondering if I could maybe have a quiet word?"

She just stared back at him and the atmosphere in the room plunged rapidly.

Anjay rose from his seat looking awkward. "Yes, well I should be off. It was lovely meeting you. Thank you so much for dinner. Take care." And with a polite nod to both, he excused himself and made his way to the door, followed by Emily.

When she returned, Emily's expression had hardened. Jack continued to struggle to find the right words, his mind racing with frustration and regret.

"Why are you here?" Emily's voice cut through the atmosphere.

Jack took a step forward, looking straight into her eyes. "I came to talk to you. I need to tell you something important."

"So important that you ruin my date?"

Jack's face fell. *Date? Had she moved on from him already? Oh God, what was he doing here?*

"Well?" she added.

He tried to muster the courage to broach the subject that weighed so heavily on his mind, but he couldn't quite do it. "Look, I want to talk about your resignation. The firm needs you back. Your expertise and dedication are irreplaceable."

Emily's eyes flickered with curiosity and guardedness. She took a sip of her wine, observing him intently. "And what about you, Jack? Do you need me back?"

His heart skipped a beat. Caught off guard, and still thinking about Anjay, he stumbled over his words. "I... I think the firm needs you, and we... we should be able to work together professionally. Once we have that sorted, we can then have a sensible discussion about our personal feelings as long as they do not hinder the success of the firm."

Disappointment crossed Emily's face. She set her glass down and with a tone tinged with anger, said "So, this is only about work then? You're not here to discuss us? You and me?"

He suddenly realised the gravity of his mistake. He had failed to fully understand her feelings and the emotional turmoil that had led to her resignation.

"I... I didn't mean to give that impression. It's just... I haven't had enough time to process everything. I don't know what I feel," he confessed, his voice full of regret and confusion.

"Well, if this is only about work, then I think it's best if you leave. I resigned because I didn't want our personal lives to create conflict in the office. If that's all you're concerned about, then there's no point in continuing this discussion."

Jack felt his whole world slip away in a wave of regret and disappointment. He so wanted to stay with her and even to talk about their own future, but he couldn't form the words he needed to unlock his feelings with her. He wasn't ready and so with a heavy heart, he rose from his seat.

"You're right. I'm sorry," Jack said softly, his voice underscored with a tinge of sadness.

Emily nodded formally and refused to speak.

With a lingering glance, he turned and walked away, leaving both of them grappling with their own emotions. As he made his way outside, the weight of his mistake settled heavily upon him. What was he doing? How was he, Jack Braun, master lawyer and brilliant tactician, messing this up so badly? He needed to pull himself together. But how?

CHAPTER SEVENTEEN
Emily

Emily stood outside the picturesque country farmhouse. The familiar scent of blooming flowers and freshly cut grass filled the air, bringing back childhood memories. She had made the right decision in arranging to come and visit her parents; their comforting presence would surely help lift her spirits. As she approached the front door, she noticed the absence of any sound. After there was no answer to her knocking, she took the door key from its secret hiding place and let herself in.

She hesitated for a moment before deciding to explore the house. As she moved through the rooms, she found herself surrounded by the memories of her upbringing—family photos on the walls, the familiar creak of the stairs, and the cosiness of each well-worn piece of furniture. Eventually, she made her way to the back garden, where her father spent countless hours tending to his plants and tinkering with various tools.

And of course, there he was, standing amidst the lush greenery in the greenhouse, engrossed in his work. Emily's heart swelled with love and relief as she called out to him. He turned, his face lighting up with a smile as he saw his daughter.

"Emily!" her father exclaimed, setting down the lawnmower

he was fixing. He hurried over to her and enveloped her in a warm hug. "It's so good to see you, my dear."

Tears welled up in Emily's eyes as she held her father tightly, finding comfort in his embrace. It was as if a weight had been lifted off her shoulders in that moment. She pulled back slightly and looked into her father's kind eyes.

"I've missed you, Dad," she whispered, her voice packed with emotion.

Her father's expression softened, and he gently brushed a strand of hair behind her ear. "C'mon Emily, it's only been a few weeks. Not that we haven't missed you too, my darling. Now, tell me, how was Bermuda and what's been troubling you?"

*

Emily took a seat at the garden table, and surrounded by the tranquil beauty of the garden, Emily began to share her struggles, opening up slightly about her complicated feelings for Jack and the uncertainty that had consumed her. Her relief at sharing was also tinged with embarrassment that despite her being a successful, experienced businesswoman, she still needed this. Her father asked her the occasional question for clarification but generally just listened as he continued to grease and assemble the various bits of the lawnmower he had placed on the table in front of him. He offered a sympathetic ear, providing a safe space for Emily to pour out her emotions. He didn't interrupt or judge; instead, he simply let her express herself, offering words of comfort and understanding.

When Emily had finished, he wiped his hands on an old rag in his pocket and looked straight at her.

"Em, I can't tell you how you feel about this chap, but just make sure you look after yourself. You've had to deal with so much in your life already. Make sure that you prioritise yourself as much as others."

Emily nodded, her eyes watering slightly.

"Now come on, I think I heard the arrival of the boss a few minutes ago, so it must nearly be time for tea and cake."

*

Emily took a sip of her tea. Her mother was describing an argument that two other women in the village had engaged in during their weekly bridge night and it was clear she had taken some enjoyment at this conflict in the village. Normally, her mother's focus on the trivial annoyed her but she found this soothing and a welcome distraction to her own situation. Her father sat in silence munching his way through an improbably large slice of lemon drizzle cake. It was a beautiful summer day, and their large garden was in full bloom offering a wonderful setting as they sat at the old wrought iron table.

"And how is the new job, dear?"

"Well, I was telling Dad. It's good, and the work is easy compared to what I'm used to…"

"…Oh, I can imagine. I mean you were the most successful female lawyer in America."

"Well, no, I'm not quite sure that's right…"

Emily's mother bristled and looked slightly hurt.

"No, it's not that I wasn't successful, but there are lots of other successful women in the States."

Her father cleared his throat.

She added, "No, the thing is, and I was explaining this to Dad. There's this guy at work."

Her mother's eyebrows raised at this.

"And well, I think we've kind of fallen for each other."

"What? You've only been there a few weeks!"

"And he was sort of engaged…"

Her mother's voice moved an octave higher. "To be married???"

Emily nodded, which prompted an unwelcome exclamation from her mother. She looked as though she was going to say something else, but then stopped and remained quiet.

As the three of them sat in silence, the only sound was the clink of her father's fork on his plate as he finished his cake.

*

Later that evening, Emily stood at the kitchen sink washing the dishes from dinner and placing them on the large, wooden drainer. As she looked out of the kitchen window, she could see her mother religiously storing away all of the chair cushions as the sun was setting and her father approaching the kitchen door.

"Shall I dry?" he asked gently, to which she nodded in agreement.

"She loves you very much."

Emily did not respond and continued to try and remove the greasy residue on one of the baking dishes.

"It's just that she cares so much about you, and she wants to fix things in her way. She can't always see the other perspective."

"I know, I know."

"You mustn't give her a hard time for sharing her emotions so freely. She hasn't had the benefit of a forty-year career in the civil service to train her in the fine art of listening and saying what the other person wants to hear."

Emily turned to see her father grinning and couldn't help smiling in return.

"Look, I'm willing to make you a bet. And you know how much I hate to part with my own money."

"What's the bet?"

"I bet that you come out of this fine. You'll get to the bottom of this Jack chap, and I have no doubt that either he'll be the real deal and you snag him, or you find out he's got a screw loose and you move on."

She laughed, "Oh, it's *that* simple. I should have realised!"

"I know. I know. What I know about courting and dating and what-not, you could put on a postage stamp, but what I do know is you. And I know that when you are determined to sort something out, one would be crazy to bet against you."

"That's true."

Her father put a hand on her shoulder and his expression became serious. "There was a time, one time only, when I thought that you might not make it. When I first saw you after the accident and you were in that hospital with tubes and pumps and everything, well, I wasn't sure. I really wasn't sure." As he spoke, he gently shook his head and looked pale. "I felt so hopeless. To this day, I find it difficult to think about those days when we just didn't know whether you'd be okay. But you were a fighter. You *are* a fighter. And my word, did you show everybody. The recovery, the physio, the rehabilitation, you nailed all of them. And that's why, I know you will be okay. And why I know your mother is secretly pleased that you might have found someone."

As he finished speaking, they both had tears in their eyes. Emily found comfort in her father's wisdom. She felt a renewed sense of strength and resolve building within her.

As they walked out together into the peaceful garden, Emily felt a glimmer of hope. Maybe, just maybe, she would find the clarity she sought and the strength to navigate the stormy waters of her heart. The sun began to set, casting a warm golden glow over the garden as Emily and her father sat in comfortable silence. The weight on Emily's heart seemed a little lighter, and a newfound focus began to bloom within her.

Her mother came over and said, "All finished?"

Emily stood up, walked over and hugged her deeply.

Surprised, her mother smiled. "What was that for?"

"I love you, Mum."

"And I love you too. Just make sure you look after yourself."

After a moment of everyone being lost in their thoughts, Emily said, "Look, I don't want to let my personal struggles affect my work. I love being a lawyer, and I will never lose sight of that."

Her mother nodded understandingly, her face full of pride.

Her father smiled warmly, his eyes crinkling at the corners. "You're our daughter, and we'll always be here for you. Remember, sometimes the most challenging moments in life pave the way for something even more beautiful."

They sat together a little longer, savouring the serenity of the garden and the bond they shared. Emily felt a renewed sense of purpose within her. She had to face her own inner conflicts head-on and find the strength to make choices that aligned with her own happiness.

As the evening sky turned into a tapestry of stars, Emily rose from the garden chair and hugged each of them tightly. "I'm so lucky to have you both. Thank you for always being there for me."

In the quiet of her old bedroom, Emily closed her eyes, finding consolation in the memories of their conversation and the love that surrounded her. She knew that she would need time to heal and reflect, but with her parents' words echoing in her heart, she was full of hope.

Piecing herself back together was like solving a jigsaw puzzle. Piece by piece. And she now considered one piece; her feelings for Jack. Drawing a line under everything else, she needed to consider this: did she want to be with him or not? And if she did, how was she going to open up to Jack without him panicking and pushing her away like last time?

As her thoughts of Jack and love tumbled through her mind, she slowly fell asleep, with a gentle smile across her face.

*

A few days later, Emily stepped out of her cozy London home, the brisk morning air awakening her senses. It was her last day in the job and the streets were alive with the hustle and bustle of the city, a symphony of sounds and sights that formed the backdrop to her contemplation. As she made her way toward the tube station, her footsteps fell in rhythm with her racing thoughts. It had only been a few weeks since Emily had last walked down the West London street towards Mariya Svravipona's office but so much had happened it felt like another lifetime. Emily's focus, however, was still mainly consumed by Jack and his whereabouts. Only an hour earlier, Emily had received a message from Sarah that Jack would not be attending the client meeting. Emily's thoughts raked over why Jack wasn't there—*was it her? Or had something happened to him?* Her mind raced with worry, wondering where he could be and whether she was the reason he wasn't coming.

Putting her concerns aside, Emily approached the large wooden door of the office. Out of the corner of her eye, she became aware of a dark figure staring at her from the other side of the road, but before she could focus on whoever it was through the traffic, they had gone. *Strange*, she thought, but conscious that it was probably nothing and she didn't want to be late, she went to the door and pressed the buzzer.

Less than fifteen minutes later, she was sat with Ms. Svravipona in the elegant meeting room guiding her through the intricacies of their case, detailing the steps they had taken to freeze Sergey's accounts and recover her hard-earned money. During these last few days of work, Emily and her team had worked diligently to resolve the case, and she was determined to see it through to the end before she left. The elegant and powerful Russian woman listened attentively, her expression transforming from curiosity to satisfaction.

"So what you are saying, Ms Taylor, is that my money is frozen so Sergey cannot steal it, but it will take time to transfer it back to me. Correct?"

Emily nodded. "Correct. It will take a bit of time, but you can rest assured now that you'll get almost everything back." Taking out of her case a sheaf of papers all carefully indexed, she added, "I just need your signature on all of these. I'm sorry. There's quite a few."

Mariya smiled gently and started to read and then sign each of the documents.

Moments later the door to the meeting room burst open and in stormed Sergey himself.

"Well, well. So, I have you both now. Good," he growled in his deep Russian accent.

Emily immediately recognised Sergey as the figure that had been lurking outside and cursed herself for not raising it with her client.

Compared with the agitated man in front of them, Mariya was icily calm. She slowly put down the pen she was holding and looked up at him. "And what is it you want, Sergey?"

"What do I want? What you think I want? I want MY money!"

A smile crept across Mariya's face. "You mean *my* money. It was never yours."

His pupils dilated and became increasingly agitated. "You witch! I work hard for the money. It's what I'm owed. You think you safe here, just cos you in nice office?" He pulled a handgun from the back of his belt and aimed it directly at Mariya, who for the first time showed a flicker of fear.

Mariya lifted her hands as if in surrender and pushed her chair back from the table. Emily was still reeling from the shock of this intrusion but instinctively wanted to protect the older woman, so she stood up slowly and stood between Mariya and the desk, obscuring Sergey's line of sight.

"Get out of the way," snarled Sergey. "Or I shoot you, too."

Emily could feel the adrenaline coursing through her veins. As the man opposite raised the gun directly at her, she was for a microsecond taken back to the moment of the car crash that had changed her life. The familiar sensation brought a clarity and sense of calm that surprised her.

"Sergey. Don't do this," she said in a level, composed voice. "This isn't going to get you what you want."

He gnashed his teeth and, gesturing with the gun, he said,

"Get out of my way, woman."

"Think about it, Sergey. Nothing you do here can change what's going to happen. The best you can hope for is to walk away and…" But before Emily could finish her sentence, there was a loud pop from beside her and she saw two wires fly across the room towards Sergey. As a crackling sound filled the air, his body spasmed and he fell to the ground dropping the gun on the carpet.

No one moved and Emily realised she was holding her breath. Exhaling deeply, she turned round to see Mariya holding a taser in one hand, detaching its nozzle and wires with her other hand before slipping the bright yellow gun back into her designer handbag.

"I got bored," said Mariya rolling her eyes. "Men. They think they are only ones with weapons. Pathetic." And at this she moved round the table and prodded Sergey with her high heeled shoes. Satisfied that he was out for the count, she took out her mobile and, selecting a familiar number, put it to her ear. She spoke in deep Russian to whoever answered and, looking satisfied, she hung up and turned to Emily smiling.

"And you. You were ready to take a bullet for little old Mariya, eh?" she laughed lightly.

"Well, I err, I was just trying…" said Emily not sure how to respond.

"No. No. None of your British false modesty. You've done a very good job, Miss Emily Taylor," she said, her eyes sparkling with gratitude. "Not just the legal work, but you show real loyalty. And you have made sure this bastard here won't be able to hurt anyone else."

Despite the bizarre situation of a body lying near her on the carpet, Emily's lips curved into a small smile, grateful for her client's kind words.

"What will happen to him?" asked Emily.

"Never you mind, dear. Now let's get you out of here. I'll sign papers later and get someone to bring them to your office.

Okay?"

Emily nodded and Mariya took her arm to gently guide her out of the room to the exit. Sneaking a final glance at Sergey's body, she wondered how concerned she should be about his future.

As the lift arrived and Mariya held the door open with one of her bejewelled hands, she turned to Emily and said, "Forget all about Sergey and instead focus on that hunky Jack. You two are made for each other and you should follow your heart."

"Thank you, Ms Svravipona. It's a little complicated..."

As Emily entered the lift and Mariya let the doors close, she smiled at Emily and replied, "Love always is."

*

Later that day, Emily sat at her desk, her heart pounding in her chest. She was still trying to process the bizarre encounter with Sergey earlier, but increasingly her thoughts had turned to Jack. She had gone over to ask Sarah where he was, but she had also been out and there was no one else around to ask.

She had challenged herself on why she wanted to see him. Yes, she needed to tell him about the case and how it was close to completion, but more importantly, she wanted to tell him herself that she was leaving and that she still had feelings for him. Feelings that she hoped he also had and wouldn't shut down now that they weren't going to be working together.

But to do that, she needed to confront the situation head-on and find out where Jack had disappeared to. She picked up her desk phone and called Annabel, asking whether Darius was free, and not much later she found herself outside Darius' office once again.

Taking a deep breath, she knocked on the door and entered when she heard Darius' familiar voice calling her in.

Darius looked up from his desk, his expression one of concern and curiosity. "Emily, my dear, what can I do for you?" he asked, motioning for her to take a seat.

Emily hesitated for a moment, her mind racing with thoughts and emotions. She needed answers, but she needed to be careful with Darius. Gathering her courage, she spoke with a determined tone. "Sorry to bother you, but do you know where Jack is? I can't find him and he's not answering his mobile. I need to brief him on the close-out of the Svravipona case."

Darius lent back in his chair and a conflicted expression flickered across his face. "Emily, I've been sworn to secrecy. Jack asked me not to say anything to anyone, but..."

"But?" Emily's eyes pleaded with him, hoping he would share whatever he knew.

There was a pause whilst Darius considered his response. Finally he spoke, "Very well. I think I *should* share the situation with you. Jack has taken some time out. For his own wellbeing. He just wanted to be alone, to sort things out on his own terms. And..."

"But is he all right?" she interrupted sitting down in the chair opposite, her face full of concern.

He gently shook his head. "Jack just needs time. I've already lost you and I don't want to lose another partner, especially one that I consider my protégé." As he continued his tone became harsher and more exasperated. "This situation is becoming intolerable. Jack offered me his resignation. His resignation, for goodness' sake! Naturally, I've rejected it and told him to take some time out to pull himself together."

"What?" she exclaimed.

"Exactly. Honestly, I feel like I'm running a couple's relationship counselling group rather than a bloody law firm." He thumped the desk. "The two of you need to sort this matter out. I told Jack to take some time out and get his head straight."

"But how could you let him go?" Her voice was angry and frustrated.

Darius' eyes lit up. "Careful of your tone, please. Of course, I didn't want him to disappear, but I'd rather get him back with his head straight than lose him completely because he thinks he has to resign."

She crumpled into the seat, and spoke quietly. "Apologies. It's just that I am worried about him. I really am."

He regarded her for a moment, weighing his options. He knew the depth of Emily's feelings, and he believed that she could be a positive force in Jack's life. With a resigned nod, he reached for a pen and a piece of paper, scribbling down simple directions.

"Jack is up in Skye, on his uncle's estate," Darius revealed, sliding the paper across his desk. "It's stunningly beautiful up there and just the right place for Jack to get his thoughts straight. Look, I know you won't want to hear this, but Jack may not be ready to face you or his emotions just yet."

She took the paper, her hands trembling slightly and thanked Darius sincerely, gratitude shining in her eyes. "I understand. And I appreciate your trust in me. I won't push him if he's not ready. But I need to let him know that I'm here for him."

He offered her a warm smile, his voice offering hope. "I truly believe that you're good for Jack. Just remember to tread gently and give him the space he needs. I wish you both the best, and for goodness' sake, get that boy back on his feet and back to work. I will remind you that I do have a bloody law firm to run."

Emily stood up, a mix of grit and trepidation coursing through her veins. She walked towards the door, clutching the piece of paper tightly in her hand. Turning back, she offered a grateful nod. "Thank you, Darius."

As she stepped out of the office, she felt a renewed sense of purpose. She had a destination now, a place where she could find Jack and, perhaps, find the answers they both sought. Skye beckoned her, its untamed beauty calling out to her adventurous spirit. With purpose fuelling her every step, she set out on a journey, armed with hope and a willingness to confront the unknown. She knew that the road ahead would present challenges and uncertainties, but she also knew that the depth of her feelings for Jack made it all worth it. As she walked through the bustling streets of London, her thoughts centred on the path that lay ahead. Skye awaited her, and with it, the opportunity to reconnect with this man who had captured her healing heart.

213

CHAPTER EIGHTEEN

Emily

Emily tossed and turned in her bed, the sheets twisting around her restless form. The digital clock on her nightstand mocked her with its unyielding glow—*03:00am*. Sleep seemed elusive, slipping through her fingers like sand. Her mind buzzed with thoughts of Jack, her heart heavy with both longing and uncertainty.

She turned on her side, her eyes fixed on the moonlight filtering through the window blinds. Shadows danced upon the walls, mirroring the tumultuous dance of emotions within her.

The room was hushed, the silence oppressive. Emily's thoughts swirled like a tempest, an intricate web of doubts and insecurities. Did she truly love Jack, or was it simply a fleeting infatuation born out of the circumstances they had shared? And even if her feelings were genuine, did he reciprocate them?

She traced her fingers along the edge of the bedsheet, her mind retracing their conversations, their shared laughter, and the lingering glances that spoke volumes in the silence between them. There was an undeniable bond, a magnetism that drew them together. But was it enough to build a foundation for something deeper?

With a sigh, Emily threw off the covers and sat up, her feet finding the cool touch of the wooden floor beneath. She padded to the window and peered out into the night, the city's glow a tapestry of twinkling lights. The stillness of the hour enveloped her, offering a momentary respite from the chaos in her mind.

But the silence amplified her worries. Doubts whispered in her ear, taunting her with their insidious voice. She wondered if Jack was feeling the same restless torment, if he too was grappling with the weight of their unspoken bond. The uncertainty of it all fuelled her restlessness, rendering sleep a distant dream.

Not truly knowing what she was doing she left her room, unlocked the back door and let herself out into the small garden, bathed in blue by the moon.

The soft glow over Emily's garden gave her just enough light to see as she sat on a weathered bench, her thoughts swirling in the quiet night. The stillness enveloped her, heightening her senses and amplifying her uncertainties. Her mind was a tangle of questions, her heart ached with longing.

Why had Jack gone? Did he share her feelings, or was she just a passing flicker in his life? The unknown pressed upon her, filling her with both anticipation and trepidation. Her heart yearned for answers, but she knew that some things couldn't be forced or rushed.

Her mind drifted back to the moments she had shared with Jack and the undeniable connection that seemed to transcend mere friendship. Was it enough to build a future together, or was it a beautiful illusion that would fade with time?

Emily's heart whispered conflicting emotions. It craved the comfort and security of love, but it also feared the vulnerability that came with it. The darkness of the night mirrored the uncertainty within her, as doubts and fears danced in the shadows.

But amidst the turmoil, a spark of resolve ignited within her. She couldn't let fear paralyse her. If she wanted to discover the truth, she would have to take a leap of faith and confront her feelings head-on.

With a newfound resolve, Emily stood up and returned to her bedroom. The quiet of the house enveloped her as she slipped back into her bed, the warmth of her blankets cocooning her. As she closed her eyes, she made a silent promise to herself—to face the uncertainties with courage, to listen to her heart, and to embrace whatever outcome awaited her.

*

Emily settled into her seat on the train, her eyes fixed on the passing countryside. The rhythmic motion of the train and the ever-changing landscapes outside provided a backdrop for her deep contemplation. Her mind wandered back to the first day she met Jack, the unexpected experience they shared, and the whirlwind of events that followed. Memories of their time together flickered through her mind like a reel of old film, each frame capturing moments of laughter, vulnerability, and shared understanding.

Lost in her thoughts, Emily realised that her recent struggles had clouded her perspective. She had been so consumed by the turmoil in her heart that she had neglected to appreciate the simple joys of life. The passing scenery outside reminded her of the beauty that surrounded her, waiting to be savoured. The vibrant hues of green fields, the gentle sway of trees, and the expansive skies whispered promises of serenity and renewal.

As the train reached its halfway point, Emily's heart felt lighter, and a sense of anticipation tingled through her veins. She pondered on the journey that lay ahead, not only the physical one from London to Scotland but the emotional voyage she was undertaking. With every mile that carried her closer, Emily's excitement grew. She imagined the moment they would reunite, the look in Jack's eyes, and the words that might be exchanged. Her heart danced with the hope that their relationship, once again, could transcend the obstacles that stood in their way.

By the time the train pulled into the bustling Glasgow Central station, Emily stepped onto the platform with a renewed energy coursing through her. The vibrant city atmosphere surrounded her, but her focus remained steadfast on the path that led to Jack.

As she waited for her connecting train to Fort William from Glasgow's Queen Street station, she found a café nearby that served good coffee and sat people watching the crowds that passed by. She allowed herself this moment of stillness.

The Skye train pulled away from the station and Emily watched the cityscape give way to rolling hills and the rugged beauty of the Scottish countryside. Each passing moment brought her closer to the moment she had been longing for, a chance to lay bare her heart and rediscover the depth of her feelings for Jack. In this moment, she was not just positive; she was full of a renewed sense of wonder and exhilaration, ready to embrace the unknown and discover what lay ahead in her pursuit of love and happiness.

*

The hire car hummed along the winding roads, carrying Emily through the breathtaking Scottish scenery. Majestic mountains stood tall, their peaks touching the heavens, while lush green valleys spread out before her in a tapestry of natural beauty. The late afternoon sun cast a warm glow on the landscape, painting it in hues of gold and amber.

As the day gradually transitioned into evening, Emily found herself crossing the iconic bridge to the Isle of Skye. The ethereal beauty of the island instantly captured her heart. The rugged coastline, the dramatic cliffs, and the serene lochs held a mystique that whispered tales of ancient legends and untamed wilderness.

With the address and postcode in hand, Emily navigated the tight bends, her eyes transfixed by the unfolding scenery. But despite her best efforts, she couldn't seem to locate the precise location of Borreraig House, the estate that, according to Darius, belonged to Jack's uncle. As dusk settled over the land, casting a dusky veil, Emily decided to seek assistance.

Spotting the warm glow of lights emanating from a nearby pub, she parked her car and entered the establishment. The interior was cosy, chock full with the chatter of a few patrons who sat comfortably in their own corners. Emily approached the bar and caught the eye of the young woman who was reading a paper on a stool in the corner.

"Excuse me," Emily said quietly. "I'm looking for Borreraig House. Could you point me in the right direction?"

The woman looked up and smiled. "I kin do one better than tha'. There's Willie Henderson himself, o'er there."

Emily followed the woman's gaze to a ruddy-faced man sat in the corner who seemed to exude an air of ruggedness and familiarity.

As she approached, William Henderson paused for a moment, a glimmer of recognition flickering in his eyes. Finishing his drink in a swift motion, he set down the glass with a warm smile.

"Aye, lass, I ken where ye're headed. Tha Darius bloke called me this morning," he replied in his rich Scottish accent. "I'm Willie, gamekeeper at Borreraig. It's nae far. Leave yer car here. I'll guide ye."

Emily followed William outside, her pulse quickening with every step. The air carried the scent of the loch and the promise of adventure. He led her to a small motorboat moored nearby, its dark silhouette outlined against the moonlit waters. Emily handed him her bag, her trust in this stranger still undecided, she remained anxious as they embarked on their journey across the loch.

However, as they sailed across the calm, shimmering water, the moon casting its silvery glow upon them, Emily couldn't help but feel anticipation and awe. Borreraig House materialised before her, an imposing structure with its grandeur and history etched into its very walls. It stood like a sentinel, guarding its secrets and beckoning Emily into its embrace. The boat glided smoothly towards the pier, and as they docked, Emily eyes widened, her heart pounding with a blend of nerves and excitement. Stepping onto the solid ground, she looked up at the vastness of Borreraig House, its turrets and stone façade rising against the night sky. It was stunning.

What strange world had she entered? Emily wondered. With every passing moment, she felt a sense of intrigue mingled with trepidation, as if she were stepping into a realm where dreams and reality intertwined. But her determination to uncover the truth and confront her own feelings propelled her forward. As she followed William towards the grand entrance, the heavy wooden doors swung open, revealing a glimpse of the opulent interior. Emily was ready to embark on a journey that would unravel secrets, challenge her perceptions, and ultimately lead her closer to the answers she sought.

Emily followed William through into the large, impressive hallway of Borreraig House, leaving the chilly Scottish air behind. As they entered, warmth embraced her, accompanied by the flickering glow of a roaring fire at the far end of the spacious, double-height room. The scent of wood smoke danced in the air, mingling with the inviting aroma of freshly brewed tea. In an instant, the slumbering figure by the fire sprang to life. It was an old woman, her eyes bright with warmth and mischief. Two large dogs at her side wagged their tails in joyous anticipation. With a burst of energy, she approached Emily, her voice lilting with an unmistakable Scottish accent.

"Welcome, lass! I'm Moira Henderson," she exclaimed, extending a hand in greeting. "Darius gave us a wee bell on the telephone and said ye might be on yer way. Come, come, have a seat and warm yerself by the fire."

Emily couldn't help but be charmed by Moira's enthusiasm and genuine hospitality dispelling much of her anxiety. She settled into a comfortable chair while William obediently carried her belongings to one of the many guest bedrooms, his robust frame moving with ease.

Moira bustled around the kitchen, clattering pots and pans, retrieving teacups and saucers with practiced efficiency. Within moments, a steaming cup of tea was placed before Emily, its comforting warmth seeping through her fingertips as she cradled it.

As they sat across from each other, Moira's eyes sparkled with curiosity. She leaned in, a conspiratorial smile on her face, as if eager to delve into the depths of Emily's life.

"Now, lass," Moira began, her voice laced with warmth and intrigue. "Tell me, wha's the story between ye and our dear Jack? I've known tha' lad since he was nae bigger than a wee bairn. Aye, I've watched him grow up in this very house."

Emily's brows furrowed slightly, unsure of how much she should reveal. She hesitated for a moment before finding her voice. "Well, Moira, it's complicated. I've been working with him at the law firm, and there's... something between us. But I don't know where it stands, or even how he truly feels."

Moira's eyes narrowed with curiosity and concern. She leaned back, the fire casting flickering shadows across her face. "Aye, lass, I've always had my suspicions about that lad's heart. He's had his share o' troubles, and it's made him cautious. But mark my words, there's a tenderness in him that only few've seen."

She stopped and stared at Emily, a hint of regret flickering across her features. "Now, I hope ye dinnae mind me saying this, but I never cared much for that lass, Kate. She wasnae right for Jack, no in my eyes. Though I probably shouldnae be speaking so openly about it," she added, a blush of embarrassment colouring her cheeks.

Emily smiled and continued to sip her tea.

Moira's expression softened, and her tone turned maternal. "Ye see, lass, I've known Jack since he came into this world. His mother worked here before me, and when she passed, I took up the mantle. The Laird of the estate thought the world of Jack and treated him like the son he wasnae blessed with. I've seen him through his ups and downs, like a second mother. I care deeply for him, and I want nothing but the best for him."

Emily listened intently, touched by Moira's genuine affection for Jack. She realised that, beneath her gruff exterior and gossip-loving nature, Moira possessed a deep understanding of the man Emily had come to seek. Her words offered a glimpse into the complexities of Jack's past, illuminating the struggles that had shaped him into the person he was today.

As the fire crackled and the dogs nuzzled at Emily's feet, she was almost overwhelmed with a sense of gratitude for the unexpected guidance and warmth she had found in Moira's presence. In this strange and captivating world of Borreraig House, Emily sensed that she was gaining a deeper understanding of herself and the man who had captured her heart.

Emily took a sip of her tea, letting the warmth soothe her nerves. The flickering flames cast a gentle glow over the kitchen, creating an atmosphere of trust and understanding. She looked at Moira, her eyes filled with gratitude.

"Moira," she began, her voice edged with a newfound resolve. "I need to find Jack. Can you tell me where he is?"

Before she could answer, William, returned from the kitchen, leaned against the countertop and joined them.

"William, I was just asking Moria where Jack is..." added Emily.

Moira exchanged a knowing glance with her husband who gave a small nod. Turning her attention back to Emily, she said "Aye, lass, we can tell ye," her voice gentle yet tinged with concern. "Jack's gone up to the bothy."

Emily furrowed her brow, unfamiliar with the term. "The bothy? What's that?"

William's voice held the rough edges of a man familiar with the rugged terrain of the Scottish Highlands. "The bothy is a remote cabin up in the mountains, lass," he explained. "It's a place where Jack retreats to when he needs time alone, away from the noise and chaos of the world."

Moira chimed in, her eyes offering fondness and concern.

"Aye, the Laird used to take him there when they went hunting. It's a special place for him, even if he doesnae hunt anymore. Jack finds peace and clarity in the silence of the mountains."

Emily nodded, absorbing the information. The idea of Jack seeking refuge in a remote bothy seemed fitting, considering his need for introspection and solitude. She experienced a renewed sense of purpose to reach him, to bridge the emotional chasm that had formed between them.

"You should get a good night's sleep, lass," Moira suggested, her voice laced with a motherly concern. "The journey up to the bothy isnae an easy one. It's best ye're well-rested. Tomorrow mornin', William here will guide ye up there to see Jack."

Emily felt a surge of gratitude towards the Hendersones for their unwavering generosity and willingness to help her find Jack. She finished her cup of tea, the warmth spreading through her body, rejuvenating her spirit.

"Thank you, both of you," Emily said. "I don't know how to express my gratitude for all you've done. I'll get some rest, and I'll be ready to face whatever lies ahead."

Moira smiled warmly, her eyes crinkling with a touch of mischief. "Ye're a bonnie lass, Emily. Just remember, love can be a bumpy road, but it's worth the journey."

With those heartfelt words, Emily bid the Hendersones goodnight and made her way to the guest bedroom that William had kindly prepared for her. As she settled under the covers, she couldn't help but wonder what awaited her in the remote bothy and whether the rugged Scottish landscape held the key to unlocking the mysteries of her own heart.

In the tranquil embrace of Borreraig House, Emily closed her eyes, the promise of a new day dawning with the hope of rediscovering love and finding her way back to Jack.

*

The morning sunlight filtered through the grand windows of

the formal dining room, casting a warm glow over the polished surfaces and elegant furnishings. Emily descended the staircase, her steps light with anticipation, as the tantalising aroma of a hearty breakfast greeted her. Moira stood by the sideboard, her eyes twinkling with warmth and genuine affection. "Good morning, lass," she greeted her with a wide smile spreading across her face. "I hope ye're hungry. I've prepared a proper Scottish breakfast for ye."

Emily couldn't help but feel a sense of awe as she took in the opulence of the room. The grandeur of the dining table, adorned with fine china and silverware, spoke of a bygone era. She marvelled at the regal splendour that surrounded her, feeling gratitude and a touch of trepidation.

"Thank you, Moira," Emily replied, her voice offering her appreciation. "It's all so beautiful."

Moira waved away her compliments with a warm chuckle. "Ye're too kind, lass. It's just the way things have always been around here. We like to make our guests feel special."

As Emily sat down at the table, Moira served her a traditional Scottish breakfast, complete with kippers, haggis, eggs, and slices of golden toast. The rich aromas filled the air, and her mouth watered in anticipation.

Just as she began to enjoy her meal, William entered the dining room, his presence exuding a sense of rugged strength and reliability. He approached with a kind smile, his eyes crinkling at the corners.

"Mornin', lass," he said. "I've put out some hiking gear for ye. We'll be leavin' in about an hour. The bothy isnae too far, but it's a bonnie hike through the hills."

Emily nodded, her excitement palpable. "Thank you. I can't wait to see the bothy and find Jack."

With breakfast finished and her hiking gear on, Emily stepped outside, her heart fluttering with nerves. The vista before her was nothing short of breathtaking. The expansive view over the shimmering loch and the rolling hills painted a picture of natural beauty that seemed to stretch on forever.

As she stood on the threshold, taking in the sight, she felt a sense of tranquillity wash over her. The crisp mountain air filled her lungs, rejuvenating her spirit and steadying her nerves. This moment, surrounded by the majesty of the Scottish landscape, was a reminder of the power and resilience of nature, a symbol of what she was embarking upon.

Lost in her thoughts, Emily was brought back to the present by the sound of approaching footsteps. William emerged from the house, carrying a backpack with provisions for their hike. He smiled warmly at her, his eyes twinkling with a hint of mischief.

"Are ye ready, lass?" he asked, his voice infused with a rugged charm.

Emily nodded, her smile mirroring his. "I am. Let's go find Jack."

And with that, they set off together, traversing the picturesque terrain of Skye, guided by the promise of rekindling love and the adventure that awaited them in the remote bothy.

*

The bothy stood in solitary splendour amidst the rugged Scottish landscape, its stone walls weathered by time and its charm undeniable. The small stone hut was only ten feet or so wide and about as high as William, but it looked sturdy and an effective refuge from the bracing wind.

As Emily and William approached, she experienced a deep sense of the moment. This was the place where Jack sought clarity, where he retreated to when the weight of the world bore down upon him.

They stepped through the worn wooden door, and Emily's eyes swept across the humble interior. The room was sparsely furnished, adorned with simple hunting items and a small fireplace that had seen countless nights of crackling warmth. It exuded a rustic charm that spoke of solitude and contemplation.

William glanced around, his experienced eyes taking in every detail. "He's probably out there, walkin' the hills, tryin' to find his way," he said, in an understanding tone. "Jack's always had a knack for findin' himself amidst the grandeur of nature."

Emily nodded, her attention lingering on the empty space that Jack would soon fill. "I understand. Thank you, William, for bringing me here and for everything you've done."

The gamekeeper smiled kindly, his rugged features softened by empathy. "Ye're welcome, lass. I hope ye find what ye seek."

He offered to stay and keep her company until Jack returned, but Emily insisted she would be fine on her own. She needed this time, this space, to confront her own doubts and fears. With a hesitant nod, William reluctantly bade her farewell and left.

Alone in the bothy, Emily took a moment to settle herself. She paced the small room, her footsteps echoing in the silence. Doubts crept into her mind like shadows, questioning the wisdom of her journey, and the audacity of hoping for a resolution between her and Jack. She looked out through the small door, gazing at the vast expanse of the landscape stretching out before her; she was a long way from Manhattan or London now. The rolling hills and majestic peaks seemed to hold the answers she sought, whispering in the wind and urging her to trust her heart.

Sitting down on a worn wooden stool, Emily closed her eyes, taking deep breaths to steady her racing thoughts. She needed to find clarity within herself, to face the questions that haunted her. Was she doing the right thing? Did Jack really feel the same way she now did?

As the hours passed, time seemed to stand still within the confines of the bothy. Each minute felt like an eternity, and doubt gnawed at Emily's resolve. She questioned the audacity of her actions, the enormity of her emotions, and the uncertain future that lay before her.

In the midst of her contemplation, a soft breeze whispered through the cracks in the walls, carrying with it a gentle reassurance. Emily opened her eyes, her gaze fixing upon a well-worn hunting jacket hanging on a hook by the door. It symbolised Jack's presence, his essence woven into the very fabric of the bothy.

With renewed determination, Emily steeled her resolve. She had come this far, traversing miles and overcoming obstacles, driven by a love that burned within her. Doubt might linger, but she couldn't turn back now.

Emily's restless spirit refused to be contained within the confinements of the bothy. With each passing moment, her impatience grew stronger, compelling her to explore the vast beauty that surrounded her. Determined to fill her time while waiting for Jack's return, she made the decision to venture into the area surrounding the bothy.

Despite wanting to surprise Jack, she decided to leave a note for him in the bothy, before embarking on a path that led her deep into the enchanting wilderness. The air was crisp and alive with the scent of pine, filling her lungs with the essence of nature. The path meandered through a grove of majestic Scots Pine trees, their branches reaching upward as if beckoning her to discover the secrets they held.

As she wandered along the winding trail, a sense of tranquillity settled within her. The forest embraced her, its ancient wisdom whispering through the rustling leaves. Lost in the serenity of her surroundings, Emily suddenly caught sight of movement among the trees. Her eyes widened with awe as a group of deer emerged, their gentle eyes meeting hers. Time seemed to stand still as they observed each other, a fleeting union forged between human and creature. In unison, the deer gracefully bounded away, disappearing into the depths of the forest. Intrigued by their fleeting presence, Emily felt an inexplicable pull to follow them. Pushing aside any hesitation, she ventured further into the woodland, her steps echoing the rhythm of her racing heart. But as fate would have it, the heavens opened, and raindrops began to fall, transforming the once peaceful atmosphere into a deluge.

Determined to return to the bothy quickly and avoid the downpour, Emily quickened her pace, her feet dancing over the forest floor. However, in her haste, her foot landed on treacherously uneven ground, causing her foot to twist painfully. She cried out in surprise, feeling the sharp sting of a sprained ankle as she fell and rolled down the hill that bordered the path.

Moments later she found herself collapsed in a crevice, with the world around her seeming to shrink. Fear gripped her heart as desperation gnawed at her thoughts. How would she ever find her way back to the bothy in her injured state?

Attempts to free herself from the confining crevice proved futile. Panic threatened to consume her, but she refused to surrender to despair. Summoning her inner strength, Emily persisted, pushing through the pain and exhaustion. But just as her resolve was waning, on the precipice of giving up hope, a faint sound pierced through the relentless rain. She froze. A single shout echoed through the forest, reaching her ears; *was that Jack?* she wondered.

She lifted herself up as much as she could, her eyes searching for the source of the sound. But nothing. After several minutes of only the noise of the rain and wind, her confidence fell away. *Had she imagined the sound? Had it just been the wind?*

But then she heard it again: "EMILY? EMILY?" It was Jack and she could hear his voice getting closer.

"Here. Jack, I'm here!" shouted Emily in response

Emily wiped her eyes, feeling a renewed sense of hope; hope that she had found her way back to him. And in that moment, as the raindrops fell around and her pulse raced, she surrendered to the overwhelming certainty that she had come to Skye not only to find Jack but to find herself as well.

And there, through the haze of rain, emerged a figure—Jack. His familiar silhouette materialised before her, his eyes showing both concern and relief. With each step he took, her heart soared, and infused her weary body. Without hesitation, Jack jumped down and rushed to her side, his strong arms enveloping her with warmth and support. He knelt down, his focus fixed upon her injured ankle. "Emily, are you alright?" he asked, his voice laced with a mix of worry and relief.

Tears of relief welled in Emily's eyes as she nodded, her voice trembling. "I... I thought I was trapped."

Jack's tender expression softened further, his touch gentle as he assessed her injury. " Don't worry. We'll get you out of here."

CHAPTER NINETEEN

Jack

Jack's heart was pumping wildly. All of his prayers had been answered and the woman he loved was here. He just needed to lift her out of this hollow and everything would be okay.

He picked her up in his arms and carefully navigated the slippery terrain. Slowly but surely, they emerged on to the top of the bank, Emily's spirits lifted by Jack's unwavering presence.

Lying on the wet forest floor, Emily found salvation in the embrace of exhaustion. She gazed up at the rain-soaked sky, gratitude washing over her. In that moment, she realised that, despite the obstacles and uncertainties, love had guided her to this very spot. Jack's arrival was more than chance—it was fate intertwining their paths once again.

With Emily nestled in his arms, Jack carried her back to the bothy, his steps sure and steady despite the challenging terrain. The weight of worry that had burdened him had been replaced by a deep sense of relief upon finding her safe and sound.

Upon entering the bothy, Jack gently set Emily down on a makeshift bed, carefully inspecting her sprained ankle. Concern etched across his face, he searched for any signs of further injury. As he skilfully bound her ankle with a makeshift bandage, his touch was gentle yet purposeful, his focus solely on her well-being.

With the fire crackling in the hearth, the warm glow cast a soothing light upon their surroundings. Shadows danced on the walls as raindrops continued their rhythmic dance on the roof. Jack's hands moved with practiced ease, tending to Emily's needs. As the fire's warmth began to seep into the room, a sense of comfort enveloped them. The tension that had previously hung between them like a heavy fog now seemed to dissipate, replaced by an air of cautious familiarity.

Sitting beside Emily, Jack's eyes met hers, his expression one of wonder and joy. The fear and confusion that had clouded their hearts in recent times began to give way to a glimmer of hope. They both longed for the link they once shared, even if it meant navigating the complexities of their emotions.

Their conversation started tentatively, as if testing the waters of their newfound closeness. Jack shared snippets of his time away, revealing that he had sought sanctuary in the tranquil solitude of the bothy. Emily, in turn, spoke of her journey to find him, the restless longing that had driven her forward.

As their stories intertwined, the walls they had built around their hearts began to crumble. The caution that had held them at a distance gradually softened, making room for vulnerability and understanding.

In the warmth of the bothy, Jack and Emily found comfort not only in the crackling fire but also in each other's presence. They reminisced about the moments they had shared, the laughter and experience that had once defined their relationship. Their conversation was punctuated by gentle laughter, as if the weight of their burdens was lifted, if only for a moment.

Yet, beneath the surface of their rekindled bond, traces of uncertainty lingered. The wounds of the past had not fully healed, and the road to rebuilding trust lay ahead. But in that tender moment, as they sat together, their guards momentarily lowered, they embraced the possibility of rediscovering what they had lost.

As the night deepened, the fire continued to cast its warm glow, illuminating the path they had embarked upon. Wrapped in the quiet serenity of the bothy, Jack and Emily watched the crackling flames and shared the flicker of hope that burned within their hearts.

CHAPTER TWENTY
Emily

Emily woke in the embrace of Jack's arms, the bothy's warming fire now reduced to ashes. As she shifted her position, Jack also woke from his slumber.

"Good morning," she whispered, snuggling deeper into his chest.

"Good morning to you too," he replied, smiling. "I'll get the fire going again so we can have some tea."

He kissed the top of her head and slowly extracted himself from her embrace.

"How's the ankle feeling?" he asked.

"Much better, thank you."

Moments later they were sat facing each other, with cups of warm tea in their hands and a slight hesitation in the air. The weight of unspoken emotions hung precariously over them, ready to fall and hopefully be embraced.

With a gentle sigh, Jack broke the silence, his voice full of vulnerability. "I've spent so much time running away from my feelings, denying what my heart truly desires. But being here with you, in this place of solitude and reflection, I can no longer deny the truth."

Emily's heart quickened with anticipation, her eyes shimmering with hope. She reached out and gently touched his hand, silently urging him to continue.

He looked deep into her eyes, his voice quivering. "Emily, I love you. I've loved you from the moment we crossed paths, from meeting you on your first day. I love your strength, your intelligence, and the way you light up a room with your presence."

Tears welled up in her eyes, emotions swirling within her. The weight of uncertainty lifted, replaced by a sense of clarity and joy. She had longed to hear these words, to know that the bond she felt was reciprocated.

Taking a leap of faith, Emily whispered, "I love you too. I've been afraid to admit it, to fully embrace what my heart has been telling me. But being apart from you, even for a moment, made me realise how deeply I feel for you."

As the words lingered in the air, Jack's eyes sparkled with newfound hope and certainty. Without hesitation, he gently took her hand in his and led her outside, where the rising sun cast a radiant amber glow over the rugged landscape.

In the dawn's embrace, he reached into his pocket and retrieved a simple piece of twine. With skilled hands, he fashioned it into a delicate ring, a symbol of their love and commitment.

Kneeling before her, Jack looked deep into her eyes, his voice offering unwavering devotion. "Look, I know this is all a bit sudden, but...Will you marry me?" His eyes welled up as he continued. "If I've learnt anything from the time I've known you, it's that life is too short to hold back. So will you make me the happiest man ever and marry me? Will you be my partner, my confidante, and the love of my life?"

Tears streamed down Emily's face, her heart overflowing with happiness. She nodded, her voice choked with emotion. "Yes, Jack. A thousand times yes! I want nothing more than to spend the rest of my life with you."

His face lit up with a radiant smile as he slipped the twine ring onto Emily's finger, sealing their love with a simple yet profound gesture. They embraced under the breaking sky, their souls intertwined, ready to embark on a new chapter of their journey together.

As they stood there, their hearts brimming with love and hope, the bothy stood witness to the power and transformative nature of love. In that moment, Emily and Jack knew that they had found their forever in each other, and their love would endure the tests of time.

Hand in hand, they walked back into the bothy, their hearts full of joy and anticipation for the future. The fire crackled with warmth, casting a soft glow upon their faces as they sat together, ready to embark on their shared adventure.

In that cosy, rustic sanctuary, Emily and Jack discovered that love had the power to heal wounds, bridge distances, and create a bond that would withstand any storm. They revelled in the magic of the moment, grateful for the serendipity that had brought them together and the infinite possibilities that lay ahead.

And as they sat on the hillside and the rosy-fingered dawn enveloped them in its warm embrace, they savoured the beginning of their forever, knowing that love had triumphed and their hearts had found a place to call *home*.

CHAPTER TWENTY-ONE
Emily & Jack

They stood on the quiet street, their breaths mingling in the crisp air as they eagerly discussed their future. The quaint house, in this picturesque suburb of London, that they stood before, held the promise of a new chapter—a place they could call their own, a haven to create memories and build a life together.

"I can already imagine us sitting in the garden, enjoying lazy Sunday mornings with a cup of coffee," Emily said, her eyes sparkling with excitement. "And maybe, someday, we'll have little footsteps running around."

Jack smiled, his face filled with love and anticipation. "Honestly, I can't wait for that. A home full of laughter, love, and family. It's everything I've ever wanted."

As they shared their dreams and aspirations, a familiar buzz interrupted their conversation. He reached into his pocket and retrieved his phone, curiosity flickering in his eyes as he read the incoming message. His expression shifted, a blend of satisfaction and intrigue.

"What is it?"

His voice had a hint of disbelief as he replied, "An email from Mariya's assistant. Apparently, the court order has been executed and Mariya has received the majority of the missing funds that Sergey embezzled. Well, that was quicker than we expected…"

Emily's eyes widened slightly in surprise, her hand instinctively reaching out to touch Jack's arm. "Great news for her, but I'm stunned it's happened so quickly…"

Nodding, Jack squeezed Emily's hand. It felt strange to recollect the case that had brought them together in the first place and consider this news that offered a sense of closure over that part of their lives.

Just as they were about to discuss the email, the sound of footsteps and a cheerful greeting interrupted them. The estate agent had arrived, ready to show them the house that held the potential to become their future home.

With a quick exchange of glances, Emily and Jack put their phones away, their minds still processing the news but focused on the task at hand. They followed the estate agent, their steps infused with a sense of excitement and possibility.

The door creaked open, revealing a light-filled hallway that beckoned them inside. The agent guided them through the rooms, sharing details of the property's charm and potential. Emily and Jack walked hand in hand, envisioning their lives within these walls, their dreams intertwined with the spaces that surrounded them.

As they explored each room, their imaginations painted vivid pictures of a life of love, laughter, and cherished memories. The house became more than just bricks and mortar—it became a sanctuary, a place where their love could blossom and flourish.

They paused at the back door, looking out at the small garden bathed in golden sunlight. A sense of belonging washed over them, as if the house itself whispered, "This is where you are meant to be."

As the tour concluded, Emily and Jack thanked the estate agent for her time, then looked at each other, their eyes meeting in a shared understanding. They knew they had found something special—a place where their love could thrive and their dreams could take root.

Emily put her hand in Jack's and they stood in the quiet street once again, gazing at the house that held their future. Mariya's message still lingered in their minds, a reminder of how much they had overcome. But in that moment, as they looked at each other, their hearts were full of hope and a renewed sense of purpose.

Together, they turned to face the house once more, ready to embrace the journey ahead. With open hearts and a shared vision, they stepped forward, knowing that this house, this home, would be the foundation of their love and the beginning of a beautiful new chapter in their lives.

CHAPTER TWENTY-TWO
Epilogue

Emily sat at a cosy beachfront restaurant in Bermuda, her eyes lazily scanning the mesmerising expanse of the sea. The rhythmic crashing of waves against the shore provided a soothing soundtrack to her thoughts. She couldn't help but marvel at how beautifully everything had turned out. From the twists and turns of their journey, she and Jack had arrived at this moment of pure bliss.

As the evening sun cast its golden glow on the sandy shores, Emily's thoughts were interrupted by a familiar cough. She turned her head and there he stood, Jack, wearing his signature smile that warmed her heart instantly.

"Good evening, Mrs Braun," he greeted playfully, his eyes sparkling with affection. "Mind if I join you?"

She couldn't suppress her delight, the corners of her mouth lifting into a radiant smile. "Well, Mr Braun, I suppose I could make an exception this time," she replied, her voice laced with playful humour.

They settled into their seats, their hands naturally finding each other's, as if they were two puzzle pieces meant to fit together. The bond between them was undeniable, a silent language of love and understanding.

In the distance, the soft strains of a calypso band drifted through the warm evening air, their melodic tunes whispering promises of enchantment. Jack's eyes gleamed with mischief as he extended his hand to Emily, inviting her to dance.

She accepted his invitation, her heart fluttering with excitement. Hand in hand, they made their way down to the moonlit beach, the sand cool beneath their feet. With the gentle ebb and flow of the music as their guide, they embraced the rhythm and began to move in sync, their bodies swaying as if in a tender embrace.

"I can't believe how far we've come, Jack," Emily murmured, her voice tinged with wonder.

Jack's eyes locked with hers, bursting with unwavering adoration. "Meeting you has been the most incredible moment of my life," he mused.

Amidst the moonlit serenity, she found herself overcome with a rush of emotions. Tightening her grip on his hand, her voice was full of passion and sincerity. "I love you, Jack," she whispered, her words carried away by the gentle breeze. "With every fibre of my being, I love you."

A radiant smile graced his lips. "And I love you too." His was voice brimming with warmth. "You've filled my life with a light I never knew existed. You complete me."

Their bodies continued to sway in harmony with the music, their dance becoming a celebration of their commitment, their unity, and the incredible bond they shared. Under the moonlit sky, they revelled in the simple joy of being in each other's arms, lost in the profound connection that had blossomed between them.

As the night unfolded, they wove their dreams and aspirations into the tapestry of their dance. They spoke of the adventures they longed to embark upon, the home they would create, and the possibility of a future filled with laughter and love.

Emily felt a sense of calm wash over her, the doubts and uncertainties that once plagued her heart dissipating with each step they took. In this moment, they were united, their souls intertwined, and the world around them faded into insignificance.

As the calypso music carried on, Emily and Jack revelled in the magic of the night. They knew that their love would continue to grow and flourish, nourished by the moments they cherished and the challenges they conquered together.

With hearts full and souls entwined, they danced on, creating their own melody in the grand symphony of life. Under the canopy of stars, they shared dreams and whispered promises, forever grateful for the serendipitous twists and turns that had led them to this cherished moment.

And so, on that moonlit beach, as the world continued to spin and the waves continued their eternal dance, the two of them embraced the joy of their love, finding solace in the knowledge that they were each other's forever.

Acknowledgements

There are so many people without whom this book would not have been possible. A huge "thank you" to the brilliant guys at Burning Chair for taking on an unknown author, and for all their hard work on this book.

To all the advance reviewers for taking the time to read and comment - too many to name everyone, but I would like to in particular thank Andrew Gordon. I have taken everything on board and know that this book is so much better for all the feedback.

And last but not least to all my friends and family for your love and support - thank you all so so much!

Eloise Fox
November 2024

More From Burning Chair Publishing

Your next favourite new read is waiting for you…!

Run to the Blue, by P N Johnson

Killer in the Crowd, by P N Johnson

Love Is Dead(ly), by Gene Kendall

A Life Eternal, by Richard Ayre

The Retribution, by Mike Wardle

Beyond, by Georgia Springate

10:59, by N R Baker

The Casebook of Johnson & Boswell, by Andrew Neil Macleod
    The Fall of the House of Thomas Weir
    The Stone of Destiny

The Curse of Becton Manor, by Patricia Ayling

The Haven Chronicles, by Fi Phillips
  Haven Wakes
  Magic Bound
  Haven's Deceit

Shadow of the Knife, by Richard Ayre

Point of Contact, by Richard Ayre

Near Death, by Richard Wall

The Spencer & Bart series, by Peter Oxley
  The Great Big Demon Hunting Agency
  The Great Big Demon of Flint Hall

The Infernal Aether series, by Peter Oxley
  The Infernal Aether
  A Christmas Aether
  The Demon Inside
  Beyond the Aether

The Sarah Black Series, by Lucy Hooft
  The King's Pawn
  The Head of the Snake

The Other Side of Trust, by Neil Robinson

The Brodick Cold War Series, by John Fullerton
  Spy Game
  Spy Dragon

Burning Bridges, by Matthew Ross

Push Back, by James Marx

The Blue Bird Series, by Trish Finnegan
    Blue Bird
    Blue Skies
    Baby Blues

The Tom Novak series, by Neil Lancaster
    Going Dark
    Going Rogue
    Going Back

The Wedding Speech Manual: The Complete Guide to Preparing, Writing and Performing Your Wedding Speech, by Peter Oxley

www.burningchairpublishing.com

www.ingramcontent.com/pod-product-compliance
Lightning Source LLC
Chambersburg PA
CBHW070627170726
48291CB00003B/913